The First Rays of Sun

The First Rays of Sun

John Brooks

Strategic Book Publishing and Rights Co.

Strategic Book Publishing & Rights Co., LLC
USA | Singapore
www.sbpra.com

For information about special discounts for bulk purchases, please contact Strategic Book Publishing and Rights Co. Special Sales, at bookorder@sbpra.net.

ISBN: 978-1-68181-615-9

The Author

I was born in South London, in the United Kingdom, in 1946, and worked most of my life in display, promotion, and design, as well as for five years as an artist and loved every moment.

Family life took over and stopped this period of self-indulgence. For most of the journey, I fairly successfully ran my own display and promotion companies until a disastrous fire destroyed the company and, due to insurance averaging, reduced life back to basics—house, cars, wife and money were all gone. "Oh dear!"

In these later year's, I spent a good deal of time enjoying Spain, with the thoughts of writing and maybe starting to paint once again. I live with my partner, Lesley Anne, in a small village set amongst the hills of Almeria enjoying each and every day.

I feel writing books is an all-consuming affair. In the beginning, trying too hard was a huge problem; it simply produced an unworthy result but with the good fortune and the help of capable friends endlessly reading the progressing chapters, *The First Rays of Sun* was completed.

Writing mainly through the night with adjacent cups of coffee and cigarettes at hand was an endless pleasure. Living the characters and situations, constantly asking oneself, 'what would happen now, what would I do', was enlightening. It was indeed enormous fun. I sincerely hope you too enjoy the journey."

I would very much like to thank the friends who have taken the time to read through the many drafts of this story and have given their valuable time, opinions and comments. It is a lonely job in some ways, albeit a pleasure, and without your input it would have been so difficult to progress and improve.

Deserving special thanks is Rosemary Johnson—thanks a million for your help, love as always.

In addition, I would like to thank Janet Steward, Joy Fairburn, and Jack Riley, together with Leslie my partner, without whose help the task would have been so much more difficult to complete.

'If you find you enjoy this story I would very much appreciate your comments and a review.

It would certainly help me improve my writing in the future.

If of course you know others that might enjoy the story, please let them know about the book.

They or indeed you may like to look out for the follow-up stories in the trilogy, they are;

'The Second Dawning' and the final part of the journey is titled, 'Innocent Reflections'.

Obviously, sales are important, particularly with a first book and your interest would be much appreciated.

Reviews and Comments can be forwarded to: johnbrooksy@outlook.com

Thank you for any interest, John Brooks.

Contents

Prologue

Garr is a woman of the future who lives in a world created by hard realities after a succession of global disasters. She, as all people in this tomorrow-world, cannot aspire to a global view but inevitably, she has her own journey and wisdom to follow in life, as does the spirit of the land upon which she lives and all who lives upon it.

Her time is a hundred years after global changes, when huge amounts of the solid earth have been swallowed by the expanding and outrageous seas. It is a time when the seasons have become increasingly extreme and a time after dramatic generations of endless turmoil, in which all the basic factors and expectations of life had changed.

The world that was, is now no more. That yesterday-world is just a vague memory, with most of the culture and artefacts long lost in the dust. It is a time almost impossible to imagine, yet dreams, desires, and ambition remain constant.

In their sparsely populated and borderless world where those harsh realities had interrupted thousands of years of human development, Garr has, like many others of her time, grown up with a focus on survival and basic instincts. These were now the key factors of life.

Survival skills took time to learn and, although knowledge from the past remained within odd books and artefacts, it had dimmed over the years. That information still existed for some, but the time to extract or re-apply yesterday's wisdom was still not readily available for the majority—hunger and conflict saw to that.

But, as it does, the wind of change came blowing over the land, generating a new and unstoppable force that humankind was unable to deny or resist. Destiny once again played its hand. For both Garr and all the people upon the land, these forces of natural progression seemed to be driving them towards a change of thinking and desire; the phoenix had risen.

Three Generations Before the Birth of Garr

During those times, global warming had been politically denied, international travel had ultimately spread new diseases, antibiotics no longer worked, medical care failed. New freedoms jammed existing systems of control; the expectations of all were unsustainable.

As the global birth rate exploded, conflicts raged over borders for resources, fresh water was at a premium. Energy supply systems broke down.

While these issues grew, the world was driven into a time of extreme weather conditions that finally pulled the world asunder.

Ultimately, the big death took over; an ever mutating virus and millions died. Borders disappeared as, one after another, governments collapsed along with security services, leaving the remaining small local communities to survive as best they could. These communities were not educated in survival techniques and community groups further broke down into family groups fighting disease, hunger, extreme weather conditions and each other.

The Origins of Garr's Family

Generations came and went. Garr's forefathers were distributed widely across the area to the east of the Pyrenees Mountains in the ancient realm of France. Each successive generation honed new skills to survive within an ever-changing environment. Some moved into the hills, while others settled into the new townships which, slowly, evolved from the old. Nature played her eternal hand and a once great civilisation was eventually hidden and broken by vines, sapling, wind, sun, rain, and ice.

It was a tribal world once more, with people only breeding with extended family or those extremely close and known to them. Men and women learned to accept death, disease, and disaster on a daily basis, and learned to kill anyone or anything that threatened their survival. The deformed or even those sympathetic to the misfortunate met a similar fate.

Ancient skills were re-discovered; humans slowly forgot much of their ancestors' civilised ways and the days of plenty they had enjoyed, returning gradually to a life of hunting and gathering—warriors in a lawless and borderless world.

Garr, with her brother Nicolas, grew from that foundation, enduring the hardship and humiliation which came with those times. Ultimately, they became accomplished warriors and survivors, who were nevertheless people of vision and unfulfilled thoughts. Both followed their own journey through life and arrived somewhere quite unexpected.

True necessity is a strange companion, whilst destiny is an unknown path, marked with endless impossible decisions, twists, and turns.

Garr's World

It was a great view, stunning in fact; the far side of the plain must have been six kilometres away at the least. There, the ground very obviously began to rise once again in dramatic stages to a very considerable height. The distant peaks were heavily capped with snowy white crowns, while the horizon they created was like a line of huge legal dignitaries, standing shoulder to shoulder.

As the eye travelled once again down to the lower levels, it came to thickly wooded areas, with clearings here and there, which formed a huge forest. Stories had been told by many about the extraordinary game that lived there, fantastical stories of giant cats, wolves, and, particularly, wild boars. The tales of their ferocious courage were the stuff of legend, generating fear and respect in equal measure.

The sky immediately above was clear blue with an odd whisper of a few white clouds, as well as a few small, dark blue and mauve clouds just beginning to claw their way above those distant snow-capped mountains. They were like terrifying forces, churning and shifting, looking down upon mere mortals and preparing them for world domination.

The temperature was comfortably warm now that the day was fully launched. An hour ago, it had been bitterly cold, with the shadows still shrouding the rocky outcrop. It would not be long before frosty fingers greeted one each morning and the land converted once more into a frozen waste.

A flat rocky platform extended some ten metres before the cave entrance and a similar distance to either side. At the centre, where a deep dip in the rock existed, grasses and vegetables of different types grew on a seasonal basis and a small but stout apple tree took pride of position.

To the far left of the cave entrance stood a number of large boulders and, between them, the ground gave way to a downward track which twisted between them and formed relatively safe steps to the lower levels. If you knew the path and each of the rugged rocks which stood proud from the track, it could be descended easily until it disappeared and dissipated into a different phase of the mountainside, ultimately, the valley floor itself. Normally, lush green existed there, but depending on the particular season, it could also be barren, baked or frozen earth.

It was nevertheless, a safe place to live—a cave where one could, if need be, defend the entrance without much difficulty. Although that need had never yet occurred, it was always a possibility.

At the cave entrance, a small fire burnt happily next to a long, ancient, and ornate bench that was supported by various shaped rocks wedged together along the outer rock face.

Over the fire, woven on a darkened stick, was a skinned rabbit, unfortunately a little over cooked on one side, due to the carer's habit of occasionally just sitting for far too long staring out across the plain whilst contemplating plans or unravelled thoughts.

With food preparation, you had to concentrate and give it a little love and attention if you wanted to take any satisfaction and delight from your effort. On this occasion, the operation was going downhill a little. Potatoes, wrapped in grass and surrounded by earth in a small indentation next to the fire also needed some care; some occasional turning would have helped the process.

Inside, the cave split into further levels. One was falling downwards, to a small fresh rock pool and trickling stream running along a rock channel to the right. The water came from deep inside the mountain, probably gathered from a thousand smaller pools and channels. Another track within the cave lead upwards to two further areas, one ideally creating a kitchen-cum-storage or working area well out of reach of nature's bad temper.

The upper area formed two natural sleeping platforms within the rock. Once laid out with interwoven pine branches layer upon layer, then covered and filled by heather, lavender and other herbs, they were extremely warm and comfortable, if a little smoky, as the heat from the internal fire obviously rose and heated the high spaces.

Nevertheless, Garr's gaze to the faraway mountains continued regardless of the wisps of smoke from the fire drifting directly over the view.

Over the past couple of hours, a turgid formation of cloud had grown considerably over those peaks and now made their own ominous mass of dark, threatening material. From this distance, one could see the initial dynamics generating within the dark cloud—flashes like little explosions on the top and beneath the growing mass.

A cold breeze now arrived over the outcrop as the sky continued to rapidly darken, followed suddenly by the cracking and rumble of the storm's beginning.

The dark mass now occupied most of the sky, with only the smallest areas of blue to the far extremes; the colours were stupendous. Purples and all shades of blue, black, and grey, and then, in splashes here and there, some shocking pink and deep reds.

The spatter of rain now joined the heavenly orchestra; large pebble-sized drops fell as the light show began in earnest, with flash after flash daggered down towards the lazy earth, mixing with thunderous booms and crashes. The temperature was dropping rapidly too as the torrents increased in intensity, appearing as if the Gods were hurling down a hundred thousand stones at the feeble creatures of the earth. The noise was deafening as the water danced and bounced off the rock, forming a thousand white-water rivulets that would help maintain Garr's rock pool.

Garr had already moved into the cave entrance and added an extra layer of warmth over the sacking drape she was wearing in the form of a skin-hooded wrap. She continued to watch the storm with interest while tending the over-cooked food, which was conveniently shielded from the torrents by a substantial canopy of rock above the cave entrance.

The storm would pass, as such things do, and life would continue as it always had. The rabbit and potatoes would be eaten and replenished, hopefully, tasting a little better next time around.

However, the course of life would change, maybe for the better, maybe for the worse, but change it must.

Garr, now fed and warm, shook her long blond hair away from her face, stood and stretched, then took to the heathery bed area to see out the rest of the storm. It was far too comfortable. With the food inside her, the sweet smell of lavender and heather blended with pine proved too much; sleep crept in and the storm drifted slowly away, silenced by dreams of a summer's day with all its delights.

When Garr awoke, she stretched her long limbs and felt the familiar ache throughout her body that accompanied each day. It was hard work fending for oneself out here: as beautiful as it was, her existence came at a price.

Loneliness was something she had grown accustomed to; she had learnt to suppress many of her feelings and memories of the past, filling her world with the richness and wonderment of her surroundings. She found if she kept working from dawn until dusk, relishing in the hard physical labour that was necessary for the upkeep of her private world, she would sleep easily. It was only at dusk that she allowed herself to drift in and out of luxurious thoughts, which sometimes took her into the painful past; so strongly and tangibly that she could reach out and touch people and places she had long left behind.

It had not been her intention to idle the day away in nothings, but sometimes it happens, and, in the end, what did it matter if it did. Nobody, as far as she could remember, would be visiting her, and that, of course, was normal, although she liked to consider the possibility. There was more than enough of all the essentials stored away safely for her not to worry.

She was proud of her reserves; they were the result of all that endeavour and constant effort.

Yes, there were objectives to achieve, discoveries to be made. But tomorrow would be fine, or indeed the day-after-tomorrow would also do nicely—she was due a little time off her daily routine.

Life for Garr was a strange mixture, her day-to-day routine, alongside the memories of her years as a young warrior and the desperate times of her childhood, still real and invasive.

Since taking up her cave life, she had found time to think and reflect. Maybe for the first time, she had found solace within herself. This, together with the wise words and kindness of her only real friendship, gave her the inward knowledge and confidence of her own abilities that, for twenty three years, had only been expressed in resentment or through her skills as an awesome and unforgiving warrior.

The next moment of awareness came with a great darkness directly over her face. For a moment, she was unable to focus, fear grabbed her heart, and the pulse quickened. Then a big wet softness was on her face and then a cold sensation nudging her into the morning. Just for a second or two further, she remained fearful and frozen, thinking it might be one of the many wild creatures that shared her world. Then a comfortable realisation dawned.

"Get out of here, you little monster. Let me wake up slowly."

The young dog walked away, accustomed to the early morning rebuff, and so took up his favourite position at the entrance of the cave adjacent to the still smouldering fire. There he could await the first warming ray of sun as it crept over and around the rocks to the far left of the cave entrance.

Garr, in slow and carefully planned moves, adjusted her position upon her bedding, whilst endeavouring to remember when she had removed her wraps. With each upward movement upon the bed, she ensured the warm wraps and skins moved with her, until she was sitting upright, and then, with a deliberate and sudden burst of energy, she leapt into a run to fulfil the first need of the day. Once relieved, she grabbed her boots and a wrap and took two bundles of dry kindling, which she gently spread out over the ash and embers. She left them there for a minute or two and looked at the day outside of her personal world. Then she bent and wiggled an air hole into the ash and blew softly. Rapid smoke was suddenly followed by a burst of golden flame spreading quickly amongst the embers; it was always the routine and it worked well.

When Garr had first found her cave and moved in with excitement and enthusiasm, she was quickly driven towards depression by her lack of ability to maintain the fire. She had devoted hours to it on a daily basis, and, on occasion, had gone days without heat or cooked food. Ultimately, the coming of summer had saved her; during that first long summer she devoted all her endeavours to the new essentials in her life—fire, food, and routines. It had of course always been important in her life, but in the new townships, it was not so essential a skill; here at the cave, there was no common interest, no companion or neighbour to assist.

Monster now stood staring at Garr, head to one side expecting his turn in the attention queue.

"So, where did you get to last night?"

Strangely, there was no answer; he just displayed that 'who-me look'.

"I suppose you were off investigating again—haven't yet learnt to bring home any food, have you? You weren't even guarding your mistress either, were you?"

This question generated the guilty look, which formed as a wrinkly frown upon his ever-growing face. Then Monster seemed to think it better to simply look in the opposite direction for a while and hope a certain somebody would stop nagging at him; anyway; what was a dog supposed to do with his time?

Garr flipped down the old metal rack across the fire and placed on it the pan of water to boil.

She reached up to the rock shelf and took down a treasured plastic container, where she had placed the spare rabbit and potato, and fed Monster.

As soon as the sounds of mealtime arrived, so did Wiz, the large white tom that also occupied the cave. Wiz simply nudged his way onto Monster's food and began to help himself. They were good companions; little Monster endured endless liberties from his smaller companion, but, if need be, he had already learnt that he should rush to his defence. Wiz gave nothing, except the opportunity to enslave oneself to his desires.

While the day ahead was contemplated, herbal tea was sipped and hard-boiled eggs were eaten.

Garr suddenly remembered that her one and only friend had said he might visit around now. He was a good person; Garr enjoyed time with him, which she could not say about anyone else. Garr had met Knap years ago in her wandering days, just after splitting with Nic, her brother, and somehow she had kept bumping into him in the strangest of places. Over the years, they mutually motivated one another and found themselves moving into the same areas, often sharing the same thoughts about life. Neither had realised this fully, until once again Garr had bumped into Knap while both were out hunting and checking traps.

Knap was old enough to be Garr's father, possibly grandfather, but that had never really showed itself as a barrier to their friendship. His keen, enquiring mind stimulated Garr and allowed her to discover new depths and abilities within herself.

For Garr, Knap had become everything and everybody in her life. Because of Knap, Garr grew. His family group adopted her as one of their own, and she once again experienced a real family.

It was such a small world, yet both thought themselves immensely lucky to have met.

Knap and his partner, Mara, were also different in that they had a family—a big family of two boys and a girl. This was a great rarity these days; the birth of healthy children was an exception, and the little ones that did appear within any group were considered great blessings and gifts, raising the parents to the highest social level.

Garr did not know the two boys well, but the girl, Sala, who was the youngest, had known Garr since birth—a firm and close friendship had developed between them. Garr was always Sala's champion, and indeed Knap was Garr's.

Apart from Garr's brother, with whom she once had been inseparable, but who she had not seen for a number of years, Knap and his family were the closest thing to friends that Garr had.

She sat for a while enjoying the beginning of her day, before her mind began to wander in a thousand directions.

Firstly, she thought about the people and faces that were familiar to her, and then those she avoided and who had to be treated with due caution, which in reality was just about everyone.

This was open country, so knowing somebody could mean seeing them once or twice a year. People were bitterly independent and tough; they had to be or they perished.

Then she started thinking of the matters to be attended to prior to the start of winter and the yearly Big Gathering of hill folk, which was due soon. The Gathering represented the only communal activity that all hill folk recognised. It was an occasion to cautiously share experiences, listen to a musician, dance maybe, trade, and compete. Also, a time for children to learn about others within the hill country; a time for flirting and courting and maybe kissing.

She was looking forward to the possibility of seeing her brother and his family, plus other old acquaintances she knew in passing. It was the occasion for such meetings and the opportunity also to share both ideas and fun.

Her thoughts began to take an analytical direction, looking at diverse aspects of her life. She found herself thinking about where and how she lived; why she was still a loner. It was jumbled thought flitting in all directions—the kind of contemplation that probed her life, who she was, and what she did to survive.

As her eyes wandered over the rock face where she lived and now sat, she remembered the other caves that existed further along the rock face, many of which she had checked out before selecting her own very special cave, some of which were now occupied. She had heard that some industrious folks had actually mined their own caves within an area of hard chalk abutting to limestone.

When she originally arrived upon the mountain, it had been only herself, as far as she knew, and she had enjoyed those lonely but hard times.

On the lower level of the valley, where the ground began to flatten a little, a few structures of varied styles had appeared and then disappeared. Even further down the mountain, as the terrain levelled into the plain, some had placed a number of structures together and interlinked them. Some of these camps had then been covered with odd materials, normally traded from those who scavenged the old towns and cities that were still lying decimated under a cover of vegetation.

Most folk who lived this way had buried their homes under the earth in natural hollows and covered them over with earth so that, from a distance, they disappeared or appeared as strange bumps on the landscape. As long as they were well constructed, they seemed to provide excellent protection from all weather. Some were further disguised with the planting of saplings or other foliage around them. Garr had noticed on her hunting trips that smallholdings had developed and spread. Some of these were quite spectacular and yet not intrusive.

She tried to remember names and visualise the faces that went with them, but it was not important in her life.

The thoughts and memories changed direction.

She did not understand why a lifestyle such as hers continued for anybody, let alone herself. It was a variety of what was once called hillbilly or backwoodsman culture that Garr remembered reading about somewhere and that existed centuries ago; maybe in her great, great grandmothers' time.

She appreciated that everyone had his or her own lifestyle, opinions, and views. Personal philosophy was strong amongst the hill folk, and yes, stubbornness and aggression.

She thought about how none of these people ever seemed to visit the old urban areas or the new larger communities. This was no longer justified as nobody had contracted the big death for years, and even clear memories of exactly what had happened were not available. She felt as most did, that the extreme years had passed; generations had come and gone. Any explanatory or historical literature still available appeared contradictory in the extreme and was hard to follow if your ability to read was limited by the lack of education and time to apply the little you had. Reading was the only skill that she and Nic had taken from their childhood and although Garr only possessed two books, she had continued to read them over and over again until she and Knap had befriended each other. Knap seemed to have countless books which he allowed Garr to wallow amongst, devouring the knowledge within them repeatedly and slowly building herself into a competent reader, which certainly stood her apart from the majority.

She realised that older folk only had misguided memories. Most had no clarity or education about what had happened in the past. In fact, that seemed to be one of the main problems for everybody; the truth about the past was buried by time itself. The explosive rate of the Big Death overtook any hope of maintaining control in the old world. Their experiences were not well recorded at that time in history, and now the ability to learn from the written word had diminished, as had the ability to re-create or understand most of the old artefacts that remained.

They were seen as mystical or religious objects, useless for education but essential for belief.

It appears that governments, borders, and security forces simply disintegrated over time, leaving folk to do the best they could to survive the violence, hunger, and decease. Indeed, that kind of life was tough in the extreme and survival was a forgotten skill that nobody wanted to have to relearn.

She, more than most, realised that survival here and now; while watching one's back, was never going to be an easy task, yet life had taught her well. Her understanding was that after the great floods, came the Big-Death—that had simply swept over the population and the great infrastructures that had previously existed.

She had also heard that those special people who remained and seemed to possess the spirit of survival had still bred with the misfortunate, the ill and sickly, those who were not resistant to the death. Mutants were often the result, or another round of deadly sickness, which could wipe away another generation. Evidently, it became the practice to destroy any with the sickness, as well as all mutants, at birth. People began, as a survival necessity, to pull away from historical breeding and care habits. Real fear became an effective contraceptive.

All this was their inheritance which, slowly turned into fantastical stories of yesteryear by the travelling storytellers—unbelievable achievements, great courage and bravery, all used to delight the rare child and adults alike around a fire. None of it truly believable, or was it?

Slowly, over time, those stories had been given colour and romance or moral and philosophical meanings; valiant maidens were rescued or the evil destroyers of their world were driven into angry seas together with their greed, and then devoured by gigantic beasts that protected the righteous.

Suddenly Garr needed to break from her jumbled thoughts, to redirect herself into her daily routines. The organising of her extensive cave was first, particularly as there was now the expectation of a guest arriving with news, maybe gossip, and maybe gifts for the store cupboard.

Broken Peace

Some twenty kilometres southwest of the lower climes of the Pyrenees, within a group of old stone hilltop buildings, Nic and his family scurried about at first light, readying themselves to work upon the land they had slowly cultivated and to harvest anything ready for consumption. They kept around half of their crop; the other half was delivered to the village.

In and around the hilltop village, twenty-five family groups had developed a community that was now well bonded. They had developed a communal commitment to each other, as well as rules and a euthanasia policy, which was applied in equally firm measure to age and illness. It was a tough policy developed over those extreme years, yet all knew that, in those times, it was right. It simply was not practical to feed or give endless time to those who could never contribute. But even then, it was problematic; judgements had to be made and then action taken upon those decisions. Somehow, they made it work; the pain made it right, like taking medicine, and yet there was a common feeling that time had changed something. That feeling was now growing within the whole community.

One building had been set aside as a common meeting place, and all were committed to gathering there one day a week to share conversation, problems, thoughts, and laughter.

A central food store existed within the village, where both ins and outs were recorded scrupulously. A number of buildings had also been committed to animals; chickens to one, goats and sheep to others. They even produced their own bread, butter, cheese, and wines; everything worked around the seasons. If there was a collective surplus, which was rare, then they traded for whatever was wanted or needed.

Their overall success was based upon a strict observance of the rules, of which there were a small but growing number. While consideration was given to genuine life problems, the harshest enforcement was applied to any who flaunted the regulations or deceived the community.

There had been times in the bad years when they had defended their hilltop homes with no mercy. If they had agreed a need prior to a conflict, young women were occasionally taken, but never grown males or older folk. It was both simple and primitive, and, somewhere deep inside their souls, they knew that. Children were always spared and normally adopted within the community. Thankfully, those days of warfare appeared to have passed, but it was part of their inheritance and had been the basis of their survival.

Nic, with his partner Sarina, and their two children, Jac and Ban, walked happily out of the village and down towards where the large fields were cut like steps deep into the hillsides, which they believed had been formed many centuries earlier.

Nic and Sarina had spent two years clearing the land they had been allocated and rebuilding walls and irrigation channels. It had been a labour of love, and now they were reaping the rewards of that labour.

While that work continued, the cleared areas were cultivated in the same way as the other members of their community had done in their fields. Sometimes they also ventured further down past the great steps towards the thick areas of trees and walked amongst them and the cacti searching out fruit or nuts.

Some days the work was pleasurable and rewarding, while others days the work seemed endless and backbreaking; the rules of their community felt tedious and bore down upon them like boulders, but they understood they were necessary. Taken as a whole, life was good, if not a little limiting, particularly for Nic.

Unfortunately, for Nic, he had too many dreams and plans, similar to his sister; the sort of thoughts that worried others within such a tightly regulated community as this. This caused him a good deal of frustration and conflict, even with Sarina who rightly concentrated upon the day-to-day welfare of the children and the security of their future. Nic saw it as a limited future for his boys, secure maybe, but the possibilities were not being considered—surely minds should be stretched not encased, he would argue.

At the communal gatherings, he would often find himself alone, both physically and intellectually, with nobody choosing to stand with him. There was no wish to explore alternative thought or even old technologies when all were gathered, and yet, individually, the villagers would sometimes express other views.

It was not that Nic was a bad man; his neighbours liked him, but were frightened by his optimistic and outgoing views, which were seen as dangerous for the community. But his openness had won him friends and his wisdom earned him respect, and, hence, he was tolerated.

Above all, they still were farmer-warriors and maybe Nic alone could see that the world they shared was changing.

The family reached their land, stopping to survey the situation and take in deep breaths of fresh air. Jac pushed Ban clear over the low wall bordering their land and a pursuit followed. Nic and Sarina sat and watched the two boys play at chase for a moment, enjoying the fruits of their family; it was a good moment that any parent would have enjoyed and here on the land that they had cleared, warm feelings and sunlight bathed them for a moment.

Nic called the boys back for work.

He raised an arm and waved to other group members working higher on the hillside, then began with Sarina to dig up and harvest the root crops now ready for the pot.

From above them, they heard the low tones of something like a horn echoing and floating over the hills and all around them but paid no particular attention, thinking it to be the fresh breeze catching amongst the hills.

They worked on steadily as the sun rose higher in the sky.

Nic raised his head for a second and shouted once again, "Jac, Ban, get back here, now."

Sarina also stopped to look about for the two boys.

"Did you see where those horrors went, Nic?"

"Up higher towards Big Brian and his lot I think, Sarina. They will be back, let us just get—" Sarina stopped Nic mid-sentence.

"Nic, look. What's happening?" Nic did not respond, his head was down once again in work.

"Bloody look up the damn hill, Nic, what the hell is happening up there? The boys, you said they went in that direction."

They both stood for a second and stared up towards the commotion, not believing what their eyes were conveying to them.

"Sarina, they are being attacked. There's some kind of battle going on. Run, run like the damn wind, get to the village now. Bloody run, woman, I'll find the boys. That's some kind of a raid. I think we're being attacked by a warrior tribe."

Sarina hesitated for but a second, adjusting her thoughts and intentions, then flew, holding the bottom of her long sacking dress in one hand, with the other arm across her front to contain her breasts. She was both fit and fast, even against the upgrade of the hillside and like the wind she flew, her feet hardly touching the ground.

She could but place her instant trust in Nic for her children, her babies, as he had just done in her speed.

Nic grabbed for a weapon then leapt to the land level above his own and frantically called again for the boys. He ran to the far end of the plot where the land fell away sharply.

"Jac! Ban!" he continued to call; nothing, there were no little voices he recognised in reply.

He again leapt over the stone wall to the next level and looked quickly to the left and right. The conflict was raging above him, and, from where he now stood, he could see what he thought were the wounds of battle and the black-red of blood.

Big Brian was exactly that. At 2.4 metres with shoulders to match, he was an awesome sight, let alone adversary. His three sons, all around two metres in height, and their partners were all large like oxen. In normal circumstances, nobody in their right mind would have picked upon such a group.

Nic ran to one end of the plot and then the other, calling and calling.

His heart was now beating even more rapidly in his frustration and fear.

He stopped and turned to look downwards once again, still nothing.

One more leap to yet another level.

He stood for one second to calm himself, then suddenly an almighty scream and holler raged at him, as two foes leapt down from the upper level and charged at him, weapons raised high.

Anger, adrenalin, and hatred surged through his veins.

His pent up fears turned to anger and strength and the pace of time changed. The two aggressors, with hair and clothing flying behind them, fell upon him.

"Bastards, bastards, bastards!"

Nic swung his staff about his head; generating both a powerful whoosh and courage within his spirit. He thrust it at one of his advancing adversaries, landing with a ghastly crunch on the side of the head. He staggered and stared, his knees crumpled, then he fell to the ground, his eyes showing surprise as blood flowed; the other foe swerved away, now a little less confident.

Nic, like Sarina, was fit, fast, strong, and accurate. The years of his youth with Garr had trained him well.

With a dive towards his fallen foe, Nic picked up his weapon—a thick double bladed sword—in his right hand and smashed it without mercy towards the man's throat.

It found its mark instantly.

His companion still faltered for a second, his confidence now diminishing quickly; it was enough time for Nic to throw himself into a shoulder roll towards the faltering enemy and enter the blade under his rib cage with the force of a man leaping into the upright position. The blade entered and reappeared at the shoulder with almost no sound.

Strangely, there was no scream and no sigh, but the momentary eye-to-eye contact belonged to another world.

For a second the aggressor stood with axe raised, unable to follow through, a statue of disbelief.

The ghastly death gargles and chilling screams of the dying men and the stench of blood and sweat in all their nostrils was all that remained. Nic gave them neither a second glance nor a single further thought. Their deaths were strictly of their own making.

Now, once again, Nic shouted for his boys, while scanning all around. His voice seemed to be failing him, he could not shout loud enough. He suddenly found himself standing alone upon an island, shouting and shouting, floating and drifting.

The screams of his foes now angered him in his frustration. He swung the sword with all his force and a head fell without dignity amongst the dirt.

Big Brian was now jumping down to Nic's level with two of his sons all wearing the blood of their own battles; their foes defeated.

Their women were apparently staying on the higher level to ensure the job was finished. From this distance, Nic could see them in his hazed vision clearly completing the job, clubbing continuously until no movement existed.

"You okay, Nic? Well done, lad. The village—come on, let's go, we must."

"Brian, Brian, please stop, please, the boys, Ban and Jac. Have you seen them?" He turned to Brian's sons: "Have you seen my boys, lads?"

Quick looks passed from one to the other indicating an obvious no.

"Nic, they are probably back at the village, come on, man, let's finish these fuckers. They've really pissed me off now."

There was no further time for thought, only action.

All four men ran up the hill towards the village. Nic took the lead and went off track to enter the village from a side alley, allowing them the advantage of the upper ground.

As they entered the village, hell was before them.

Fire, smoke and screams, blood and shouts hit them from all sides. It was surreal. The group stayed together, acting as one, as if they were veterans, like a machine, as if they had been in battle as one forever, each totally understanding the others' movements and intentions.

Striking to left and right, to head then legs. The grunts and moans of pain vanished from their ears.

Their adversaries were generally longhaired, bearded, and wild, running about the village shouting, screaming, and killing whomever they confronted.

Picking off the enemy one at a time, Brian and Nic were cold and efficient, attacking each opponent from opposite sides where possible—one attacking high the other attacking low.

Occasionally, they would come against two foes, then Brian's lads, if free, would swing around and cut them down from behind.

There was no honour involved now, only victory. Their world was at stake and they would not let it be taken from them.

They moved from alley to street, from street to house. Checking, killing, cutting, and dragging their foes into the street for disposal.

The enemies were mainly concentrated on plunder and destruction, but rape was always upon their minds. Poor young Garia was found crouching in a corner, bloodied and in a trance, gathering around her what was left of torn garments, her naked skin cut and bruised.

John Jameson lay slaughtered while Molly was spread on the ground naked, held by two and abused by another who viciously struck her about the head as she made a valiant effort to defend herself; Nic and Brian arrived at the scene with her wild screams echoing along the lane.

Luckily, Brian's sons were on their toes and, between them, the three abusers were put to rest, spilling their blood into the gully at the edge of the lane and causing small rivulets to run between the flagstones. At her salvation, Molly collapsed into a faint; her defenders moving on, into further conflict.

Not once did their power appear to falter or be challenged; it appeared that none had the ability to stand in their way.

Then it suddenly appeared to be over.

A few of the remaining enemy ran from their village screaming and hooting wildly, still swinging their weapons above their heads and carrying booty under their arms.

It appeared pointless, a drug-inspired craziness with little gain apart from fear.

The smell of battle filled their nostrils—fire, thick, languid smoke, blood, and their own sweat. The sounds of battle were replaced with heart-breaking screams and sobbing and the crackling of burning wood.

For all the noise, there was a stillness, a sad quietness.

Nic, Brian, and his sons stood looking around, weapons hanging at their sides dripping the blood of their foes. Victorious or defeated, they did not really know; that it was a disaster they were sure.

Slowly, their hypnotic state began to slide away as their companions and neighbours wandered magnetically into the small central square where they now stood. Others were rushing to the aid of the wounded or abused.

Normally, when the square reflected sunshine, it created a comforting feeling. But the ancient flagstones, the small still fountain at the centre, and the buildings forming the square with their arched coach yards and balconies were now in shade—grey, dark, hard, and austere. Thick black smoke billowed from windows and doors, forming dark, ominous clouds above them.

Exhaustion was replaced by emotion, as the devastation around them sank in.

The only thoughts that now existed in each of their minds were of their loved ones. Where were they? Were they safe? Were they alive?

Some, who had found one another, grabbed, cuddled, and held each other tight, tears running over dirty skin; their strength and bravery depleted. These were embraces that should last forever; never-to-let-go embraces.

Others simply dropping the weapons from their dirty blood-stained hands, ran towards home, calling names, fear echoing through each syllable uttered.

Nobody spoke. Only a lurking anguish hung silently in the stifling air.

Nic jerked himself back into full reality and then raced, his heart beating faster than in battle.

'Sarina, Sarina, Jac, Ban!"

He burst against the oak door. It was partly open, and straight through he ran, into the hallway, into the main room, seeing instantly the upturned furniture that had been obviously kicked aside; the place was in total disarray.

"Jac? Ban? You here, Sarina?" He paused for thought and through fear of what he was anticipating.

"Please be here, be hiding somewhere. Just be here, please, please."

He could no longer move forward. He stood with his head looking downwards, his hands gripped tightly into fists, nails cutting into palms.

Tears now just ran down his face, gushing and unstoppable. His head spun faster and his body lifted into the mist of momentary despair.

"Nic, Nic, we are here, Nic, upstairs. I can't open this bloody door. Can you hear me, Nic?"

Nic leapt four of the large stone stairs at a time and threw his shoulder at the heavy door; it budged a little, just enough for fingers, Sarina's fingers, to appear around the edge.

"Are you okay, are the boys okay, Sarina; are they all right?"

"Nic, I thought they would be with you, they're not here, Nic. Yula and Hose are here with me, that's all. Oh Nic, Nic, where are they?"

Nic's heart sunk once more. Yula and Hose, their elderly neighbours, stood in silence. Intense, menacing fear entered the atmosphere again.

"Sarina, I'll get you out of here, then I'll run back to the fields. They'll be there, I know they will. They're bright and smart. They'll be there. They'll be okay."

"Hurry, Nic, please hurry."

A stout pole was quickly found, and with one almighty tug and grunt, the door was freed. Nic grabbed Sarina close, kissing her head tenderly and quickly pulling Yula and Hose into a group embrace. Then he loosened the embrace and for a second they looked eye to eye, neither saying a single word. He turned away quickly and raced from the house.

Yula took the place of Nic, embracing Sarina with affection and caring, and Hose reached forward to gather the group in close once again. For a moment or two, they allowed some stress and emotion to be released, and more tears trickled down all their faces. Then Sarina re-gathered herself. She wiped away her tears and passed her hand gently over Yula and Hose's cheeks, signalling both care and the need to move on, then took a deep breath or two.

"Come on, you two, the boys will be fine, I'm sure, and we have work to do."

Within, her heart was pounding with her lack of conviction in the words she had spoken, but to loiter was to fail. Time for self-indulgence, as short as it was, was over.

Garr's Visitors

Monster twitched, his ears swivelling in all directions. Slowly his great head raised as he checked the air, the call of duty dawned within him. As young as he was, he understood his duty. Now energised by his mission, he silently padded across to the cave entrance, turned his head to alert Garr of an imminent visitor or intruder, then padded back and took his position at the top of the downward track.

Anyone previously unaware of his existence would have been horrified coming face to face with this creature. His warning call resounded along the cliff face.

Normally, his disposition was that of the gentle giant; now his hackles were up and the whole of his body turned from loose to firm and muscular, swelling as he tensed.

'Monster, shh! Quiet, boy."

"Garr, Garr, it's Knap. May I come forward without being eaten?"

Garr laughed, expressing her delight of company.

"Knap!" Garr moved towards the entrance, stood next to Monster, and shouted down to her visitor. "How wonderful, please come into camp, Knap. Okay, Monster, it's ok, boy. It's Knap, and you behave now."

Knap very carefully approached the camp together with Mara and their daughter Sala. Garr greeted the party while firmly holding Monster, who still subsequently gave them all the full security check, with endless figures of eight, loud pig-like snorting and sniffs, and occasional deep concerning and threatening growls.

When recognition and memory slowly dawned, his tail proceeded to wag slowly, then faster and faster it went, for now he remembered Knap as a friend and bearer of gifts. Then suddenly, without any further ceremony, he flopped back down at the camp entrance, apparently feigning instant sleep, head upon paws with one blood-red eye permanently open and observing every movement and action.

His display was rapidly adjusted as Knap retrieved the anticipated gift—a giant bone from his backpack. Tail a-wagging yet again and drooling disgustingly until receiving Garr's approval, he lumbered forward gently taking the bone and returning to his designated position.

The small party settled down around the fire at the cave entrance, initially all talking at once. Soon the chatter turned to laughter, and they all sighed and took a moment.

"Well, young woman, it's been quite some time since we've been able to do this. We've been thinking of you. So, how have you been and what trouble have you been up to?"

Mara, ignoring Knap's initial question, addressed Garr herself.

"Garr, we are bearers of gifts for you, my dear. Just what do you think of these little offerings?"

With that, she started to undo the backpacks fully, revealing so much it was magical; so many wonderful gifts started to appear. Soap, a colourfully woven jumper, salt, peppers in real glass jars, pears, tomatoes, lemons, matches, and two excellent joints of meat. They looked like pork packed in salt. Without a doubt, it was a wonderful array of gifts, a real fiesta. So much, in fact, that it was almost too much; it was unexpected and a little embarrassing, as Garr felt she had little to offer in return, apart from her hospitality.

"Mara, all of you, this is so wonderful, but too much. I have nothing to offer that would be worthy in return."

"Garr, my dear child, say no more," Knap insisted. "How about letting us stay over for a couple of nights. There's been some trouble reported further south and our place isn't best placed for security these days, especially now the boys are no longer with us. I think it might be wiser, if it's okay, to be here. "Changing the subject on you for one moment, Garr, do you realise that when I was a child, there was no such thing as a lemon?"

"Yes, Knap, that is very interesting, but, staying with the main subject for a moment, you know you are always welcome here, all of you, as long as you like. It is never and will never be a problem. What's the trouble? What exactly has happened or what have you heard, Knap?"

"It doesn't sound good, Garr. A mixed group, mainly from far over to the east, we've been told. When I say group, I really mean a small army of meandering, murdering bastards. Evidently, they have been wandering their way across the south as many tribes do, and then they started northward when they reached the Pyrenees. Obviously, this is all second hand or third hand hearsay, but too many folks have been talking about them. We met a small group of travellers from the south just two weeks ago and they confirmed the stories. It appears there are about two hundred of them this time, women, children, and all. They work normally in small raiding parties—the normal routine, rape and pillage, then moving on. As far as I am aware, there is nobody or no community ready or capable these days to deal with these bastards. We really should get ourselves better organised—it's about time."

"That kind of story is always worrying, Knap. I have a brother living somewhere down there. But listen, what is the chance of them passing your way? The odds must be well on your side."

"You're right of course, Garr. Those living on the plains are far more at risk—easy small targets I am afraid—but the likelihood of trouble passing directly our way, or indeed their way, is very small. The problem is the feeling of menace and threat that these stories create. In the end, it is simply about fear. Fear exposes all our inadequacies and insecurities. Suddenly every single tiny sound at night is the enemy at your door, standing beside your bed. Every story you hear keeps going round and around inside your head. Mara and Sal wanted to be somewhere else until this current threat had passed, and, indeed, why not? It makes good sense."

"You're right, Knap. This is one situation where you have to admire the shufflers in their townships, I guess. I gather they rarely have these problems anymore—too many of them and too well organised. I think they are a very weird lot, but I have heard they do stick together. Regardless, I don't think I'll be moving into a township—way too crowded and restricted for the likes of me."

Sala interrupted the chatter. "Any chance of a drink, Garr?"

'Sorry, forgot my manners. Let's get some water boiling and some food in the pot for later. I have to check out some traps and if you fancy keeping me company. I will show you my new fish-store. It's been a real success, far better than any I've built before."

"Okay, sounds good to me. We'll look forward to that."

The water boiled and some strong nettle and rosehip fusion with honey was sipped slowly as the party of four exchanged stories and thoughts. The day was turning into a pleasant one. The surface water from the storm had dried, leaving the rocks, air, and greenery clean and fresh. There was a good-to-be-alive feeling. Garr translated this into energy. She was ready to take that walk, although her guests were still recovering after their early morning start and long hike.

"You guys ready for a wander?"

"If you don't mind," Sala answered, "I'll stay here. Had a rough night and very early start. To be honest, I could do with having a laze around really or even a doze, especially after tramping over here with all those gifts of yours."

They laughed and Garr was unable to think of a worthy response.

Mara took the same position as Sala and elected to remain at the cave and prepare some food for later, so Knap joined Garr and Monster.

Garr grabbed her shoulder bag that carried all the essentials for the exercise, added a small pouch of water, and picked up her favourite staff and bow.

"Let's get to it, Knap," Garr said with enthusiasm and started to descend the track. "I'll close the entrance off, Mara. We should be about a couple of hours—back before sundown."

They descended along the track that turned one direction, then another, at times enclosed on both sides. The floor was mainly solid rock with loose boulders which regularly fell from above after storms; the track formed irregular large steps when you looked carefully, they zigzagged around enormous boulders, which occasionally created blind alleys between the sharp vertical faces of the cliff.

About half-way down, the track turned sharply to the left and then, after another thirty feet, started to level and clear before it descended steeply once more; at this point Garr stopped to lower her defences.

Two years ago, Garr had spent weeks creating this delicately balanced masterpiece of engineering and had continued since that time refining the operation. In principle, it was simple; levers, balances, and good fortune. The good fortune was that sometime in the past a substantial tree had fallen beside the entrance track. With levers, Garr had slowly moved it into the ideal position, attached a heavy rope to the lower end and then took that over an outstanding edge of rock, which created a sharp turn down the track. At the upper end, the base of the tree was wedged into a crack in the rock face, allowing it to act as a hinge due to its weight.

The main problem Garr had at the time was creating a smooth running surface over which her rope could move without constantly causing it to wear and break; creating just that had taken her over four weeks, rubbing rock against rock, working hard each day with sore and blistered hands. But, in the end, it was achieved. At the end of her rope was a heavy wire net she had found upon a dump and she had formed it into a bag with logs that held the mouth open wide. Inside the bag were boulders of varying sizes. By adding only one selected boulder to the bag, the tree could be lifted with relative ease and, once passed, could be lowered down once again. The rope was nicely concealed behind the turn in the track and the heavy branches. For further security, the tree could be fixed in position from either side by the insertion of a single long flat rock that acted like a bolt. Added to this was the fact of the incline; to approach it from the down side was steep, very steep, and attempting to move the tree or pass it would be almost impossible if one was not aware of the magic rock key.

Rightly, she was very proud of her endeavours but of course could only let selected people into the secrets of her mechanics, and Knap was indeed the only one.

At times, she would sit and stare at her creation with much pleasure and pride, while conjuring improvements, and would then lie in her bed adjusting every detail until she decided the idea was ready to be implemented.

Garr, with Monster at heel, led Knap upon one of her favourite walks, as she liked to call them. Occasionally stopping to check snares, pits, and other types of traps, always assisted by the enthusiastic Monster by her side, she took Knap down towards the small river that ran throughout the valley; it was here she was able to catch the majority of her meals. Excluding her home, this was Garr's favourite place. During some winters this meandering river turned into a dangerous waterway of considerable depth or solid ice and, yet, at the height of some summers it could contract into a stream. Even then, the small ponds and lakes remained, always allowing her to catch fish and other fresh water delights.

She had created a small, dammed pond. The river water was fast moving at this point due to a narrowing bend. The entrance to her pond was within a little riverside bay around which the water swirled. At that entrance, where it separated from the river, was a kind of sluice gate, which could be removed when required, and, situated within the actual entrance, she had installed a basket weaved funnel, surrounded and supported with stones beneath and dammed over at ground level forming a bridge. Once an unfortunate fish had been washed into it, or chosen unwittingly to enter, there was little to no hope of escape even when the gate was up.

She took from it only what was needed. Some fish had been captive for weeks; one unfortunate carp that had mysteriously appeared within her pool had now been there for six months and was now double its original size. Others swam round and round or lay mournfully at the bottom, awaiting their inevitable fate.

Garr expertly gathered half a dozen unfortunates, which she intended to preserve by smoke or alternatively use for tomorrow's breakfast. Monster looked on keenly, awaiting a possible treat that did not appear. He clearly understood that anticipation was part of a dog's duty. To that call of instinct, he would always adhere.

Her two main methods of preserving her meats were by smoking or placing them deep into her salt chest; vegetables and fruit were kept in containers, in either brine or syrup. When the weather was favourable, sun drying was a good alternative but, of course, nothing beat fresh produce, but that was no easy option and committed her to hunting, gathering, or tending her small vegetable patches on a daily basis.

She had located fruit and nut trees and endeavoured to isolate them from the eyes of others by camouflage. Overall, she had a good diet; it was obviously seasonal in the main, but that she enjoyed.

The two friends wandered a little further along the riverbank, then moved upwards and away from the river once more through a lightly wooded area.

"Arr, hold on, Knap, I needed to grab some nuts from the river. Give me five minutes and I'll be back."

"Okay, I'll be on the top of the ridge."

"Here, take these, but be very careful with them." She handed over one of her prized possessions—a pair of binoculars.

"Wow, Garr, I didn't know you had these. They're incredible—wish I had a pair. Don't worry. I'll treat them like a salt mountain."

In five minutes, Garr had run back down to the riverbank, thrown herself down flat and fished around with one arm. Having made her collection, she was soon back at the top of the ridge once again without even a heavy breath. With Monster bounding by her side, she looked around for Knap, her backpack dripping river water from the fish and large amount of blanched nuts that she had been processing in the river for well over a week.

He must have wandered along the ridge a little, thought Garr, looking in all directions.

Further along the ridge, she found Knap, safe and sound, contemplating the magnificent views over the plain and valley and generally playing with the binoculars. They both sat for a while and spoke of the Big Gathering to which they would all be going and how things around them generally appeared to be changing. They mused, or rather Knap did, about why Garr hadn't found herself a man for company. They contemplated the weather and oncoming winter period. Eventually, they spoke again of the warriors and how such villains could be brought to justice or, alternatively, into order and harmony. They had few real detailed answers, only the hope that one day a common desire for a set of rules would exist and the will amongst folk could be found which could allow peace and security for all. With their chosen lifestyles, it was almost impossible to see such things happening. They were all too isolated and intent on survival.

Their chatter was abruptly halted by the raising of Garr's hand.

Stillness fell over the small gathering. Then Garr slowly pointed towards a small buck standing alone some fifty metres off.

It was a truly beautiful vision, standing there downwind with head raised among the brilliant rays of sunlight penetrating through the canopy. Its light fawn coat turned to gold, while all around endless woodland birds sung and butterflies fluttered.

Monster knew the routine well and dropped down on his belly amongst the bracken, head alert and awaiting an instruction.

Garr crawled on her belly two metres to gather her bow, then with care and in a well-practised manoeuvre, loaded an arrow and gently raised her body until it was in a kneeling position. She thought again, realising it was too long a shot for a certain kill. Dropping down once again on her belly, together with Monster, she crawled forward. Halfway to the buck, she once again prepared her shot—there would probably be only one chance.

Her heart rate had increased, as had Knap's as he viewed the developing scene before him.

Luckily upwind of the buck, she slowly drew back the arrow while taking an instinctive aim and then steadied herself for a second before letting fly the deadly bolt.

In a moment of slow motion, the arrow flew, arcing slightly towards its victim. The spirit of the forest appeared to stand stock still, sensing the imminent sacrifice. The arrow entered the buck at the rib cage; although in reality there was no sound, they heard a thud as the arrow connected with the deer and a parallel pain entered their own souls.

Energy was released, and slow motion suddenly changed to fast forward.

A mournful grunt was heard, one of shock and pain as the creature staggered in all directions trying desperately to stay upright. Its great eyes flashed helplessly in all directions. After tossing and shaking its head rapidly, it slowly fell to the ground.

Garr, with the bow at her side, slowly straightened herself, followed by Knap.

Monster was up and awaiting instruction to collect, yet before the command was given the heroic buck had staggered back to its feet. Vainly and sadly, it attempted its escape, but its legs would no longer do its bidding. A rear leg was shaking violently, uncontrollably, and then once again the fragile front legs collapsed as bellows echoed through the woodland, silencing a thousand birdsongs and insect calls.

With incredible instinctive courage, the buck once again began to push its body into the full and upright position. It urinated, now totally out of control of its bodily functions, then suddenly and without ceremony it was smashed to the bracken by forty-five kilos of pouncing mastiff. Teeth now dug deeper into his throat, suffocating, closing, finishing.

Stillness again surrounded the sorrowful scene.

Garr walked over to the creature, where Monster still lay with a firm and deadly grip upon the creature's throat; she knelt and stroked the creature in a gesture of respect, its spirit floated away amongst saplings and woodland flowers, and then birdsong slowly filled the air once more. First one, then another, until the small area of woodland was once again a riot of choruses.

The dead buck was hoisted to hang from a low bough and, within fifteen minutes, its innards were gone and buried. Normally, all would be used, but, with guests in camp, time was limited. The carcass was cut down, trussed, and laid over Knap's shoulder for transporting back to camp.

Now they moved with extra caution for upon this land there was many creatures interested in fresh meat.

They walked in silence for some time; here, in this lifestyle, respect and thanks to Mother Nature were everything.

As Garr and Knap made their way back towards the cave, their path took them along the edge of the plain, where there stood a large rusted tower upon a small rise. Knap badly needed to rest, for as strong as he was, the carcass was a considerable weight for him.

After five minutes, he was recharged and decided to scale the structure. Forty-five feet from the ground, he could stretch his eyes and play yet again with Garr's binoculars. He looked along the length of the valley and over much of the plain. It was a distinctive view he was familiar with but on a different scale. It contained just about everything in nature that one would choose to rest one's eyes upon.

The craggy rocks along the northern flank, where Garr lived, were so different to the southern side of the plain where rocks grew sure and slowly into mountains footed with that thick and lush woodland. Those foothills ultimately merged into mountains which, through the winter, wore thick white caps. The plain between was not flat but interspersed with small outcrops of treed rocky areas and the river with small brooks adjoining. Way in the distance, Knap could see the edges of Dartell, a fortified town, probably the largest along the full length of the valley. Garr always chose not to look that far and particularly in that direction; it gave her no pleasure.

"There's a lot of smoke above that place," shouted down Knap.

There was a small pause prior to Garr answering.

"I don't want to know anything about it. I hate the place, Knap."

"As a very clever young woman, Garr, you should. I don't need to tell you that."

"I have my reasons, Knap. Painful reasons."

She thought for a moment and then looked back up at Knap high above her.

"Perhaps one day I will take a trip there again, possibly you can come with me. I wouldn't want to go on my own—I don't think I could do that."

"You're on, Garr. I'd be interested to see what is happening there these days." Knap now paused for a moment.

"Now, after thinking about it, I feel nervous, but we should mix more often with other groups—the town folk, the wanderers. We should mix more freely and exchange ideas. It's the only way the things we spoke of earlier will ever progress, Garr, you know that."

"I know you're right, Knap. This little world we live in needs some serious work done on it. I like where I live. It is beautiful around here, but life could be a lot better for everybody with the sharing of ideas. In fact, I've been thinking through many issues of recent times, my life as it is, and where it's going. If we have the opportunity while you are at my place, I'd like to share some thoughts and ideas with you. Apart from that, I know one can't live like this forever. It's tough; really tough at times, and alone I will lose the battle."

Life in Dartell

Within Dartell, around three thousand soles eked out an existence. They were safe through numbers and had the facilities established for just about all they needed.

People like Clark, together with his family, lived in the smallest of areas. In the winter, it was not cold, and, in the summer, it wasn't too hot.

Food was issued each day for the following twenty-four hours.

Everybody worked and everybody had to contribute.

Each had a quota allocated to them dependent upon age, sex, health, and work undertaken. It was a fair but restrictive and over-complicated society.

All inhabitants were used to queuing, waiting, or appearing on queue, so to speak; no argument expected, none allowed.

For the hill folk, that was not living.

Nonetheless, it appeared to offer a reasonable and secure way of life, and, for those born to it, it was hard to impossible for them to visualise living as the hill folk or nomads did—an unreliable and insecure life with all the many hardships it involved.

In Dartell, there were daily chores to be undertaken, as with any existence, and some individuals flipped from one occupation to another once consent had been granted or orders issued by the council. Others, or indeed all, were allocated tasks aimed at any experience, talent, or physical abilities they had.

The rules applied to every age and both sexes alike.

The young worked hard, although they were given regular tuition on basic academic and trading skills unless trained in warrior duties.

Illness was their biggest problem. If you could not carry out your task, the council gave you a health pass and, while unable to work normally, all your time was spent at the health centre. It seemed to work but it was the biggest area of dispute amongst the community.

Yet, it all seemed to work. Nobody owned anything, everybody owned everything, and the council members were changed yearly by selection.

Clark had been a council member twice before; he was respected for his fairness and decision-making abilities. At the time, he wasn't one and spent his time as instructed, tending the community fields and carrying out administrative work.

All had been comfortable within the community for over two years; that is, excluding the odd crime. And even crimes had never caused any dissent among the council or community; suspects were tried fairly, and, if found guilty, the punishment was either death or rejection. In both cases, they were never to return to Dartell.

At the end of a long day in the fields, Clark sat around a small fire while his two partners rushed around in their second room cooking a meal over a small open fire.

The conversation flowed freely between the three family members. The normal things of life were discussed, along with odd jokes and jibbing.

In this home, it was usually meal then bed, as their days started early. Occasionally, there would be some kind of activity at the community centre, which gave a welcome change to the routine.

Clark began to relax, and, as he did, his head started to nod and jerk as he fought off the inclination to sleep. The small child that lived nearby was visiting and gave him no mércy, pulling at his sleeves, asking endless questions. Clark could not refuse to help; he only wished that he had been blessed with a child of his own.

His meal arrived; vegetable stew was it normally, and on occasion, a little meat was added. He forced himself back into an awakened state and loaded the child's bowl with hot and steaming vegetable stew accompanied with hunks of flat bread. It smelt good and was consumed eagerly by the hungry group.

Their meal complete and the child dispatched, it only took a few minutes before all were in bed and falling into peaceful slumber.

What Clark and the others didn't know was that out in the fields where they had been toiling, enemies now gathered; wild ones, nomads; a different culture completely to their own. Rape, plunder, and death meant little to them; it was their way. They had their own sense of honour, their own rules.

There were crops to be gathered, stolen, and, more importantly, tethered livestock just waiting to be led away. Although not the norm, after such a long period of peace in Dartell, even the committee had begun to take its security for granted.

The warriors of Dartell were called upon by the night guards and they gathered. They left the township in a long single column under the walls, which linked all the ancient properties. They travelled through great pipes that had once served other purposes and entered covered trenches that ran all around the fields where they toiled.

It was a long line of warriors armed with bows and swords, and armoured with heavy leather chest covers and helmets. They moved silently, knowing exactly what they were about, generating the courage and the detachment for battle. By nature, theirs was a slow moving culture, in which they were accustomed to queuing, shuffling, and obeying the rulers, but this way of life also bred a simple efficiency.

The blue-white moon was conveniently full, determining their plan of attack.

The long line of warriors divided several times within the trenches before reaching their pre-allocated positions.

Quietly, sections of the trench cover were lifted and moved upon the grass banks that ran parallel with them. This allowed them to access and view their enemies from a number of positions.

They prepared and readied themselves. The order was given and arrows began to fly into the night; dozens of deadly silver darts flew towards those enemies from one side and then another.

Arrow heads twinkled like fireflies with a deadly whoosh and an awesome sting.

Surprised heads turned in the stark moonlight to search from whence they were being attacked.

In shock and panic, they began to flee, still pulling behind them the stolen cattle together with sacks of other valuable booty from the fields.

In that instant, it was a difficult decision for them: drop the booty or save their souls.

The booty began to be dropped; cattle scattered.

They fled away from the arrows that were reducing their number only to meet a new and unexpected onslaught from the opposite direction.

There was no escape; this was the plan. No one should ever be able to reveal their defences, their security.

Ultimately trapped in an impossible position, the remaining turned to fight, but the arrows were endless.

From still further positions, the warriors of Dartell climbed from the trenches, now blocking all routes of escape.

Maybe the warriors of Dartell were not great athletes, or even great warriors individually when compared against others, but they were as one in body and spirit—one large body of well-rehearsed and determined people.

But one of their foes was allowed to run the gauntlet through the warriors of Dartell. He was the messenger. He would be allowed to escape with his life so he could deliver the message that Dartell was not a place to plunder ever again. This marauding tribe of nomads would select easier targets in the future.

Many of them lay dead, many badly wounded. Some crawled hopelessly, others groaned with their pain whilst feeling their lifeblood drain away.

That night, prior to the moon being replaced by the sun, all would be slaughtered and stripped of any valuables and weapons. Their naked and bloody bodies would be dumped in piles at each of the entrance gates of Dartell, displaying and clearly warning any others of the risks involved in attempting to attack their world. Over the course of the following days some heads would be removed, with bodies delivered to pits far away. Those heads were smashed upon stakes and displayed alongside the tracks leading to town.

It was an awesome message, marketing the resolve of Dartell to retain its security and way of life to visitors, residents, and foe alike.

Clark awoke at around six the following morning; stretched, and started his day. Later that day, he was of course told of the event that took place overnight.

The council called him to attend a council meeting.

He was, after all, the main author of many of the community plans and rules of recent years. Never a dictator, he had proposed, suggested, and explained his thinking, and now a review was called for, so he had to be in attendance to guide and advise.

Most members within the community knew of his value and, although it went against so much of their thinking, he was an established leader who often went against so many of their primitive inclinations, adding wisdom and civility to this restricted society.

Physical Comforts

Garr and Knap wandered their way back towards the cave in relevant silence. They had been gone longer then Garr had intended.

Monster loved their wanderings; he would have been quite happy to stay out for days, as they often did. He zigzagged his way ahead, smelling and checking, occasionally raising his head to visually double-check his other senses, then looking back for Garr, ensuring her safety and wellbeing.

As such a young dog, he was simply amazing. He was almost human in his understanding and communication with Garr and, although there were larger creatures that lived within this world, with sharper and longer claws and fangs, his aggression and pack instincts born and bonded via Garr already made him the ideal companion. Only time would tell whether he would remain bonded or eventually drift into the world of wandering packs.

As the three approached the cave, they shouted ahead and were pleased to find that all was safe, fires were burning merrily, and most importantly, food was ready for consumption. The two women were wrapped appropriately, sitting at the fireside deep in chatter; it was a good and comforting sight.

Bonding reconfirmed between all, Garr lowered a large leg joint from the cave ceiling and threw it to Monster, who caught it effortlessly in his gigantic mouth and waddled off to his favourite position to enjoy a well-earned supper.

The women had obviously spent time sweeping and tidying for Garr. So much so that Garr couldn't remember the last time she had seen her abode look so organised. She stood in amazement with hands on hips looking and re-looking, a little concerned that items may have been moved into unknown locations but thankful and impressed by their effort.

"Have you guys had a good time out in the wilderness? It certainly looks successful. What are you going to do with that, Garr?"

"Tonight I'll just hoist it up in the ceiling funnel and let it smoke and dry. Tomorrow we can remove the legs and I'll salt them. The rest can be on the spit all day, and by tomorrow evening we can feast to our hearts content. Oh yes, and fish for breakfast. Does that sound good to you?"

Everyone smiled at the thought of indulging in so much meat.

They all ate around the fire as the sun completed its effort for the day. Garr attended to the fires for the last time, rinsed her mouth and followed the others inside the cave, then called Monster to her side.

"Sala, you better bunk in with me—is that ok? Knap, you know where you and Mara are. I checked it over yesterday and everything is comfy for you."

Just beyond Garr's risen bed area was a lower flat area where Garr bedded any rare guests. It was always wise to check out the heather and pine branch bedding as creepy crawlies could become your companions—sometimes something larger, but that was generally when they were in the change of seasons or extreme weather conditions came to visit.

Garr, who normally slept naked, retained one of her of wraps and Sala, following her lead, did likewise. Both cuddled down into the deep comfort of heather and lavender and lay quietly for a while. The aroma of lavender mingled with the smell of wood smoke and dampness acted quickly upon the senses, and soon Garr reached to her side and blew out the candle, patted Monster who lay at her side, and closed her eyes.

"Goodnight, Sala."

"Night, Garr."

For some time both women lay warm and comfortable, listening to the noises of the night; nearer to hand was the snoring of Knap and Monster.

A wind had suddenly kicked up and the noise of it travelling over the rock face was considerable and yet peaceful; similar to that of waves to-ing and fro-ing upon the shore, sliding over a million pebbles.

As sleep began to wash over the two women, they naturally fell towards the centre area of the bed. The extra warmth this offered was welcome; it was not necessary, but the nature of the warmth was different. Neither was accustomed to sleeping so close to another; this was the heat of a person, experienced via skin and flesh. It felt good, even special.

Both were forced into an awareness of one another, and neither pulled back from the now electric feeling they experienced.

Nevertheless, slumber still crept further into their beings, and they fell into the darkness and floated away.

Sometime in the middle of the night, Garr woke a little. She stretched out a hand, touched Monster's warm mass, and then turned over.

Garr's arm reached across and embraced Sala's body; she cuddled back towards Garr, and they lay there spooning for some time.

Garr found her hand upon the softness of Sala's stomach under the loose garment; it was erotic and irresistible. Her thumb stroked the skin, touching also the exquisite softness of a breast.

Sala moved instinctively a little, allowing m?
her garment. Her hand reached backwards and
leg and squeezed it gently.

Garr nestled her face in close amongst Sala's neck and
hair. The smell was wonderful. She was aroused and breathing
heavier.

This position changed little for some time. Both were held
captive to the moment; it was erotic and sensual. Neither woman
was sure of their feelings or what to do next.

Then, without realising, Garr found her hand between Sala's
thighs, a single finger running slowly amongst her thick bush
of pubic hair then moving her fingers around slowly, touching,
stroking. Her fingers ran deep through the tangled cluster.
Almost without thought, her other hand slid under Sala and
began to stroke her soft upper thigh, whilst her buttocks nestled
in closer causing sensations deep within.

Sala, hardly moving but making small adjustments, welcomed
the exploring hands, breathing deeply and slowly, full of intensity
and nervousness.

Rubbing and stroking, Garr's' fingers travelled deeper. Sala's
legs parted and fingers ran down the moist lips of her vagina,
causing her to shudder.

Garr was surprised by the amount of wetness she found
there; smooth, warm, thick wetness.

She noticed again how thick and youthful her pubic hair was
and pulled at it gently.

She couldn't have stopped now, even if some wild creature
had entered her cave.

All inhibitions abandoned, Sala half turned towards Garr;
they kissed slowly, long and soft kisses—kisses which released
such feelings that they took over all else. They couldn't stop
kissing, but hands and hearts were on automatic as each caressed

47

the other. The kisses continued, on and on; arms holding and possessing, hands and fingers discovering.

The thick juices were spread between the others' legs, between their buttocks; fingers entered, withdrew and re-entered; stroking endlessly.

Noises belonging to feelings were reluctantly muffled; gentle groans were lost to the night.

Exhausted, happy, and satisfied, both gave way to slumber once more. The morning would be different for both of them, possibly the world.

Monster and Knap snored on, unaware that indulgence and necessity had changed something for Garr and for Sala, possibly now neither would ever feel lonely again. The expressions of love, of desire, of belonging, were a vital experience for all *homo sapiens*, even in this strange world where they existed.

The Search Continues

Nic and Sarina stretched simultaneously as light streamed in through a gap in the wooden shutters.

It was cold and the fire had gone out.

It had been a torturous time for both Nic and Sarina. Their moods fluctuated from deep depression to false cheer, both attempting to bolster the other on particularly difficult days. On other days, their conversation went around and around in ever decreasing and depressing circles of *why*, *how* and *where*. Sarina occasionally took to sitting upon a chair all day in silence, holding something belonging to her boys. Often, on these days, she would be accompanied by others of the community, all of them sharing the heartbreak of the lost children, a treasure shared by them all and a gift they all indulged in.

On this particular morning, there seemed to be something different in the air. Possibly it was misguided optimism, but it was good to wake with these feelings for a change, and Nic hoped that Sarina also felt this way.

Nic, using his optimism, tried feigning sleep, but Sarina was on to his ploy. She cleverly snuggled down close to him, displaying affection, seducing him into her trap built out of similar feelings. Of course, for a moment it worked.

With one almighty burst of energy, she thrust against him, causing him to roll clean from the bed.

Nic was her equal now, and, as he tumbled, he grabbed at the bundle of wraps that made up their bed covering and turned them around himself. She was tumbled, exposed and cold. Initially Nic was wrapped within his own trap. He knew Sarina well, therefore he needed to free himself rapidly, or she, without doubt, would be following through with further pranks. She assessed the situation rapidly. "Nicky, darling please, I'm sorry, pretty, pretty sorry—honestly."

They both laughed a rare laugh, and then, as suddenly, the day began in earnest and the mood reverted to seriousness, worry, and heartache.

Nic, with reluctance, slowly threw the covers back over Sarina, then bent and kissed her affectionately on the forehead.

"I'll get the fire going, Sar, you troublesome little female."

It was now almost impossible to maintain and display the initial feelings of lightness and optimism that the morning had given them for but a moment.

Their souls were back into seriousness. The burden of their lost children was, as usual, boring itself through both their hearts and the hearts of the other villagers, making them heavier with every passing second. It would be yet another difficult day to endure for all in Prallian.

Around the hilltop village, there had been little peace or comfort since the big battle.

All hearts ached as they mourned the dead and missing.

The burials had been many, the searching and pain long. They all understood it would take many more months or even years before Prallian was once again a happy place. Beyond everything, the children were the treasure of the village; their pride, their joy.

It was not long before Nic had set forth once more upon his constant searching. He had another idea where to search. Sarina would again try to fill her time with comforting others.

The older members at the village who had lost partners were now lost souls.

No matter what remedies had been created to allow them all to move forward, they seemed to fail, and yet the situation was generating many new questions about the rules that applied within their community. Without group discussion, feelings and actions were beginning to change. The losses were a kind of antidote to that familiar resistance to change. Circumstances were allowing settled and contained re-adjustment.

Nic stood at the brow of the hillside track. He truthfully had no ideas left. His head hung downwards for a moment as he considered again if he should express his doubts and thoughts to Sarina. In reality, he knew he could not take away the hope she had—the hope she hung on to desperately. Or did she also have other less optimistic thoughts? Yes, of course she did; she was a bright, practical, sensible woman, but her pretence, her hideaway, was all that she held on to these days.

He let out a long and heavy sigh, then set forward yet again, off track, up and over many hilltops. He wasn't concentrating on the possibilities around him. He had walked many long journeys to other communities, asking the questions, looking for clues, all to no avail.

He then stopped once again to subdue the despair that constantly resurged.

He ate some food and took a mouthful of water.

It was a rocky and sterile terrain he found himself in, yet a positive feeling suddenly began to generate from nowhere, pumping and flowing through him. With new heart, he gathered his belongings and moved towards an area where the rocky formations appeared to promise the possibilities of caves.

It was tough climbing over the loose rock. Steep inclines and surface water trickled over yellow lichen and green moss-covered surfaces. A number of times Nic stumbled, knocking knees and knuckles. Then before him was a level area containing, as he had thought, the openings of many a cave. It was an interesting formation and for a moment, he stood in wonderment, yet apprehensive of what lurked within.

He was surprised how despair and wonderment could sit together so closely. Possibly this was the formula for hope, or was hope simply blind belief? He wasn't sure.

Nic returned to his task of checking the entrances for any signs of the boys. He cupped his hands and called down each opening, waiting for the echoes to diminish before shouting a second or third time. He entered the large caves but little of importance was to be found. There were signs that at some distant point in history people had occupied these caves, maybe temporary or permanently, who could tell, but there were no signs of recent lodgers.

Dark shadows started to descend over his mind once again. He stood upon the flat area and found himself once again giving a deep, mournful sigh.

He started to make his way around the rise in the cliff. There appeared to be a track running along the front of the cave entrances. This left the flat ground before the caves and then clung to the rock face and disappeared from view. Possibly a goat track, he thought. At certain points, it was necessary to hold to the damp cliff face due to its narrowness, which together with the loose rock underfoot made it treacherous. The rock face now plunged to a considerable depth and the view made Nic feel uncomfortable. He continued to edge his way forward, now sweating continually, for what must have been two-hundred metres. He thought it might never end. Eventually, it began to widen and slowly blend into regular terrain. And there it was—a small piece of cloth, a recognisable piece of cloth. It beggared belief that here upon an almost unreachable track in this most inclement of weathers was a sign of his beloved children.

Before he could think it through properly, it was necessary to sit and sob his relief. Holding the small piece of fabric, which was the remains of Jac's cuddle cloth, the tears ran down his face whilst he passed audible sobs. Jac had been inseparable from this relic of his babyhood. He would be struggling without it; somewhere he would be struggling badly, and this was the most wonderful news.

Suddenly no doubts clouded his mind and his spirit flew high to the heavens. Standing now amongst the changing weather of torrents of rain and gusting winds, he raised his arms and shouted his thanks until his throat was hoarse and his undergarments soaked.

Back in Prallian, Sarina worked on, filling her mind with things of the moment to block out her loneliness and heartache. She was an intuitive person, but time and sadness had dulled those senses.

She began to be concerned for Nic, as the night was drawing in—an awful night which hid the surrounding hilltops. She wouldn't worry, she decided, and turned her attention back to the work of caring for the elderly ones with whom she now spent her time, helping them to recover before unpleasant decisions would have to be made about their future in this tough community.

After the battle for Prallian, the council had agreed to maintain a building to be occupied with the elderly. In particular, those who had lost a partner would now have company and care when needed. This was a drastic change in the community's rules and outlook. It placed upon all members a new and heavy burden, which many doubted could or should be maintained.

The evening turned to night and Nic had not returned.

There, now alone in her home, which had once been so happy and full of life, Sarina loaded the fire high and pulled the covers up tightly around herself. The whole night was a restless and cold experience with nightmarish visions that circled around and around within her mind.

'Please come over the bridge. I've been waiting and waiting so very long. Where did you get to? Has there been any sign of the boys? You must be soaked in this mist, Nic, and completely exhausted.

'Nic, Nic, is that you darling?

'What is that over your shoulders, Nic? Is that the children, Nic? Are they well and happy, Nic?

'I can't cross this silly old bridge, darling, it scares me, you must come to me, come to me, come to me.'

The nightmare went around and around, annoying, frustrating, and threatening in a dark and sinister way. She couldn't escape and she couldn't understand.

'I suddenly can't see you properly now, Nic, and I can't hear you either. Don't go away from me, please bring the children back to me, come towards me.

'Look, the mist is blowing away now, darling, and look, the sun is beginning to shine through. Are those people your friends standing either side, Nicholas?

'Look, Nic, who are they, who are they, who are they, who are they?

'Please don't turn away, Nicolas, you're so close.

'Please don't walk away from me, darling.

'NO! Please come here, towards me. Please!'

The intensity increased, and she was aware of herself jerking and turning where she lay. She was perspiring now. Uncomfortable shivers travelled continuously up her back as the nightmare grew into new dimensions.

'BRING ME MY FUCKING CHILDREN, YOU BASTARD, FUCKING FUCKER! COME HERE!

'Please sweetheart. Come across the bridge my dearest, my dearest, my dearest.

'Please come over the bridge, I've been waiting and waiting so very, so very long, where did you go to, has there been any sign of our children?

'Look, you must be soaked in this mist, Nic and so completely, completely exhausted. Nic, Nic, Nic.'

Not a lot of sleep was experienced. When eventually the light broke through the shutters, it was cold and steely, mean light that reflected her inner feelings, her frustration, and her pain. She lay there for an eternity, shivering, awaiting a positive feeling to flow through her thoughts and her heart.

The Journey to Dartell

Garr awoke with a great stretch. Monster nestled his head in under the covers. Garr rushed to relieve herself. She was naked, which instantly drove her mind back to Sala and the night's closeness.

All her guests appeared to be still deep in slumber, which was convenient and allowed her to adjust her thoughts. Standing at the cave entrance, she stretched fully while admiring a splendid early blue sky. She loved the view across the valley towards the far off mountains, and she often wondered how she would ever be able to live without such a view.

Her lean and athletic body was completely tanned and weathered; her dark blond hair hung down to the middle of her back. The only real signs anybody could see of her lifestyle were the skin and broken nails that were on her hands and lower legs—they were covered with bruises and cuts; her feet, although straight-toed, needed more care. The boots she ran and lived in were once properly constructed, but over time they had been repaired so often with leather sewing and wrap that, in reality, they barely did the job any longer. She badly needed new waterproof footwear that reached to the knees and could be turned down when need be, with soles that gripped and protected her feet. It was but a momentary dream at the end of which she imagined two pairs, one in use and the other hung to dry.

She attended to the fires, and, in no time, both had responded correctly, bringing her attention to the need for restocking her enormous wood store. This took so much of her time, particularly as the seasons moved towards colder and wetter.

Sala was first to join her at the cave entrance. There was no look of reproach or guilt, for she too was naked, her thick and long black hair a mass of tangles.

Her first act of that morning was to wrap her arms around Garr. She was shorter than her idol and less athletic in build. The arms around Garr spoke a million words for both women. Garr responded; it was a wonderful good morning greeting. For both, life had reached a new spring, a new happiness. Closeness was hard to find and wherever it was found, it was treasured.

Soon enough, the site was busy with activity. Monster contributed by gnawing once again at the remains of last night's bone.

Once again, all four of them sat around the fire drinking and making small talk, Sala sitting alongside Garr.

"I must check some traps today. I'm sorry about all this business. I also have to collect wood. Could you possibly help with that one?"

"You just tell us what needs doing, Garr. We're not here for a laze around my friend."

"Okay, thanks, Knap. Well, first, one pair of new boots while I check out the traps, and, if you don't mind, Sal and Mara, could you collect some wood for us?"

"As it just so happens, young woman, you're talking to the right person when it comes to boots and leather work."

"That is right, Garr. Our man here is quite the master when it comes to leather. Seriously, let him take some measurements and you'll be amazed with what can be done by the time you get back here."

"Really, I was only joking. I didn't really mean—"

"Garr, stop right there. Did you say boots—yes, you did. So boots there will be."

"Knap, this is so wonderful." She raised herself and flung her arms around him, then commenced a small jig of excitement.

Garr left the cave with Monster at heel.

She returned to camp five minutes later to sit and spread out her long legs and remove her old boots.

Neither Knap nor Garr said a word, then both broke the silence and fell about with laughter. Measurements and imprints were taken, and Garr once again made her way from the cave, still holding a broad smile upon her face, a leather back pack slung to her spine with all she needed for the day's activities. She was walking into a world that she loved, fearlessly and competently.

"Good hunting, Garr, see you in a few hours."

Without turning, Garr raised a long waving arm which held her bow and disappeared from view.

She fared well. Fish was waiting when Garr returned. Mara, with the assistance of Knap, had placed yesterday's catch upon the spit. The sides of the fire had been built into small walls, earth piled against them, old hide soaked and laid over to create a slow oven.

Sala had excelled at the wood collection, and Garr's fire supplies were growing well. To the rear of the internal cooking area was a cavernous space slowly filling with drying timber? Garr knew from experience the enormous amount of timber one could consume, particularly if the winter period proved to be one of ice and snowstorms. She had learnt to live within the smallest area, where timbers were wedged from ceiling to floor and then woven with any flexible materials she could locate, stuffed with dried bracken, heathers and palm leaves, and finally draped with skins.

Upon Garr's return, Sala unashamedly gave her the warmest of return greetings.

As they talked that evening, arrangements were made between Knap and Garr to visit Dartell. They planned a two-day trek, there and back, one night at Dartell, maybe two.

Sala fancied the trip, but Knap would not leave Mara alone.

"That's not wise, Sala. What do you think, Garr?"

"I'd love to say, let's all go, but it's a serious trek. What about drawing straws?"

"No, no, you go with Dad, Garr. There will be other opportunities, so I will stay with Mum. That makes good sense really, it's okay."

Both women felt regret in the decision, but common sense had to prevail. They both understood that above any personal desires or wishes was security and survival.

That evening, the travellers packed the essentials. Tomorrow, they would be gone at sunup. Monster would stay at the cave, it was agreed.

The only regret being, as yet, the new boots were not complete, but Knap had achieved a great deal more than was expected, and it was clear already that these were going to be the best of footwear.

The night was spent in ecstasy, warmth, and comfort. The rediscovered delights of closeness; of being able to share oneself totally now added a further dimension to both Sala and Garr's existence.

Family and friendship was always important, but the freedom and wonder of sharing oneself extended one's spirit and soul, allowed one to fly.

Speaking in low tones, they agreed that night that Sala would stay on when it came time for Knap and Mara to return to their own place.

"Let's not expect too much, Sala, we'll go slowly."

"Yes, I agree. We can see where we are by the time we all meet up for the Big Gathering—yes, that's the right thing to do."

Moreover, with that decided they both slept a peaceful sleep, contented.

As per the plan, Knap and Garr were striding forward at dawn. The two other women were still wrapped up cosy, and Monster was wandering the entrance of the cave somewhat agitated by the instruction to stay, which contradicted all his instincts, and yet once again he accepted his instruction, albeit reluctantly.

At this time of the day, there wasn't a requirement for conversation. They walked in single file, Garr out front, staff swinging to offset her stride. They followed vaguely trodden paths, which were occasionally crossed by others. After an hour or so of dedicated walking, they stopped to eat and drink a little. Sitting on wayside boulders, admiring the surrounding landscape, they watched as a small herd of deer passed their way.

A host of green finches darted over the coarse grasses and between the trees like a swarm of bees. Two wagtails came to join them, ducking their heads and twitching their tails as they darted hither and nether upon the track and were rewarded with crumbs.

The sun still shone weakly through a few whispery white clouds.

If the sun had been stronger, their walk would not have been so invigorating, particularly for Knap who was already showing signs of falling behind a little. Garr discretely decided to adjust her pace.

They continued their journey, crossing many a small and cool stream that tumbled onward to the main river to which they were generally aiming.

At one point, a small herd of cattle were gathered to drink at the stream's edge. It was a strange mixture of colours, mainly browns with patches of white and black. Garr and Knap stopped to watch them from a distance for a few pleasurable moments. Amongst their number were two young bullocks jostling with one another.

Suddenly they stopped their play fight. Inquisitive by nature, something had caught their attention in the shrubbery. Garr and Knap strained to capture their vision but initially could see nothing. Then they managed to focus upon the mystery; it was a large cat of some kind, orange in colour with markings that wrapped it in a magical coat of camouflage.

Garr had seen such creatures a couple of times before; they were secretive and rare but earned respect. Stories were abundant of their sudden turn of speed and power, let alone their ability to take down a child or man.

It wasn't only these large cats one needed to be aware of, but there were bears and packs of wild and strangely coloured dog, all of which warranted caution and deserved respect.

They continued to watch the scene unfold before them, full of intrigue and anticipation. The large cat appeared to have selected its meal, a small heifer standing alongside its unaware mother. The two young bullocks wandered towards the crouching creature, the agitation clear to see in its twitching tail and general body language. Suddenly, like a spear being released, it leapt from its cover towards the smallest beast, and the bullocks scattered in confusion causing the small herd to do likewise. The parent, now panic-stricken, turned back towards the scene in a desperate effort of protection. The cat was upon the young creature, claws gripping and swinging its weight, its mouth searching for that suffocating hold.

The heroic parent charged into the mournful scene issuing bellows of intent. It had fortune on its side as a timely sweep of the head sent the cat flying in a summersault into the edge of the stream.

The scowling cat, now unsure of its powers, crouched for a second, and then, upon reflection, decided to look elsewhere, while knowing that this wasn't supposed to be the outcome.

The scene returned quickly to a riverside paradise. Knap and Garr both took deep breaths and walked on.

The terrain through which they travelled was fairly level, now moving along a more definable track, which loosely followed the small river running through the valley that in turn was joined by those numerous small streams. At places along the edge of the river and higher up amongst the rocks or raised land, trees grew in clusters, sometimes thick and intermingled with climbers and vines.

They walked through rocky areas, where at times great smooth and black rocks lay half exposed from the flat earth around it, like sleeping whales waiting for the return of the tide; rust and sand-coloured rock burst from the ground and rose to a great height like stone monsters.

As the sun burnt away the last whispers of cloud, the going become slower, and the rocks doubled their colour range as deep shadows and highlights were created. By early afternoon, the largest part of the journey was behind them, and the two comrades decided upon a second pause while the sun appeared at its strongest.

Under the shade of an ancient yew, they lay side by side, looking down mesmerised at the flowing water. Then they spent some time viewing the great tree above them, looking for convenient timbers that one day could be converted into something of a different value.

Knap had been performing better as the journey had continued, and the necessity of slowing the pace had been reduced. Overall, they were used to physical output; if Garr had been travelling alone, no doubt the journey would have maintained a steady pace. Knap reflected how once he too would have done likewise; it only seemed but a few years ago.

Now sitting and talking of serious things whilst working their way through the meat and fruit they had brought with them, a gentle breeze grew to the beckoning of the falling temperature upon the riverbank.

Without a change or pause or facial expression, Knap spoke out of sync with the flow of the conversation.

"Don't move your head, Garr, but I think we have visitors." He paused for a moment to allow time for his message to be absorbed. "There appears to be two bodies behind the bushes to your far left."

Garr, without overreacting, gathered herself and slowly made adjustments to her position in readiness for whatever came her way. Knap had already adjusted the position of his staff and withdrawn his knife discreetly.

"When I say, Knap, we'll both dart behind the tree. Are you ready?"

"Whenever you say."

In a move that could have been practised, both stood and moved swiftly behind the trunk. It was a worthy girth, and now Garr was standing with an arrow loaded and primed for action. The air stood still and all was frozen for a moment in time.

"Is your view clear, Knap?"

"Nothing to see here, Garr. Have you got sight of them?"

"I have … Hey! Show yourselves or die."

Even the breeze and call of the birds were still.

Garr raised her bow. She was a very capable archer and a fierce adversary when tested. Life had taught her that, if nothing else; as a younger women, she had been both the victim and the destroyer of many a foolish warrior.

Both Knap and Garr were as tense as they needed to be, their bodies pumping adrenaline to the far reaches of their bodies.

A sudden movement within the bushes brought Garr's bow up and to the release position, her fingers struggling to hold back the keenness of the arrow.

A crouching figure started to move towards them through the bush.

Garr now stood away from the yew a little so her shot would be true. She pulled back a faction further, her heart now racing.

All her warrior instincts were now analysing every tiny movement.

"Hold back, hold back. No harm. Friend, no enemy."

She could see that two open hands were being held out in front of the crouching visitor as he moved cautiously towards them.

"The other one! Both of you come forward, hands out and very slowly. Both of you ... now—move."

They did as they were bidden. Slowly, the two figures, now both crouching, as they moved forward, passing under the low hanging branches towards Garr's position.

As they straightened, it was clear they were nomad warriors. The second of them, a woman, was carrying a child upon her back. From ten feet away, the smell of them was awful.

"Are there any more of you? Weapons—where are your weapons?"

Knap had moved to flank them, his staff raised and in an attack posture, feet astride and shuffling.

"Weapons in bush. No harm. Friend. No harm. No harm."

"What do you want? Why were you creeping up on us?"

"Woman dry, no food for child. We no problem, the child must eat. We no trouble and be gone."

The nomad woman came slowly forward a little, her hand held out before her in a begging posture. She presented a strange vision of warrior and mother.

She was indeed a contradiction in terms as nomad women were well known to fight equally as their menfolk, and yet here before them was a warrior turned mother, displaying all the motherly traits of all peoples.

Her hair was in tight plaits, heavily beaded. Her ears were also heavily decorated, and her chest leather likewise. From either side of her leather chest plate extended some kind of loose sacking material that also formed baggy pantaloons, which were decorated in dull-coloured patterns with beads hanging in small clusters.

He was full-bearded with long thick hair blending into his beard, and his hide clothing looked uncomfortable and dirty, with the soiling of time and possibly battle. In his eyes, one could see a detached dignity and possibly pleading.

Knap moved in close now, ordering them to sit. They obeyed.

"What do you think, Garr? They seem okay—just after the food I think."

"We'll give them some food for the child and send them on their way, I guess." She placed her bow against the tree and took out her own knife while gathering a little of the food from Knap's shoulder bag. She moved towards the woman and handed her the offering, which she took eagerly after the male had nodded his consent.

Immediately biting from the apple and rabbit carcass she crammed it in her mouth, which caused both Knap and Garr to flash a look at one another.

She chewed the food then rejected it from her mouth and straight into the child's, who seemed to take it readily.

The situation began to relax as the feeding continued.

"Is much good, is good you do. Wait. Look, no problem, no harm." With that being repeated continually, the male slowly rose and moved back towards the bushes leaving his hands extended and obvious all the time. Garr once again picked up her bow while looks were exchanged between Knap and herself.

The warrior male slowly bent into grass and their bundle of belongings, and, taking the blade of a small knife in his extended hand, moved back cautiously towards the gathering.

Once among them, he slowly bent forward placing the knife before Garr. With waving actions, he indicated it as a gift. Garr, relaxing again, kicked the knife towards Knap, who picked it up and nodded his appreciation.

"It's good, Garr, really nice—too good really." Nodding towards the warrior, he said, "It's good, very good, thanks, okay."

"Ya, is good. Food good para nina. Tanks, okay, many tanks."

There was honour and dignity in his manner.

Garr replaced her bow with her staff and drew a line through the dirt, indicating that they should stay behind the line.

"Where are the other warriors, the tribe?" Knap asked.

"We travel man woman only, seven day. Warriors no many friends, small food, many, many enemies, big cold soon, me child much important, tribe and women need new life. Many warriors need new life, me many good women." He turned and smiled at his woman now cradling the child in sleep.

Garr spoke up. "If true, I help tribe, you and women."

"And da child?"

"Yes, of course the child. You know metal tower; metal tree under double mountains?"

"Me know, ya." He grabbed a stick with enthusiasm and immediately drew a rough map in the dirt. He obviously knew the lay of the land well.

"Okay then, three days, Knap and me, Garr, meet you and tribe and child by metal tower. We meet and talk."

"Ya, much good. Three da, much good, talk, good."

With that said, they began to back away. Knap called at them. They stopped dead still not knowing what was about to happen, the woman clutching the child close to her. Knap took the remaining food and threw it towards them. Their pleasure and gratitude was clear. Nodding yet again, they backed away and slowly vanished amongst the trees.

"Well, I'll be!" expressed Knap as he took a deep breath. "We knew we were on an adventure, Garr, but this trip is turning into something special. What's next? I got your drift straight off; you're thinking the Big Gathering aren't you?"

"I'm glad you saw it. This could be the beginning of something good for all of us, something towards the things we have spoken of so often. Maybe we will be able to find a likeminded person in Dartell. Just maybe, my friend, your thoughts, dreams, and visions can become reality."

"They are also your visions, Garr, we will work on this together."

Their journey had been eventful. They had enjoyed their time together and they expressed it to one another as they now walked abreast, talking over many things and clarifying their thoughts.

Before too long, they left the woodland and riverbank and began to cross an area which consisted of strange flattened debris—it appeared to be broken remains of buildings from a time long before. In front of them, they could see the walls that enclosed Dartell, and, at the centre, directly before them, they could make out the great gates.

No doubt, over time the outer buildings had fallen into disrepair, collapsed, then slowly and naturally spread, possibly with the aid of Dartellians, some of those materials being used to create the walls that linked the remaining structures and formed the outer perimeter.

It was a secure stronghold; an awesome sight, displaying power and organisation and certainly a threatening place for warriors or hill folk.

Now walking upon a risen track above the height of the flattened debris and fields, they approached the entrance gates. On either side of them as they walked were varied traders showing their goods. They stopped at one to trade for food and water with the salt they carried for that very purpose. It was all they really had to offer, and a deal was struck between them and the portly trader.

Stalls sold a multitude of goods, including some that neither of them had ever seen. Some stalls displayed coins and old pieces of jewellery. Others sold metal containers for cooking or carrying, and another only had for sale six pairs of glasses; ancient things of great value. Further along the track they saw glass jars, and yet another trader had a mixed range of ancient things: a beautiful wooden chair—neither of them had ever seen something so wonderful—books, odd knives, other eating tools, and strange unfathomable items in both plastic and metal. It was a paradise of wonderful goods, the sight of which excited them both and generated many questions about the reality of the past.

Prior to the main gates were small stout temporary gates through which visitors filed one by one. Carts and horse traffic went through another. At both sets of gates were guards who checked everybody and everything, both in and out. It was obviously a long and cautious process which nevertheless allowed conversation or aggravation to develop.

It wasn't clear exactly what their criteria was for preventing entry; they were friendly enough and yet firm. All visitors were issued with discs of varied colours and shapes, with numbers upon. A stay within the township could not be extended without express permission; that was made very clear.

As Knap and Garr were intending an overnight stay, they were given a special tag. "You must find this place to sleep, there is no charge." They were again impressed, but they assumed this was based upon control rather than generosity.

As they walked into Dartell, they looked around in amazement; how different it was to their own existence. It was busy and bustling, crowded to capacity. The people of the community could be seen at a glance in their uniform attire of brown heavy sacking cloth, belts, and pouches. They were generally overweight and used to the habit of shuffling slowly around.

"Knap, I'm feeling harassed already. Memories are making me feel very nervous—I do not like it here. Remember that I grew up here, well, for six or seven years anyway."

"No, I didn't know that. Possibly one day you will tell me all about those memories. They aren't good memories for you are they?" Garr ignored the question and pulled Knap to one side of the track, pointing to the sign above the door. They entered a community building, which appeared to be some sort of library with meeting halls.

"Tags. Tags. Show your tags." The details were recorded. "You only have a short time as we are due to close up shortly and it's a little dark inside now."

As it was now twilight, torches were being lit everywhere.

Within the library rooms, they both again looked around with amazement—books and books and books. Neither of them had realised that so many of these precious items even existed. In turn, they picked different titles from the shelves.

Both Garr and Knap had books, especially Knap. They were lucky; they could both read. These were items of great value, but they had never seen so many.

"Look at this, Garr, there are books about just pigs here."

"Take a look at this one—an atlas. I have an atlas but not like this one, and just look at that one."

"Philosopher's Stone, what is that all about?"

They opened one after the other, feeding their eyes in continual fascination and wonderment.

"Replace, replace, replace the books now. The library is closing. Replace your books now. The library is closing." Garr and Knap responded to the instruction; another, who was probably deeply engrossed, did not respond.

Guards descended upon the unfortunate soul, and without ceremony, he was ejected from the building. It was a sharp lesson in community law. The conflicting aspects of Dartell were dawning upon them both. They made their way out into the twilight, where they could see the last few visitors moving quickly towards the exit and looked around for an appropriate sign to lead them in the direction of their sleeping place. There were so many signs, so many instructions. Each one was supported by images, which was by far the most common form of visual communication.

As they moved along the crowded tracks and alleys, they managed to catch sight of the signs for their sleeping area; as normal, here it was associated with a number. They edged their way through the crowd and turned in the direction the signs indicated. The smaller track into which they had turned was less crowded and, at times, it was possible at last to walk side by side. They passed a variety of small shops, with many doors displaying bold numbers above or to the side. They noticed how clean the track was; they saw no rats, no cats, and no dogs. Where are the children, where were the people all disappearing to? The tracks were now emptying rapidly. Only the torches affixed to the buildings remained to represent life and movement; flickering and sending their wobbling light in all directions, giving both vision and dark eerie shadows which echoed a threat.

"There it is, Garr—Bed Twenty—the sign and the tag are the same. Looks a bit of a rowdy place to me, my girl. Oh well, come on, let's have a look inside." He led Garr through the entrance.

Inquisitive eyes looked in their direction, yet they were not really threatening. The lighting was poor and the room was very smoky. In front of them, behind a bench of thick timbers, was a large fireplace, flames dancing within it. To either side there were arches and beyond they could see what they assumed was the bedding stalls.

"I need to see your tags folks. Okay, they're fine. Not been here before then?"

"No we haven't. Are there rules?"

"That's easy, yep—no fighting, no sex, no stealing, and no arguing. Here just for the night, I assume you know you must be gone from Dartell by midday tomorrow. Okay, what do you trade in? I assume you want a drink."

"We have salt." Garr, with relief, took out a small bag of salt and placed it on the wooden bench in front of the man. He was not impressed.

"Two drinks each then, okay."

"There's at least a kilo there," Knap spoke up, "feel the weight my friend. How about three drinks each?"

"Ouch, okay, friend, I'll agree five between you. Is that fair?"

"A deal, friend." The man threw five small metal discs on the bench. Knap took them and placed them safely into his pouch.

"Your beds are marked seven and eight back there. They're fresh and clean today, okay."

Garr and Knap moved to a table, the only one unoccupied and to the left of the room. They piled their belongings to the far side of the seating.

"It's good to unload, let's have that beer, Garr. I'm all in, my friend, and I need to sit for a while." Garr moved back to the bench and requested two tankards of beer.

Through the entrance came three community members, shuffling forward, as they all did, and approached the front bench, staying deep within their conversation. One of them absent-mindedly bumped into Garr. He broke from his conversation.

"So sorry, friend, so sorry."

"No problem," Garr responded, with her usual smile and nod.

Garr returned to the table where Knap was already looking rather sleepy. It had not been the distance, he commented, but the pace. He was not used to that pace these days.

"Come on Knap, wakey, wakey—a couple of beers and bed. Tomorrow, we'll be up early, have a good look around, and be on our way home by midday. It will be real late by the time we reach our mountains, but I guess there'll be hot food awaiting our arrival. I think I can smell it now," she said as she raised her head and sniffed the air.

While they started to chat seriously about what they had already seen in Dartell and the excitement of their journey, in particularly the meeting with the warrior couple, the three men standing at the bench approached them.

"May we sit on this side of the table, friends? No more room at the inn, I'm afraid." Knap and Garr nodded simultaneously.

The group of three sat and continued deep in serious chatter, as Garr and Knap did.

Knap gathered himself and continued with Garr to discuss their trip so far; between pauses all became aware of the other group's topics of discussion. That was intriguing, so ears were straining.

As Knap was refreshed, Garr was showing the signs of being intoxicated. She wasn't used to alcohol, and she started to alternate between rapid chatter and periods of staring into open space, nodding at the wrong moments, her timing badly off. Knap took advantage of one of Garr's silent moments and turned to the group opposite them.

"We're sorry to interrupt your conversation, but couldn't help hearing you talk of the attack you experienced here the other week. We hear of these attacks from time to time and I think all static communities fear these people. They obviously have such a different culture. If I may explain for just one moment, I'd like to tell you about a strange experience we had travelling here today. I think it's relevant."

Garr perked up and supported Knap's statement. The group of three looked to each other and indicated for Knap to speak on.

"Yes, please do, if your information is of value."

"We had stopped to rest and eat and suddenly were aware of people creeping upon us. We thought we were about to be attacked. There were only two of them plus a child, nomad warriors that is. The conversation with them was difficult due to language, but they were more able to talk to us then us to them. They mainly needed food for their child, but as we talked to them, they expressed that generally many of their community wanted to change their lifestyle, to be peaceable, more settled, and stable. It was not what we were expecting from them, they appeared caring and thinking people— so much so, that we have arranged to assist them and help them gain the trust of the hill folk. They may even settle, who knows?

"We agreed to meet them in three days and take them with us to the hill folk's Big Gathering. There, they may be able to explain their position and begin the process of that change. It felt to us that it was worth of a try, anyway. Of course, they could well have been together with the group that actually raided your fields, but nonetheless, it was an interesting and unexpected experience and, as I said initially, may be of value to your thinking."

The three colleagues looked at each other in silence and then nodded at Knap's comments.

"Mmm. What you say does have interest, my friend. Firstly, let us introduce ourselves. This is Councillor Gable and this, Councillor Deck. I am member Clark. We are all community members here at Dartell. May we ask who you are? Are you leaders of some group or tribe as you seem to speak with some clarity and knowledge, maybe even authority?"

He paused for thought and then continued.

"As you may have gathered from our discussion, we are trying to formulate some changes that appear necessary since the last attack on our little township. It was a surprise and warning to us and your story may offer us an alternative view or additional route—indeed, a new consideration. Gable, Deck, do you agree?"

His comrades, who were the people of authority, nodded their approval, as they would after Clark had made his point and led the way.

Garr lent forward to respond.

"Friends, we aren't leaders of anybody. We are hill folk. We live our own lives and are hopefully a friend to all if they are peaceful."

"Listen my new friends," Clark said, "may I make a suggestion? You both appear good people and people of integrity, leaders or not, and I believe a chance and a gamble should be taken here. Although we will adjust our security and defences anyway, I and possibly the central council would be very interested to see how all this develops and, I for one, if the council approves, would welcome an invitation to join the discussions either at your meeting in three days or the Gathering, which we have heard of."

He paused and looked around at the others, took a sip from his jug and waited patiently for their responses. Everybody around the table was thinking. This was not conventional; therefore, an un-thoughtful response would not be appropriate. All sipped at drinks while making their considerations.

"What does everybody else think then?" Clark spoke up again, obviously a little frustrated by the slowness of their response.

"If we all wish to take this seriously," Garr responded, "I suggest the full meeting should be at the Big Gathering. It is right and smart to move with caution. There will be major compromises to be made by all, risks to be taken, and possibly help and assistance needed for a long period. And even if we accept that, the question is if this is affordable for the hill folk or even Dartell and others. I have no doubt that we all work hard to maintain our lives—our time is valuable."

"You are correct to say all you did," Clark said to Garr, "but nothing is achieved apart from the growth of egos and memories if you don't act, and, indeed, action always generates risks. My grandmother used to say to me, 'actions speak louder than words'. I always liked the sound and sense of that little saying."

Arrangements were made quickly, as Garr and Knap were now badly showing the effects of drinking and tiredness. Neither party truly knew whether their conversation was serious and whether either party had the power or will. Was it anything other than an embarrassing and drunken interaction?

After Garr and Knap bid their new friends a good night after exchanging details with promises to reconnect, they then gathered their belongings and staggered quietly towards the sleeping areas feeling somewhat surprised and confused by the pace and outcome of their conversation and indeed the events of the long day.

Now they found themselves squinting in the dark through aching and smoke filled eyes. They managed to locate the sleeping areas seven and eight. Both of them viewed the bedding with glee and relief. Then, after storing their goods, the sacking curtains were pulled around their area, and they both collapsed willingly.

The night passed in undisturbed peace.

All five comrades pondered all that had been spoken. Each turned over and over in his or her mind the conversation, each trying to decide the reality of their dreams.

If even a small part of the suggestion was accomplished, it would be an enormous achievement. If only the thinking then spread, it would be the achievement of a lifetime. If a true desire existed to improve the lot for all and then it was pursued, it would be the start of new and open thinking—a new beginning. That was an exciting thought. They had all felt the power and potential of their commitments.

It was a good day.

In the morning, with sore heads, Garr and Knap once again joined the hordes in the Dartell streets and tracks. The sun had just risen above the horizon, and conversation was limited to grunts—movement was slow and painful.

They visited the central area of Dartell, looking over the stalls covered with many goods neither of them had ever seen. They revisited the library and then; time was gone. Trading their final supply of salt for bread and fruit for the return journey, they left Dartell hoping desperately for the recovery of their energy and wellbeing.

"Why, oh why did we drink beer, Garr? We must be stupid—that's your fault really."

"What! What! How did you get to—?"

"Only joking, Garr, only joking, but ... Garr, you did start it."

"Knap, you scoundrel, it was you who bought the beer—you. You caused this headache. Not I. I'm an innocent princess."

"I am only joking, Garr. And anyway, you're not really a princess, you live in a cave. Princesses were people who lived thousands of years ago and slept in great buildings and wore gold and jewels and had slaves, servants, and armies to guard them."

"You're simply a nomad, you really are. Guess we can't say that anymore now. Just keep walking—it's all I can deal with right now, Knap, and I don't want to speak to you anyway. Horrible man, it's all your entire fault."

"I fancy a beer, Garr."

"Shut up, Knap."

The return journey seemed long and hard, as most return journeys do. They stopped briefly to rest and eat.

Recovering, they sat, then walked and talked about everything, a little pleased that at least the return journey appeared uneventful so far.

Garr started to explain some of her very personal feelings about Dartell. She had moved there with her parents and brother; she was about nine and her brother seven.

"In those days, Knap, there weren't endless rules, no walled community, just a lot of people choosing to live in close proximity and working, hunting, gathering, and fighting as a group. "Slowly but surely, there were more attacks from outsiders. More people began to steal, cheat, and take advantage of one another. "My brother and I were a rarity. Within the whole of Dartell, there were only six other children of our age group. "People started to isolate themselves and barricade themselves in at night. People were killed—women were raped and taken as workers or sex slaves. As young children of seven and eight, it was a nightmare every single day and every single night. Every strange face and every untrustworthy smile scared us.

"Knap, I was kidnapped, taken away, and kept prisoner. I was used and abused for a long time."

There was a very long pause while she gathered herself. She was handling her hidden past well. She had never spoken of any of this before, to anyone accept her brother. Knap listened patiently, understanding the enormous cost the telling was placing upon Garr's shoulders.

"I was chained up at night, but eventually I managed to escape. By the time I got back to Dartell, my parents were dead and my brother had been taken and was now living enslaved and in awful conditions. After a long while of searching, I found him. He was different, changed—he had endured a lot, as I had. We returned to where we had lived with our parents. The place was unoccupied. Amazingly, it had not been plundered after all that time. It upset us greatly being there. We took a couple of odd items for keepsakes, odd things of use or value, my binoculars and books came from there. We stayed together for over eight years. Some of those times I am ashamed of. We did violent things to anybody, Knap, anybody and everybody that got in our way. That was until he found someone he wanted to be with— Sarina. She was lovely, really good for him, so eventually I gave them their space. It seemed right, and I moved towards the hills alone."

Another long pause occurred; one that drifted on and on painfully. Garr stopped walking.

"Arr, what the hell. It's all old history now, Knap. I don't know why I started to tell you all that rubbish. Sorry for going on, but perhaps you can see why it was strange for me going back there. I didn't really think I could handle it—all those years thinking that I couldn't. It didn't really affect me much in reality, and, anyway, the place is so very different from the one Nic and I grew up in. I think so much of that change within me is down to knowing you, Knap."

"What do you mean?"

"Your friendship and wisdom over the years. I was aggressive and defensive when we first met, but you were patient with me, gave me time to think, took me seriously, and allowed me to grow."

"My dear Garr, you always had an interesting point of view and an enquiring mind, always remember that you have also helped me in many ways to develop as a person. Even though our journeys have been very different, our souls are much the same. Our enduring friendship proves that. With your youth and insight, you can achieve great things, if you choose to."

"You're not so old, Knap, maybe I will be your lieutenant."

"No, I don't think so—I haven't the firmness you have within. There is no true warrior in me. You have it all and a good heart and head. Maybe, one day you'll see that in yourself, young woman. Then I'll have the greatest pleasure in watching you fly. I have great faith in you. Always remember that we are the whole of our experience, if we choose to use it."

The Plan Grows

In Dartell, the council was in session. Gable and Deck were seated together amongst the other council members. Clark sat outside of the council circle, upon a long and rickety old bench, where other valued community members were seated.

They had been deep in discussion on security issues for some time.

As in any similar discussion, some were in favour of the strong and aggressive approach, while others preferred a gentler but progressive way forward. Both camps understood the other's view, therefore compromise was called for.

"Councillors," Clark intervened, "may I suggest we initially take a two pronged approach. If I attend the Big Gathering which the hill folk will be attending shortly, and where I know a group of these nomad warriors will be attending, I will be able to discuss a way to improve the relationship between the various communities. We may be able to forge the basis of a way forward, which could be a fine example for others to follow. Simultaneously, we can strengthen our farming security arrangements once again and bring all our stock into the walled area each night, as well as re-establish daytime security. Maybe we could also build security towers. We would give ourselves the best of all worlds. Do you agree?"

There was a silence in the hall as all considered the suggestions, each knowing that such an ambitious plan involves resources.

It was a difficult choice. Working towards the future was something new, especially doing so alongside other communities and enemies. Such plans involved great care, valuable time, and effort.

"We could simply double our defences and stop allowing outsiders into Dartell," suggested a councillor. "Would that not be simpler"?

"Yes, my friend, it would," replied Clark, "but our future would be the same as our past."

A vote was organised. They elected to carry out Clark's idea, and, as anticipated, Clark was elected to travel with a council member to the Gathering.

Hope is a Gift

Far to the south of Dartell, the wind had been blowing hard for some days now. It was a cold wintry wind that cut through a soul to the very bone.

While Sarina's spirits plummeted further downwards, Nic's were still high, in fact they were higher than they had been for some time.

It had been an uncomfortable night for Nic, snuggled within a cave, facing away from the prevailing weather. When he awoke, he was as cold as ice, stiff, and aching. He stamped and shook the cold from his body, rubbing his hands together the best he could. Then he took the last small piece of hard bread and cheese from his pack and, while continuing his journey along the track, munched happily, concentrating on the hope of finding Jac and Ban.

The track began to descend on the far side of the cliff. His coat was pulled up as tight as possible to provide a little more protection against the cutting force of the wind that he now walked into. Before him, there appeared nothing but mountain scrub as far as he could see.

He bent into the wind, which occasionally wobbled him from his determined stride. After two hours, he found himself walking the lower edges where at least the weather was a little more clement. The track now wound gently downwards, winding around the footprint of those mountains and rocks.

He had a good idea of his position, although he didn't know the area.

After a tight turn in the track, he came upon a group of stone buildings. There were signs of an old mining works, but it looked deserted and desolate. He stood and took a deep breath. Then he began the serious task of searching all the buildings, never sure of what he might find hidden or lurking within some dark corner.

It was a task full of anticipation and disappointment; each and every corner offered choices of optimism and pessimism, happiness and despair but it simply had to be done.

At each turn, he readjusted his eyes due to the lack of light and called aloud the names of his beloved children. He announced himself over and over again.

The search of the main buildings must have taken him a good few hours. He saw no signs of Jac and Ban.

His spirits now began to sink once more; he had felt so near and so hopeful but a few hours ago.

He considered his own situation, querying whether he should return homeward to Sarina and then return once more when recharged. He would have to soon, regardless—he had Sarina to think about and he must survive to continue the search.

He would look and search the mine entrances, then he would travel home as fast as he could manage, gather more food and clothing, and then return to continue his search. Maybe Sarina would choose to join him.

The thought of Sarina on her own, not knowing where or how he was, concerned him.

After another hour passed by in completing his search and as he continued to control his emotions the best he could, he decided to strike out for home.

He wasn't looking forward to the trek, as the harsh winds continued and were now combined with driving light hail, which had the ability to find its way into the smallest gaps where his clothing overlapped or closed. It was unpleasant, it was freezing cold, he ached all over, he was very hungry, and now, very tired.

The route back was shorter than the outward journey and, within four hours, he would be able to see Prallian.

He began his walk through the lonely group of old mine buildings, still flicking his eyes to either side.

"Dad."

He thought for a moment that he was hearing voices, or was it his heart's desire he had heard? Or was it the wind teasing him wickedly.

"Dad, is that you?"

The words sounded clearer, more distinct, and more real.

As he turned to search for the direction of the voice, he saw Jac appearing from the shadows of an upstairs loft opening.

He steadied himself, shaking his head to double-check his sanity. It was Jac; it was really Jac, with Ban now kneeling just behind him.

"Jac, Jac, I see you. Stay there boys. Don't move! Don't move!"

In a moment of release, his hands went to his face. Deep, deep sobs broke from within; quite uncontrollably. For a moment his legs wouldn't move and his body shook. He looked once more towards his beloved children at the hatch; they were gone. The illusions faded into the shadows, like mist in the breeze.

The Plan

Garr and Knap spent hours telling Mara and Sal about their adventures. Monster was also happy to snuggle up close to Garr and appeared to listen to the stories of adventure. It brought a welcome change of conversation around the fire in the evening. When they all retired to sleep, the two travellers, now exhausted by adventure and talk, slept deep and long.

That night, Monster managed to sneak upon the edge of Garr's sleep platform allowing just enough room for Sala and Garr but that was no issue for them.

The following morning, refreshed, nobody felt like undertaking strenuous activities, so a day of pottering was agreed on. It was the correct medicine.

Knap and Garr knew that soon was to be the meeting at the tower with the nomads; there was little preparation to be undertaken, but some clear thinking was needed; they needed to anticipate any potential problems for themselves or complications that could arise both at the arranged meeting and maybe, just maybe, sometime later at the Gathering.

Garr now felt a little foolish and presumptuous over her suggested meeting.

"This is a rather silly idea really, Knap. I really don't know why I suggested it. Do you think we should attempt to warn any leaders about our intentions?"

"Garr, it was brave and ambitious. Remember, fortune favours the brave. As for warning people, who would we tell? Who does anybody recognise as a leader amongst the hill folk? Actually this is another subject that should somehow be brought up and discussed, as we both have said so many times— leadership is badly needed. You have to believe in something to make it work. It's the belief and hope that you can transfer to others. The rest of the process is down to luck or timing or natural progression."

"You're right, I guess. Possibly areas could be divided by rivers or mountain ridges, each with a leader or representative. They could be chosen initially and then elected by the people in time, similar to the method in Dartell, but larger and wider. In turn, they could vote for a chief, a figurehead. Somebody that would be able to negotiate and speak up for all the areas or tribes. I think that makes good sense, do you?"

"The only question is do you? It won't be easy. Setting this up could take years. It could take us, you and I, years. It could consume our lives. All the folk we know are bitterly independent and fiercely self-sufficient, but if they too could be given faith, then who knows what could be achieved."

"We can only try if we are given the chance! Starting the process will orient people together, surely. Some will obviously resist, but others from all communities will welcome the ideas we've spoken of and see the great possibilities and advantages. It will give all of us some order and security."

"You're right, and a warrior's heart will be called for. This could be the greatest battle ever fought."

Throughout that day, many subjects were thought over and discussed, with Sala and Mara joining in and adding different perspectives to their discussions. At the end of their recovery day, Knap and Garr both felt mentally exhausted, talked out completely. They joked that if such discussion became a regular feature of their lives, they would all need many recovery days.

Meals were taken from the stores and plenty of wood was at hand, which, together with many hands to make light of the daily tasks, made this the first day Garr could remember that did not require her to leave camp for something. She stacked the fires and then spread earth lightly over them, then stretched and yawned, clearly expressing her readiness for bed. Knap and Mara were already there, while Sala had wandered to the edge of rock lip and was staring at the brilliance of the starry sky far above and across the valley to the moonlit mountains. In these moments, nothing was of importance apart from that beauty before them, which could be freely absorbed and enjoyed. Its magical powers soaked into them, giving strength to the soul and peace to the mind.

Garr moved up behind Sala and wrapped her arms around her soft middle. Together they relished the wondrous site before them until yawning once again and moving to their bed, closely follow by Monster who had already tried to settle a number of times only being drawn back to duty with a look that said, "Come on, I'm sleepy. Let's go to bed."

They slept later than intended and, as a result, all were fully refreshed. The cloudless sky over the valley was again wondrous, this time the most exquisite shade of blue. The sun was already above the mountain, throwing its warmth over the small encampment.

Monster, who had disappeared early, now returned with a fat rabbit between his jaws and was proudly presenting his catch to Garr. Amazingly, he had not chewed his prey before presenting it at camp. Once praised, his pleasure was clear as he joyously chased sticks and other favoured items around the camp floor.

The fires were eagerly rekindled and potatoes were thrown amongst the embers for breakfast to be eaten later with some homemade cheese. Lime flower tea was brewed and an excellent start to the day was experienced eventually by them all.

The Meeting

Sala and Mara joined Knap and Garr on their trek to the tree-tower; the meeting place that had been agreed for discussions with the people of the nomad tribe.

They were undecided whether or not the family of nomad warriors would appear, but if they did, they were well prepared mentally and indeed physically for whatever might come their way.

It was an interesting occasion but experience and fear took hold of their minds. History had educated them all that nomads were normally both unreliable and untrustworthy; it was an enormous risk. They were suddenly unsure of why they were involved in such a meeting, their dreams and thoughts appearing foolish and unrealistic.

What was it really to do with them?

It wasn't a long hike down the side of the mountain to the valley bottom and then eastward for an hour or so. Just before the river was the old metal tower which Knap had recently climbed with binoculars in hand to view Dartell. A lot had unexpectedly happened since then.

The sky had clouded over and the winds that often affected this area were doing their worst, when the little gang of four gathered to await the nomads. They decided to generate a fire and make themselves as comfortable as possible while constantly checking the sky for signs of the passing time.

So they sat comfortably out of the wind around a crackling fire, eating the potatoes prepared earlier and fresh soft cheese; of course, including Monster, it was five who indulged in the same meal.

They talked quietly while Knap continued working on Garr's new boots with Sala's help. Garr whittled at a new staff and Mara generally cared for everybody's needs and tended the fire.

Time passed quickly. The weather deteriorated and then light rain began. It didn't look as though the nomad people were going to appear.

"What do you think, Knap? How long do you think we should give them? We can't all just sit here waiting in this weather." "Look, if we all move over towards those trees, we can leave a cape tied to the tower as a sign and watch from a distance. My heart still says that they will turn up."

"I agree with you, Garr," Sala spoke up. "It's not smart sitting here, anyway. We're very exposed against attack, and now this weather—well, come on let's move."

Both Knap and Mara agreed, so the camp was instantly moved, fire and all. Some of the fire was scooped back into the carrying bowl; the top replaced and held by rewrapping the cord around it. Sala allowed it to swing happily, feeding it with air as they relocated.

Re-organised and now protected to some degree against the weather, they once again took up the task of waiting.

Once again, time passed slowly. Then for the first time during their wait, Monster stirred, his head up, checking scent upon the wind. His ears twitched, swivelling a little from left to right, the muscle firming under his handsome coat.

"What's up, boy?"

He became more alert, standing and continuing to sniff the air. He moved towards a small rise in the ground, issuing a couple of low growls. The others watched his movements, taking up weapons in preparation for whatever was forthcoming.

Garr called him to heel, the two of them standing and waiting in uneasy readiness. Without a word spoken, the others were now also standing and looking around to cover the possibilities from all directions.

There were moments of silent anticipation, edging upon fear. Whatever Monster was aware of, he was not happy about it. Garr trusted his judgement; in fact, she trusted nobody more than Monster, not even Knap.

Time continued to hang in the damp air, and then slowly growing above the horizon line of the small rise was the head of a warrior. Slowly the single figure grew as if being ejected from the earth until the full body of the nomad stood upon the grassy, wet rise.

Monster pulled hard against Garr's hold, barking and growling. She could just keep him back; he understood her commands, yet had the need and instinct to protect.

The nomad held both hands forward in a gesture of caution.

"Wow, wow, no problemas, Garr. Much grandi chien. Me Volka, here talk to Garr."

"No problem, Volka, we're pleased to see you. Come forward slowly, no fast movement, Volka."

Looking extremely nervous, he laid down all that he carried and moved slowly and tentatively towards where the group stood.

Knap walked forward towards the nomad and took his arm, then turned and walked back towards the others. He leaned forward and stroked Monster's enormous head; Monster ignored him and pushed his nose at the nomad, sniffing hard, making him pull back in a natural reaction.

'Stay still, Volka. Let him smell you. Just ignore the growling, Volka, it's okay."

'Stay, Monster. Stay, boy."

Slowly the matter calmed; Volka stopped sweating and could seat slowly upon a small rock.

Monster's attention was now pulled between Volka and another possible threat. He resolved the matter by trotting between the rise of the hill and poor Volka. Each time he returned to the group, he issued a gurgling growl straight into his face and then chased back towards the rise to issue a volley of deep barks across the valley.

"Volka, is your family out there, or others?"

"Ya, family, brothers, more tribe."

"That's the problem, Knap. Will you look and beckon them here? Monster won't stop until he knows all is well. There's no point in trying to tie him up, as he'll just break anything we can conjure up."

Knap walked towards the rise, with Sala following at a short distance. Mara continued to look all about.

"Garr, I can't see anybody," he shouted back to them. "Volka must call them." Volka understood the dilemma and slowly rose from his rock, not for a second taking his eyes from the movements of Monster. Garr moved closer to him, and together they walked to the rise. Once there, he cupped his hands and shouted a message into the sodden valley. He repeated his call a number of times before eventually they could see a sizable group beginning to stand and move in their direction.

Monster stood proud upon the rise and issued forth his warning. They stopped.

Garr held high her bow, which had been held in one hand during the unfolding scene; Knap and Sala followed her example; they placed them slowly down upon the ground.

The nomad warriors appeared reluctant to do likewise but Volka again was quick to understand the requirements and shouted his instructions across the sodden grassland. Slowly and with obvious reluctance, they stacked their own weapons and belongings and again moved towards the rise.

Garr turned to Mara. "Build that fire up high, Mara. There's about twenty of them coming towards us."

"We didn't really anticipate this," Knap enquired, turning to Garr. "Do you think this is safe?"

"I think so. Anyway, I don't think there are many options now, my friend."

They returned to Mara and all five joined in the effort of building two fires, one around which discussion could be held and the second around which the families could gather. By the time the first nomad stood upon the ridge, the fires were beginning to burn satisfactorily.

The first upon the rise was a tall, good-looking warrior, with unusually light-blond hair. Instantly he displayed authority, a kind of grandeur. The others gathered about him.

Garr walked towards them, holding hard on Monster, who seemed to be now understanding the situation a little better. As Garr reached them, the majority moved back, leaving only the blond warrior to the fore. He neither flinched nor looked at Monster. He smiled softly at Garr and, still without looking down, offered his hand towards Monster, who calmly sniffed at him and sat.

"I am Idor, and you are Garr—is this correct? What do you speak, Garr—Frances, Espanola or Engla?"

"Idor, I am pleased to meet with you and your brothers. The English word is good for me. You speak many tongues."

"Garr, our lives are difficult. We travel great distances. It is important many tongues."

Led by Idor and Garr, the group moved at last to the fires, where, immediately, the women and children gathered for warmth by pulling large skins over their heads.

Sala and Mara had brought food for both themselves and others but not enough to satisfy so many. Nonetheless, it was passed around to all. The warrior folk also took food from their packs and passed it along, and there was now a banquette to be had. The bad weather had receded, as did suspicion. The fires danced happily and people began to relax and mix a little, as Idor, their leader, spoke quietly with Garr and Knap.

"Our families and our tradition has always moved us from place to place. Our world is changing. Our tribe, my brothers and I, need more security in our lives. We need more friends, more peace. It may take many years. But you both see need for change as we. Let us begin this change together."

"Idor, your brother Volka told us of your desires," said Garr. "It is fate that we met. Maybe we will make changes, maybe not, but if the changes are for the good of all, then we must try. There will be resistance and trouble, some will fall against our thinking, some will never compromise, but their children might one day."

"Let us talk of our visions", Knap spoke up, "let us speak of small ideas that are possible to implement. Let us speak of the problems we can see for all and any of the peoples upon this land—ownership, trading and justice."

Volka then spoke after receiving Idor's approval.

"We should start with simple plans; plans that do not create problems but only good things and easy do."

Time moved on and they discussed many things. As Volka had suggested, they concentrated on simple changes that anyone would find acceptable: mixed markets for trading, competition among tribes and villages. These were changes that would benefit all with fairness in mind.

It would not be too long before the darkening of the sky would be upon them all. The talk had been easy between them. They were all surprised

"Why hasn't this ever happened before?" It was a sentiment felt by them all.

This wasn't how the meeting had been visualised, but a very real meeting it had become. With many obvious matters agreed in principal, they agreed that together with their new friends from Dartell, they would meet up and spend the time together at the 'Big Gathering'. There they could talk to others and move ahead accordingly, based upon the feedback they received and the friendliness displayed throughout the many competitions and social activities that would be available. Who knew where this might lead?

While all of those at the meeting had generated good feelings and a little unanticipated respect, Garr had experienced a number of strange feelings. She was not sure whether they were good or bad but she somehow knew that she must consider them carefully.

The Search

Nic eventually staggered into Prallian some seven and a half hours after his return trek had started.

Tired beyond belief, the cold and wet were no longer of consequence. He couldn't feel his body; it belonged to another, as did his hunger.

He reached the outskirts of the village and dared to stop, leaned against a wall with his hands upon his weary knees and took a deep breath, not noticing the ice-coldness of the air that he swallowed into his exhausted lungs.

If he had stopped there for more than a moment, he would have fallen into a deep and fatal sleep. Now his home and Sarina were in sight, his exhaustion felt even more pronounced. He called upon his very last resources; pushed himself away from the wall, steadied himself, forced his eyes to stay open, and then staggered the last few steps to his stout and familiar front door, where he pounded repeatedly upon that welcoming oak. He could not have repeated the pounding, but luckily Sarina was at the door immediately.

Taking Nic into her arms while quickly scanning behind him in hope and anticipation, she helped him through the doorway and towards the fire. He fell into the comfort of a soft chair, his legs stretched forward toward the fire.

She looked down upon her man with tears of relief and sorrow running over her face. There was no time for thought or those obvious questions, so with great difficulty she removed his sodden clothing and threw over him blankets and covers, anything at hand. By the time this had been done, and extra logs thrown upon the already blazing fire, he was already sliding fast towards exhausted sleep. Such was his relief at seeing Sarina and being within that safe environment, he was quickly drawn into a deep yet soft abyss.

For the next six hours, there was nothing to do apart from stacking the fire and staring down at her exhausted man while she repeatedly ran through the endless questions that burned desperately within her mind.

When at last he moved from his six-hour static pose, he smiled a happy and long smile and then disappeared once again into slumber.

Sarina prepared some food for his reappearance into the real world. Then she also let all the worry of the last two days fade away. As sleep came upon her, the last thoughts were of Jac and Ban. Nic would soon be telling her of any news, and she could only trust in his judgement and effort. She sent her boys love and, in her mind, kissed them tenderly while pulling them both close to her breast as she snuggled down next to Nic in slumber. For Sarina, all four of them slept warm and cuddled together in safety.

They both roused around midday. As they sat around the large wooden table, Nic told of his adventures, excitement, and sorrow. Mainly the story was of hope. The recovered cuddle cloth reduced Sarina to sobbing, from which it took her so long to recover. Nic ate everything placed before him and could be seen to recover as he ate, Sarina continually replenishing his plate, sobbing both to and from the stove. That was not her nature.

By the time Nic had emptied the whole contents of the large stew pot, they had resolved to trek back to the mining village together and stay upon the trail until either their children were found or their fate discovered.

Considering the task ahead of them, they decided to allow a further two days for preparation. They explained the situation to Big Brian, James, and others, so that, by the due time they left at sunrise, a small group stood within the central square. Nic and Sarina were humbled by such a farewell at such a cool and early hour.

"To all of you, our thanks," Nic told them all. "Your kindness will travel with us and keep us safe. Upon our return with the children, we and you, our friends, will have the celebration of celebrations. We thank you." They turned to move on, but Big Brian also spoke up.

"Nic, Sarina, do you think that we would allow you to go alone? We have our children to find—children belonging to our community—and find them we will. Together as brothers we stood and fell, and so we will share all our sorrow and laughter from here on. So, let's be going."

A group of five left the little village. The numbers made up by Big Brian, Maggie; a woman of similar age to Sarina who had lost both her man and a child in the conflict, plus Stony. He was a strange character, according to most, for he had always lived alone with Regge his dog within the community, and nobody really knew too much about him or his past. But he always contributed willingly and, indeed, gave more than his fair share. Nic enjoyed his company. It was a worthy group.

The weather was now reasonable—fresh but not cold. They walked away under clear skies with optimism and a determined stride upon the grassy tracks.

They reached the mining village in good time, without a pause and little talk.

As Nic stood there once again, horrid memories of illusions that tricked his vulnerable soul flooded back. He said nothing.

He had his Sarina to think of, his wonderful Sarina who stood so loyally by his side, trusting his ability and judgement.

Stony now took the lead.

"Come on, Brian man, let's search these buildings." With that said, he knelt before Regge and allowed him to sniff the remnant of the cuddle cloth and two other items belonging to the boys. "Go boy, find 'em, boy. Go go, go!"

To everybody's surprise, Regge leapt into action, running initially in circles around the open square. His instincts led him towards the building where Nic had seen the images of his children. Nic was amazed and troubled by the dogs' action, but again he said nothing.

While Stony and Brian followed Regge as best they could, the remaining group of three stood there in amazement of the dog's ability.

Regge ran back and forth outside the building, tail a-wagging and nose to the ground. He entered the building, zigzagged, paused to sniff; zigzagged again, and then with no apparent warning bounded up the rickety staircase to investigate the loft. Regge was without doubt on a mission. He returned to the front of the building as if something was falling in place and repeated his checking routine. He stopped and stood with nose to the air and barked repeatedly.

"What does it mean, Stony?" Nic asked. "What is he saying?"

"Absolutely no idea to be honest, Nic. I was unaware that he could do anything like this, man. I'm gob-smacked the same as you lot. I was just hoping he may be able to help and it looks like he actually knows what to do."

Despite the seriousness, they all managed a welcome laugh as Stony shook his head in wonderment and disbelief. It released the tension and, with a little humour in the atmosphere, they followed Regge as if he now had the status of leader of the pack.

There was obvious excitement and anticipation amongst the group as they scampered over slag, boulders, and thick clumps of coarse hillside grass in an attempt to stay close to Regge. They weren't his equal, but Regge understood that, hence his patient waiting for them to catch up once again; normally standing proud upon a large rock with tongue hanging and tail still a-wagging. The group would be stumbling and panting as they reached him, at which moment he would turn excitedly and charge forward yet again, occasionally dropping his head to scent the ground.

The pursuit went on and on, Regge not tiring, but the group realised that a break was called for as they hadn't yet stopped since the early morning.

It was late afternoon and they were making their way downwards now towards a valley none of them had ever visited before.

"Listen to me, everyone," Sarina said as she stood for a moment gathering her breath. "It won't be too long before the day will be turning so we'll need to look out for a sleeping place."

"Okay, I agree," Maggie agreed with Sarina; she was obviously becoming tired. "Look, as we haven't eaten yet we might as well wait until we stop. One more hour or as soon as we find somewhere suitable. Do we agree?"

All agreed and continued in pursuit of Regge. They followed the downward line of the small valley, hopping from one side of a surface stream to the other as the landscape demanded, Regge's haste drawing on their final reserves of energy.

"Look up above, man." Stony had noticed the very thing they didn't need. A small group of nomad warriors stood upon a high ledge looking down upon them. They all stopped dead and looked upwards. Nic, his brain working overtime, raised his hand in greeting and salute. They awaited a reaction; they continued to wait patiently. Then one of the figures returned the salute and they disappeared from sight.

"Well, man," said Stony, "I guess we've got problems, best prepare."

"Not necessarily, Stony, they may be okay," Sarina replied. "Let me go ahead and, if they show up down here, I'll speak first. That's not confrontational, they'll see that surely? You lot keep weapons well out of sight and hands clearly in view."

"Hang on, Sar, I'm not keen about this," Nic insisted. "There must be another way. I really don't like this. I know there's some sense in it, but, no Sarina. I will not allow you to do this."

Everybody else stood in silence, not wanting to interfere. Then Maggie spoke.

"Let Sarina and me go forward, Nic. Would that be alright?"

Nic thought for a moment. "Okay, that's a compromise, Maggie, thanks. But please be real careful. They're not to be trusted—these may be the bastards that attacked our village, and we all know that."

The two women moved out in front of the small band, knives tucked in the rear of their belts, and then continued on their route, with Regge out front leading.

After some nervous and tentative minutes, the women noticed a warrior seated upon a trackside rock ahead. Between them, they agreed to increase their pace a little, extending the gap between themselves and their group of friends. A little sweat appeared on their brows and palms, but they maintained their steady pace. Nic, Brian, and Stony had seen the nomad warrior but couldn't reduce the gap without displaying their concern; the distance had now grown to thirty metres. All were wondering where the others were and if there were more of them hiding behind rocks and lurking in the shadows, ready to pounce and relieve them of any goods of value and maybe even worse.

The two women quickly and quietly made a plan of action, and, acting upon their agreement, Sarina moved ahead a little until she stood but a metre from the seated warrior. Regge was now growling and generally making a brave defensive display.

Sarina hoped her action showed confidence and not foolhardiness.

She turned to face her group ready for the pain of a dagger in her back but it was not forthcoming; she raised her hand as if to bid them halt, and they did so. She was desperately trying to show power and authority. She turned back to the seated warrior who appeared to smile softly whilst totally ignoring Regge's aggression.

"Where are your fellow warriors? Why can we not see them?"

"We no harm to you. Me brothers go to camp, I alone." He stood slowly and continued to speak. "Greetings, friend. Look, see there, weapons."

Sarina looked where he indicated and, sure enough, some four metres away was a small pile of his personal weapons.

"Me see you search. You loss people, loss animals?"

"No. Well, yes, my children. You people invaded our village and killed many and took my children. They were lost to me some months ago."

"No me people. We hunt, we trade. Some nomad warriors bad. They attack, kill, take you things. No we. You and friends also dog, eat with me tribe. I ask questions about children, maybe help, and maybe able find."

Sarina spun the thoughts through her head. If genuine, it was a good offer. If not, they would be walking into a trap of sure death, possibly an unpleasant death, but she knew she must take the chance. Even so, she was unable to decide for her colleagues. She called them forward, asking the question of them as they approached. Brian did not need any time to consider the options. "All for one and one for all say I. This man's eyes say he is a good man. What do you lot think?"

They nodded their consent as Nic moved forward to shake the warrior's hand. As he did so, he placed a loving arm around Sarina's shoulders.

"Are you leader or is women or big man leader?"

"There is no leader. We make agreements together."

The warrior looked and stared hard at the group, showing his disbelief of such an outrageous idea.

"No leader? Mmm."

As the night began to draw in upon them, they followed the warrior, while Regge, a little confused, skipped and ran between them. Then ahead in the dusk could be seen a gathering of many small fires and nomad tents. Faces reflected the golden light of the flame as the people of the tribe grouped around the fires, either eating or chattering vigorously, while a small number of children ran and played between the tents. Most looked up as the outsiders entered the encampment; some stopped what they were doing and stood, but there was no overreaction, no threat. Only the children moved in closer, full of curiosity.

Looking around the camp, the visitors could see that about a hundred people constituted the tribe or at least this encampment.

They followed their newfound ally towards the central area, constantly looking left and right for danger of any kind, and then found themselves duly standing before the leader. He appeared a portly man whilst sitting, his knees spread wide with huge hands resting upon them, possibly in his late forties or early fifties. As he stood, that portly figure re-shaped into the widest man they had ever seen, which also disguised his very considerable height. His long hair and enormous beard gave him an awesome appearance. Like the other members of the tribe, he was dressed in draping wraps, loose and flowing, which the womenfolk wore with simple yet heavy long skirts that both reached the ground and covered their heads.

He stretched out a great and dirty hand, which they all duly took by way of greeting, before sitting as instructed on small stalls before the fire.

The leader, whose name was evidently Teo, spoke to the man they had met on the track and who, they now learnt, was called Vora.

Vora appeared to be explaining their plight—the lost children and the details. Teo nodded with seriousness and apparent understanding, uttering occasional grunts and affirmations. Throughout their conversation, the children ran amongst them, evidently enjoying a game of tag or something similar. Women brought over drinks of an unknown concoction and food in the form of flatbread and meat.

Nic and his group were humbled by the hospitality and concern afforded them. Vora turned to face them.

"Children oy or gir. Aj and color." As he asked his questions, he used sign and body language, indicating to them that he wanted to know the colour of their hair, their sex or height.

Another warrior was called into the discussion as more children charged into the circle.

"Voom, voom," Teo stood once more, clapping his hands, and women immediately appeared. Grabbing at the children and repeating the instructions, "Voom, voom tu", the women led them away, presumably to bed and sleep.

All this happened while Regge had been nestling close to Stony's legs, avoiding the stares and growls erupting from an array of large and fierce looking dogs. But none would venture into the magic Teo circle. On one occasion, one took two paces forward until Teo raised his head, giving him the harshest of looks that instantly shattered the dog's confidence and caused him to look away with nervous respect.

The discussion appeared to be coming to a natural end. Vora turned to them all and spoke, "Garta has an idea for find children. Problem, many children slaves with many tribes. Morrow we go look for you in brother tribes but now we must sleep. Tu follow."

They duly obeyed and were led to a small tent containing skins and other covers. It would be very friendly and warm. There was a flooring sheet raised all around the edges and tied to the support poles so it created a kind of circular hammock.

After thanking Vora and Teo, they squeezed into the tent, firstly allowing Brian to lie down rather than have him fall upon them. They fitted around his big frame with jokes and happy jibes; Regge leapt around the tent over everyone, causing further chaos while trying to seek a small area adjacent to Stony. That was just about impossible, so he settled for lying on Brian, head to feet, which didn't impress Brian very much with a long night ahead.

In time, the jesting reduced and everybody found his place in the jigsaw puzzle. Then sleepiness began to take over, all being aware of the potential nightmare which would occur when somebody attempted to turn.

They survived the night, albeit with an occasional, "who did that?" and "Regge get out of here, you smelly thing"; as all dived under the available cover.

Regge took any comment directed at him as a compliment, inducing wild tail wagging, which, at least in some reckoning; mixed and diluted the offending air.

When they started to awake, the time was early, but the sky promised a fine day. As one after another they peered and then staggered into the world surrounding their tent, there was nothing but activity. It was, after all, like any community. There was food to prepare, find, or hunt. Children had to be organised, and there was chatter to be shared. These people had amongst them rare strangers, and that was indeed quite an event in their lives.

Being amongst these potentially fierce and feared warriors was not as they had imagined it. In fact, their flowing costumes and apparent carefree way of life made both them and their lifestyle look solid and attractive. That being said, there still lurked that underlying uncomfortable feeling—the possibility that everything could change at the flick of a finger.

Teo approached the group and began to talk to them.

"Warriors gone search for children. Tu sleep good? By midday, we know. Ya, is good."

Nic responded and thanked Teo.

"Can we work with you, help you in some way?"

"No no. Tu stay camp. No problem. Food, ya."

As they ate bread with meat and drunk the strange liquid, they spoke of how kind these people were to them. The search felt hopeful and, although sitting doing nothing was the most difficult of tasks, they all knew it was the only thing to be done. Sarina, with Maggie, bravely decided to play with the children; the men sat and talked of what to do if the warriors search came to nothing.

Time passed slowly, but the sun kept rising and eventually midday was upon them. They all became aware that this was the time Teo had said the search groups should return. The anticipation was heavy, and although nobody spoke of it, there was a noticeable lull in their talk and play.

Time moved on and nobody returned to camp.

Sarina was, once more, deep in thought. Nic sat quietly while the others subtly tried to raise his spirits.

106

The children, fascinated by the group's clothing, hair, and general belongings, moved between them touching and pointing. Possibly the biggest puzzle was how these strangers spoke. They stared and listened in wonder at the endless gobbledygook, then asked questions but could not comprehend that their questions were not understood. At least in play, all were equal.

By late afternoon, there was still no news.

Teo and two women that had befriended them during the difficult day were now also trying to maintain their spirits, but hope was fading fast and their optimism appeared misplaced.

As their spirits diminished, the sun began to spread its evening rays into an awe-inspiring sunset. The distant horizon of red and gold threw ever-growing shadows over the sun-kissed hills.

Nic and Sarina stood together watching this wondrous scene, his arm around her to give comfort and ease her pain. Brian, Stony, Regge, and Maggie also stood together with a clutch of children around their legs, viewing the golden-red sunset. The tribe had also stopped for a moment so that all looked towards that glorious horizon.

Suddenly, amongst those growing shadows, figures were approaching. Possibly a search party. Sarina dare not think hopefully. The others also held their thoughts.

The long shadows grew nearer, misshaped twenty-foot shadow figures holding staffs and bows, slowly emerging from the blazon hallo formed by the setting sun, transforming mythical men into real men.

Once in view, the warriors stopped, and then standing together, they shook their arms in the air and jumped in a sign of victory. Sarina now shook physically. She bent forward holding her face for a second, then was erect once again, before she ran forwards toward the returning group with Nic at her side and the others at her heel.

"The children, you have found the children?" She spoke so quickly it wasn't audible to anybody. She spoke again but couldn't contain her words. Nic turned to Vora, who was amongst them.

"Have you managed to find the children, Vora? Are they alright?"

"Ya, children good. Moment, you see. On moment, tu see. Much talk, much trade. Children good."

Sarina flung herself at Vora's feet. She stood and hugged him; she took his hand and kissed it humbly, thanking him repeatedly. Her face awash, she moved between the warriors delivering equal gratitude and homage, eventually collapsing to her knees and crying like only a mother could. She was quickly joined by Maggie and other women of the tribe, all in tears, celebrating that miraculous moment.

It was a bond beyond bonds. Their tears could have flowered the greatest of deserts or created a tidal wave.

Brian spoke up loudly as he pointed once again towards the fading sunset. "It's the boys, Sarina. It's Jac and Ban. It's our boys—they are back."

A small group of warriors approached with Jac and Ban both perched upon strong shoulders. When the boys saw their parents, they leapt down keenly. As the family ran towards each other, all hearts melted and not a dry eye was to be seen.

Many of the tribal women had dropped to their knees and raised their arms in thanks.

Nic, Sarina, Jac, and Ban rolled into one another's embraces. Love and family.

They were re-united at long, long last.

Sometime soon, there would be stories to be told about this day and celebrations to be had with these wonderful nomadic people, who but yesterday always looked so fierce and were assumed to be untrustworthy. This day would never be forgotten, but now, right here, on this special day, there were no grandiose celebrations. This day was simply about a re-united family, tears and expressions of love.

The Big Gathering

Most mornings now were accompanied by a light groundcover of white frosty crystals, and, although Garr's cave enjoyed the benefit of sun for most of the day, it now took a little longer to share its warmth with earthlings.

Sala and Garr had lived in harmony for a while, both working hard to maintain and enjoy their existence together.

In that time, they had the added pleasure of a new and regular visitor into their world, the warrior chief, Idor.

Idor had taken his tribe and established a temporary camp at the foot of Garr's mountain. He had obviously taken to Garr in particular, and was somewhat confused by the addition of Sala within what he saw as a serious courtship. He avoided all the obvious questions and, with great difficulty, accepted that his courtship would have to be with both women. It was not that he didn't have loyalties to other women within his tribe, it was that he normally was the one to choose or order how things were to be and this change of circumstances obviously caused him some difficulties. The three began to enjoy hunting, eating, and endless talk around a fire together.

He had responsibilities to his people whom he had now instructed to establish a permanent encampment at the foot of the mountain. Initially it caused some small problems of dissent, but due to the general disposition of Idor's people and the power of his position, the problems were quickly smoothed away.

On many nights, he elected to sleep upon the guest bedding that Knap and Mara had used. He lay there awake, restlessly thinking of Garr and Sala. His heart was full of lust, love, and desire, and yet confused by the awakenings within himself. While Garr and Sala often did likewise, they were still able to indulge in the pleasures of their closeness. Even for them, the speed of the changes and growth of emotions and feelings sometimes gave them concerns and confusion.

Just prior to the journey to the Gathering, and after a day when Idor had spent a long time in their company hunting, the subject of their relationship at last found its way to the surface.

"Idor, we both enjoy your company and the time we spend together so much. We also understand that your great responsibility to your people, together with knowing both of us as almost strangers, is a difficult position for you and your tribe to accept. Sala and I have spoken many times of our affection for you, and you seem to understand the affection we have also found between ourselves. Could we not be closer, like man and wives? It would make us happy, and, if you can bear that, we think you might find some peace when sleeping here within this cave."

For a moment or two, Idor stared at the two women not knowing readily how to respond.

"Idor, if you cannot answer Garr's question, there is no pressure on you to do so. We are happy to see you whenever you wish to be here. We are happy to be your women, but our ways are different—we are independent women. We hunt for our own meat and build our own fires. Our families do not stay by our sides, and yet we love them. Our friendship must be a compromise as indeed is the friendship between Garr and I."

"I wish to answer Sala. To be here as my heart requires is not possible. We can occasionally be as one. My tribe and womenfolk will accept my word always, so perhaps to be as one in that way would be good. It is true that I need to treat you as my women—my heart tells me this. For me that means that you do as I say when we are together. Could you live in that way when I am here? Maybe not, but that is my way. It is not possible for me to share you with other men—no, no, this would not be possible, I would have no alternative but to kill. Yet, there are other women in my tribe. Do you understand this?"

The two women could feel the difficulty within his words and see the dilemmas clearly upon his face. This majestic lord of his people, this tall, powerful, yet gentle man was clearly in love and tormented with the impossibilities presented to him. He wanted it all but saw nothing but problems.

Garr stood and then moved towards him, feeling both his emotion and her own, she wrapped herself around him. She kissed him softly upon his cheek. He, as they were, was almost in tears, with their hearts torn and confused.

Sala responded also and taking the large wrap, which both she and Garr had been under, she rewrapped it around all three of them in silence. They stayed enwrapped for a while until all were able to speak clearly once again, albeit very slowly.

"We will try this. I will speak to my brothers. I will try and change, as you must. Now, I should go to my tribe."

"You know you can stay if you wish, Idor."

"Ya, I know and I thank you, but a night of thought is required for all of us. Both our hearts and our heads have much to consider, much to resolve."

He stood tall and straight and looked up towards the moon.

"You women have taken my heart, like I did not understand was possible. Our heads, though, are as one, filled with many dreams and possible problems, and yet the night remains as ever and the moon shines its silver light as ever. We also must be strong and constant and find a way to shine our own light upon this land. The future for us all is compromise and understanding. We will try and shine that light."

With that, he threw a skin around his broad shoulders and drew them both close to himself once more for but a moment, then he patted Monster roughly on his head and walked slowly from camp, displaying all the dignity he could muster.

It was not the ending to the evening that either Garr or Sala anticipated, but in reality their relationship was never going to be easy.

At least they had spoken of their feelings and in fairness, Idor had not had the same opportunity to digest and think about the new situation with any other person.

Garr and Sala sat in quietness at the fireside for a few more moments and then turned in for the night. Monster, fully aware of tension in the camp, was allowed to accompany them on the bed that night, at least until the warmth of one another generated the need for tenderness and touch. They both badly needed comfort and love to hide within.

The following day had an air of mixed feelings.

Neither of them could help but think about Idor and how he was feeling; had they said too much, or been too forward? Only time would tell.

They needed to prepare for long hikes and a further two or three days at least to enjoy the Gathering, as well as having to think about how to bring together the different communities invited.

The arrangements with Idor, Clark, and Knap had been made. They and their comrades or partners were to meet below the great white horse, which was some twenty kilometres away, about half the distance to the Gathering site.

Monster knew what was coming and didn't really like being a beast of burden but, with some pressure from Garr, he succumbed to wearing the leather harness and the two attached side packs and drag bars. From Monster's point of view that was bad enough, but then to load them fully was adding insult to injury.

He displayed his disapproval by refusing to look at either Sala or Garr. Wiz, the large white tom, appeared to be enjoying Monster's humiliation by sitting immediately in front of his face and purring loudly. It was simply all too much; Monster growled deeply at him and pushed at him in response but to no avail. He simply relocated a very small distance away and continued with his musical purring and sickly grin.

The women were feeling a little harassed and needed to be on their way.

"Come on, Sal, let's make a move. We can't take everything. We've enough food, warmth, and loads of salt—we'll trade for anything else we want."

They finally loaded Monster a little more with bows, staff, and further poles and left camp ensuring that Garr's security was firmly in place. They made their way down to the floor of the valley and around the warrior's encampment, where they searched for Idor. But he couldn't be seen.

It wasn't the best of days, and it reflected their mixed and strange moods.

"Look at it this way, Garr, if Knap hadn't made those new boots for you, this would be a much harder trek and, if young Monster there was half the size, we'd be carrying a load more gear. Anyway, the sun will soon be out."

"Sal, you're right but why don't your words make me feel happy and at peace. I'll tell you why anyway, to save you thinking—it's because I have committed to the impossible as regards these warriors, Clark and the hill folk. It's going to be complicated and probably will all fail badly. Then, all of them will end up hating one another even more and probably go to war and destroy each other and you in the process with burning arrows and axes. That is, of course, if they don't decide to burn you, Knap, and Mara in my tent. I can't afford to lose this tent, you know that it is the only one I have."

"How come you aren't getting burnt or slaughtered in this wondrous vision? Seems a bit unreasonable from my point of view, since it was you and my father that started all this. I guess my father could be burnt, but I don't like the idea that much. Anyway, knowing my mother, I would expect her to use the flames to cook something—she's very practical that way, you know."

Sala thought for a further moment.

"On top of that, I don't think it's right that I should lose both parents at the same time. And why isn't Monster burnt alive? That's the big question, Garr."

"No, it's the Big Gathering, Sala, and you are talking rubbish. It's obvious. Who is going to carry the unburnt gear home, through the battlefields, across the rivers, and over the mountains? In this story, one of us should survive. I just happened to think that if it was me, it would be a good idea. It's not personal—you know that surely. Why are you making such a big deal out of this? You're always so critical about my visions."

"Garr, darling, you're indeed, so lovely."

"Here we go, on cue—that old emotional angle. Knew you'd use dirty tricks in the end and employ emotion."

They laughed heartily together at their silly talk and walked on.

By now, their bright nonsensical chatter was matched by an even brighter day. They had covered a good distance without realising it and apart from Monster having some difficulty in peeing over every bush due to the drag bars and the weight loaded upon them, their progress was pleasing. Occasionally, Monster's effort to leave his mark dislodged the packing and chaos ensued, necessitating re-gathering and re-packing.

On the track, they occasionally passed people they recognized, family groups carrying great piles of produce or items they had made for trade.

Sharing talk for a while with everyone they met, both spread the message of their quest and attempt to build more unity between themselves, the shufflers, nomadic warriors, and other groups. Garr said that she thought leaders of other groups might well be at the Big Gathering, but she avoided talk of creating rules or leaders. She was surprised at how she spoke so cunningly and politically. It was not pre-planned; it just flowed out that way.

"Did that sound deceitful, Sal?" she asked afterwards. "I felt as if I was lying, somehow misleading those people, but what I said was actually true. There was just no point in complicating the issues."

"I don't think it was deceit. You said what you needed to, no more. They can say or think what they like, can't they?"

"You're right. For ages everybody has talked or muttered on about more security, co-operation, and all those things. It's just going to be difficult to actually do something about it. Talking about everything is oh so easy. I'm not really sure I want to continue with all this but since your Dad and I seem to be responsible for starting this, we better carry it through, whatever the result.

"I am beginning to see that all this thinking and talk is going to change my life, your life, and maybe everybody's life. The question is do I really want that? Could I cope with the responsibility of seeing something like this through to the end?

"Walking along here, knowing I am a free person is a good feeling. I'm beginning to feel real worried, Sal, scared even of what we may be starting. I want to run to the hills, just you, Monster, and me. I must have been quite mad."

Garr walked off track and sat upon the ground. Thoughts chased through her head. Sala could feel her concerns.

"Look, we're doing okay together aren't we? If Idor wants to be closer, that's up to him. If folks want change, well, it will happen, with or without you or Idor or my father. Personally, if somebody is going to push these changes, maybe even show leadership, Garr, I for one would rather it was somebody I trusted—you or my father. Yep, it's going to change everything, but surely isn't all this talk simply talk calling out for change? Haven't the people of Dartell and the warriors shown they want these changes? Of course they have. Just be yourself. You do have options, and you or others can always say yes or no. Listen, my lovely Garr, the principle here is freedom to choose—majority rule and freedom for all. Come on, let's walk on, relax, and make a clear decision. We can turn around and walk back if you so decide."

Sal had spoken sound and wise words. It was strange for Garr to be taking advice from Sala; normally it was the other way around, but she appreciated her input and couldn't wait to meet up with Knap, who would also be able to subdue her fears, unless of course he was also experiencing doubts. Sal was certainly her father's daughter. Neither were sure that they would arrive at the Gathering.

By late afternoon they were sitting under the white horse, a great carving upon the chalk hillside. Monster was relieved of his burden for a well-deserved rest. Much to their surprise, they were the first to reach the meeting place. Further doubts crept into Garr's head. In an attempt to shake her head clear, she suggested that they build a sleeping tent, as they would need to stay overnight by the time everybody was gathered.

They bent saplings into a dome and tied them off, then threw skins over the top and within. The sleeping area was finished within an hour, which was still well before the others arrived.

Clark arrived with a party of four, all heavily loaded, with the advantage of mules. Idor with two others, Volka and a direct brother of Idor, Yegor, arrived on foot.

Introductions flowed easily and within moments of meeting, everyone appeared to be interacting freely, even with Monster, who now had many people to keep his guarding eye upon.

It was some time before Knap and Mara arrived. Sal was pleased to see them again, as it had been some weeks now and it was indeed the first time they had ever been apart for so long.

Garr was carried along on the tide of cordial greetings and enthusiasm, delighted as always to see Knap. She had missed his input and calming influence and always enjoyed his easy company and friendship. He was somebody with whom conversation simply flowed because they shared similar values and ideals.

The central fire grew as people disappeared on unsolicited wood collection missions. Food appeared and skins spread as the evening began to draw in upon the mixed party.

Garr wondered if there had ever been such a gathering.

She explained to those around the fire that she had spread the thought that different community representatives might well rise up to reconcile as many of their differences as possible. She made it clear that neither Knap nor she knew how they would be received. She expressed her thought that the party must try to establish a central position at the Gathering in order to reach and be able to communicate with as many folk as possible. If they became the centre of any disputes, arguments or aggression, they must resist responding in kind, and at all times retain self-control. Regardless of anything, Garr concluded, they would stand together as a united family, shoulder to shoulder.

In different ways, they all appeared to pledge their resolve and loyalty.

At this, Clark brought forth a small cask, and as many drinking containers as possible were rounded up. Then Clark stood and slowly looked at each and everybody there, catching the attention of all, and very slowly raised his drink in a salute and spoke.

"As one family we will stand and as one family we will fall. I raise my drink to you all." It was an emotional moment, and they all truly felt that they were at the beginning of something very special.

In a rare moment, Mara then stood and expressed that she for one felt privileged to be standing there under the great white horse at this moment in history, and all others agreed and hooted their approval.

As the chatter and discussion went on and on, all joined in and re-committed to their quest time and again.

Monster took up the most central position possible, though always at Garr's feet, like a lion at the foot of a throne. His great red eyes opened immediately anybody twitched or stretched.

As the evening turned to night, coldness descended over the gathering. With burning faces and freezing backs, they huddled closer together. Clark's cask was duly emptied; the mead of some type, sweet and deceivingly alcoholic, was doing its covert job. Mara, who didn't really like alcohol, had indulged and was now sleeping heavily against Knap, which in itself was fine, but her snoring was of great amusement to all. For a woman of her age, all agreed that she was a marvel, and the whole party was beginning to treat her with reverence, assisting her with everything she attempted to do. Idor helped Knap escort her to the tent, and, even as she crossed the ground in a semi upright position, she let out an occasional high-pitched snore.

The party began to break up, ready for sleep, leaving only Idor and Clark in deep conversation at the fire's edge.

As Garr and Sala crept into their sleeping area, followed by Monster forcing his way past them, it was a pleasure to hear Idor and Clark laughing heartily together.

Garr lay for some time thinking how strange it was that people like Clark or Idor—serious leaders in their own right—were here laughing and joking around a fireside with nobody like themselves, en route to an impossible mission.

Sala mumbled something inaudible and turned over to spoon against Monster, who now had established ownership of over half of the tent space. Garr followed them and cuddled up close to Sala, feeling her softness and touching her womanhood, then drifting softly away into a wondrous sleep.

Sala and Garr woke later than intended, as did Knap and Mara.

Mara entered the camp with endless apologies and obvious embarrassment about the previous night, which all ruthlessly ribbed her over, uttering snore-like noises, accompanied by sad shakings of the head. Others had already started to dismantle their sleeping tents and a hot fusion was standing adjacent to the rekindled fire.

Sal, decidedly still in recovery mode, stood next to the fire, needing more time for her body to catch up via the good intentions of her head.

The morning was very fresh, and the sky was clear and promising.

Idor had found a little time and space to share with Garr; they walked slowly away from the gathering and eventually sat upon a large flat rock. Neither said a great deal, Idor with his arm around Garr's waist feeling her warmth and her softness. As they stared out across the narrow valley, Idor turned and lent forward and kissed her gently. His kiss was loving, as were his thoughts. Their skin tingled at one another's touch; they were both aware of deep feelings. Was this love? He took her head within his hands and slowly stroked her hair. She found herself frozen in pleasure by his touch. He looked deep and long into her eyes, and she into his. They both knew that the moment was special; they saw the future and it felt good. Words seemed inappropriate, unnecessary.

"We must join the others."

In silence, they wandered back, and other matters began to intrude. The magic dissipated as they found themselves re-joining the rest of the group. Idor called Sala to join them. She shivered her way towards them. The temptation for all to touch was immense, but diplomacy was now called for and they compromised by standing close, while Idor explained that he would be spending time with them when the Gathering was over.

"It will not be easy, but it is my want. We will be happy together I think. Now, the Gathering is important for many people—we must all do the best we can. I wish for love and good luck. We talk later."

"That's wonderful news," Garr replied. "Listen, you like Clark I think. We heard you laughing last night, which was a good sign."

"Ya, good man."

Throughout the following conversations, Garr's body was split into a thousand pieces. Her mind flicking between thoughts of love for Idor, then Sala, and then her mission. But somehow, from her mouth, words just flowed, good words, real words that others responded to. She fought hard to retain her sanity and composure.

The remaining journey went well, with the day eventually warming up a little and the track they followed becoming easier. An obvious effort was made by all the group to interact, and to Knap and Garr's surprise, not once was there any confrontation between their fellow travellers.

Spirits were high and anticipation ripe, despite the weariness. Folks wanted fun, talk, and trade. They wanted to hear some music, drink a little alcohol, or take some light herbal relief, and then hopefully dance away the harshness and realities of their lives.

For the younger amongst the hill folk, this was a time for play or courting. Here you could find love and maybe sexual experience; you heightened or fulfilled your dreams.

To the very young, this was a riot of freedom; it was a time to meet cousins and family they had never seen or heard of, to build camps and swing upon ropes that hung from trees. Here you created memories that lasted forever.

As they strolled their way across the gently undulating plain towards the centre, Garr spent some time thinking of her brother. She missed him and his presence in her life. Once they had been inseparable and indispensable to one another. Rushes of love flowed through her. She had managed to see him here once before, but it was not an easy task to find anybody amongst so many. Regardless of her other commitments, she decided that she must dedicate time to seeing him and his family. Maybe at last, it was time for them to be closer once more, to act more like the family they were. She knew that she would like that and in many ways needed it. Furthermore, the children would be with him. She realised that would be the beginning of many changes that she had been thinking of.

A hand appeared upon her arm, making her jump from her thoughts. It was Clark.

"Look, Garr, how about setting up over there. Knap and Idor think it looks like a good place. There's that wooded area and the ground is raised a little. Shall we?"

"Excellent, it looks perfect. Do you agree, Sal?"

"Yes, it looks perfect to me as well. Come on, Mum, let me give you and Dad a hand setting up."

"It's not a problem, thanks," Mara replied. "Volka and Yegor have already volunteered, sweetheart. I am being treated like a queen for some reason. I could get used to all this."

"It's a cultural thing," explained Knap. "They are obligated to respect the oldest member of the family within their own tribe."

"What? But, you're older than me, Knap."

He shrugged his shoulders as though he didn't understand the implications of his words, turned, and smiled widely, winking at Garr and Sala. They all turned away, while Mara dealt with the conflict of being treated like royalty and having servants, set against being treated as the ancient one.

Within a couple of hours, all the tents were erected. Over to their left, people had already repaired one of the stone circles within which dance and music mainly took place. There, some musical groups were already playing, and a group of children looked on while others ran races around the circle or zigzagged and chased between the campsites. Within most of the established camps, small fires burnt, some with large pots suspended over them. Brightly coloured fabrics had been attached to the top of tents and separate poles, which had been located around there camp sites. When the wind caught the banners, they flapped and twisted, dancing merrily in the breeze.

Mara and Garr had thought ahead and went about the business of decorating their encampment. They were used to the yearly requirements and had brought with them endless lengths of silk, a thin and light fabric much valued. When this was done, they issued long thin sections of the fabric to all in their party. Some wore it around their waists; the women generally took the thinner pieces and wrapped a number of them around there heads and arms, tying them off in a traditional manner with a cluster of ends left to hang and flutter.

An air of jollity began to grow around the camp but Mara, Sala, and Garr were not happy yet with their efforts. Knap was dispatched to the woods behind them with Volka to gather creepers and vines, which they twisted and wove nimbly together. Then they tied sections of silk around the garland, converting it into something quite splendid. This was then looped from pole to pole, with further sections twisted down the poles. Clark and Idor's groups were impressed with the speed at which that little area of empty ground had been converted into a palace of gaiety and grandeur.

With the camp spirits high and most things well on the way to being completed, Garr mentioned to Knap that she would stroll around the grounds in search of her brother. Sala joined her both as company and to gain some one-to-one time away from the busyness of the camp.

Clark's companions had already taken food from their packs and were producing a large pot of something, while Knap and Mara went about the mission of gathering wood.

Idor, Volka, and Yegor were happy to sit by the fireside, taking a little rest while obviously causing interest among some of the passing folk. Occasionally, one walked over to them and joined in welcoming or asking difficult questions. Sometimes, there was a touch of aggression lurking within their tone or attitude. The fact that children found them an interesting bunch appeared to ease the tension.

Idor was, in particular, a regal man, capable of generating immediate respect, peace, and tranquillity; if ever a natural diplomat existed, it was Idor. With his natural ease, he entertained children with tricks and fun, while speaking clearly of his wishes for better relationships with the hill folk.

Yet again, the day dulled but tonight the Gathering would be alight with many campfires, and in the background, music was played and children jumped and moved to the rhythmic sounds that floated over the constant hum of chatter and laughter.

Nic and Brian led their group onto the Big Gathering site. Behind them followed Sarina and Maggie, with young Jac and Ban. Stony, Regge, and both of Brian's sons, together with womenfolk and children followed at some distance.

Theirs was a weary group, and it was too late to establish their tents and camp. Therefore, it was decided to create a quick and temporary set up for the night, so allowing the children to sleep and the parents to recover. It was hard to persuade the children to go to sleep with so many new and exciting discoveries around them. But nevertheless, it wasn't too long before the parents felt as if they were in control and their treasured little bundles were far away in another dreamy world.

These days, special attention was required in putting Jac and Ban down to sleep.

Sarina or Nic needed to sit with them, stroking their brows and talking softly until this extra security generated adequate comfort, allowing them to relax into peaceful slumber. If either awoke during the night, the process was repeated once again; there was still some time to go until the nightmares would be wiped from their young minds.

Garr and Sal had strolled through some of the site until the light defeated them, but they did not see the weary men and women that had appeared nearby and slowly unpacked their tents while shouting at their children. Neither did they notice the two quiet children who sat upon the travel packs away from the other more boisterous boys and girls or the man bending before them deep in comforting talk.

This group would sleep well tonight, the music not touching or interfering with them.

Although the main activities at the Gathering had not yet started, the music certainly had, and family groups bobbed and swayed rhythmically. Occasionally a "whoopee" was heard as somebody moved quickly or swirled enthusiastically.

Garr's group had discussed a plan to promote their intentions. As Idor's group was made up of three members, they decided to split into three groups so that each could contain a member from each community. Once the little delegations had been elected, they planned to spread out around the site to explain their thoughts and both gauge response and gather support prior to trying to engage a larger crowd. If particular enthusiasm was picked up in somebody, all had agreed that they should be encouraged to join forces. If appropriate, they should be encouraged to take a leading role.

It was a sound plan, the likes of which none of them had ever been involved in before.

"I'd rather be dancing," Sala whispered to Garr.

"So would I, Sal. There'll be time. Anyway, this is a bit like dancing but with words."

"I'm not convinced, but it's a good line for the uninitiated."

Knap overheard their banter.

"I've got to agree with you two girls. What are we all doing? I tell you, I'm really not sure, I've many doubts. I know its Garr's fault, that's all."

"I don't like you any more, Knap I thought you were my friend. You're a horrible man, be gone with you and do your job."

"Okay, Garr, see you later," and he blew her a kiss as he left.

As the three groups wandered off into the night, they smiled at one another and Garr noticed that the others were beginning to understand their humour, which initially had confused them badly. They simply could not understand how, as friends, they would speak to each other in such a manner. Clark in particular was starting to try his hand at such humour. He was not a master yet and some attempts were quite bizarre, which caused even more laughter.

There was, unfortunately, a weakness in their plan; it had failed to factor in alcohol. They knew that folk at the gathering let their hair down but they did not expect or anticipate that it would affect their mission. At most of the individual camp sites where they paused to talk, they were obliged to partake in at least one drink, usually more. Independently, they all tried to limit the assault on their clarity but all were failing badly. None of the group was used to the habit of drinking alcohol in volume; it existed in the larger communities but was rare elsewhere. So, after their tiring journey and with minds full of thoughts and confusion, drinking was not going to help.

As fuzzy words turned to fuzzy knee joints, accompanied by much giggling, they all appreciated their task this night had been ambushed by the devil drink. With each group feeling guilty, they attempted to wander back towards their own campsite, food and sleep.

_ chuckling Clark and Idor supported a staggering Garr, laughing profusely at her jellied legs. Monster was mystified and concerned by the goings on, as was Mara who had worked religiously to prepare a great pot of stew for the hard-working teams.

If they had been in a bad state, it was nothing compared with the return of Sala, Volka, and Smithy, one of Clark's delegation. Formed together in a caterpillar, with the good intentions of maintaining dignity and staying upright, they weaved their way towards the campsite, through an amused throng of onlookers. As sound as their thinking was, they had gone well past the point of stability and as they approached the entrance to the encampment with whoops and laughter, there was an obvious and unstoppable leaning to the right. Wrapped in vines and garlanding amongst two broken poles, they struggled in vain to scramble to their feet. In doing so, they knocked over yet another pole, sending it sideways towards the centre of their encampment, with the top end of it unfortunately catching the stew pot that Mara had prepared. The pot tipped towards them, causing a cascade of meat, carrot and lentils. Realising the impossibility of their endeavours, they relented and lay there in a twisted and carrot splattered heap. Resigned to their humiliation, they slid into drunken slumber.

Tutting and shaking her head in disapproval, Mara saved what she could of the stew pot.

"It'll be soup in the morning. Well, well! I really don't know what's going on with all of you."

Mara decided it was time for her to sleep too, and she left them where they lay.

Garr, in the meantime, had staggered to her feet at the appearance of Sala, who held her and then eased her towards their tent, and unceremoniously pushed her inside. Once in the tent, Garr curled into the foetal position, causing Sala to crawl over her feet, which she had not managed to push inside, only to be met by Monster, who snored happily with complete disregard for the whole predicament.

Knap and his crew were, by comparison, doing better than the others. Maybe it was the thought of Mara awaiting his return that allowed him to remain a little more sober, but somehow time had escaped him.

They now sat together with the fourth group of hill folk that they had visited and to whom they had managed to explain their thoughts. A long discussion had followed, supplemented with food, which helped to subdue the effects of the alcohol they also consumed but developed a desperate need for sleep. About the same time as the music was beginning to end far across the site, their heads were nodding and their necks were jerking in their attempts to stay awake. A couple of times, Knap had commented that they must be on their way but nobody moved, so the nodding and jerking and chatting continued, interspersed with jokes and jest, until one by one the whole party curled upon the cold ground in partial sleep.

Sometime later, Yegor roused and stood. He was chilled to the bone. He shook Knap, the others, and also their hosts, thanking them sleepily and dragging his comrades back towards their own camp.

On arrival, Idor and Clark managed to move themselves to their tents but at the entrance, still entwined in garlanding, were Volka and Smithy. They tried to awaken them, but to no avail. Yegor picked a large lump of meat from Volka's forehead, which he could not resist, before throwing covers over them and finding their own tents, just as light appeared over the surrounding hills. Knap crept into bed as softly as he could manage and lay down silently next to Mara, who now slept and snored happily.

The following day did not start until sometime after midday. Mara had been up early and was busy tidying up the site; she had also moved poor Volka and Smithy to somewhere more comfortable. That was after Smithy had found it necessary to crawl painfully towards the nearest shrub to empty his stomach. Indeed, it was a sorrowful sight.

There were few smiles around, a lot of grunting and embarrassed glances, and feeble good morning greetings as one after the other they appeared to make their apologies and fanciful explanations for their behaviour.

"It wasn't me."

"I was okay until—"

"They just wouldn't listen."

"I know, but I had no food yesterday."

"I must have eaten something real bad."

By the evening, most of them were sworn to abstinence, and all were thoroughly embarrassed, particularly considering the intent of their mission. Now, credibility seemed unlikely with any of the folk they had visited. Fortunately, they were not the only ones to have started their Big Gathering badly. Like them, most of these folks were not used to the freedom of so much alcohol. Fights had occurred, people wounded, some deaths, and generally disorder in all directions. It would be some time before they would re-gather their senses and revert to being the people they could be.

All around the Gathering, stalls and displays of goods were appearing. The archery competition was being organised in which Garr, Idor, and Yegor intended to compete. In other corners, boulder tossing and hoop throwing was in progress. There were races and spear throwing competitions.

Brian had entered the boulder tossing; he was big and strong. In the past, he had nearly won, but of course nearly was never good enough.

The organisation was a miracle of mayhem but showed that the ability to organise and lead certainly existed when need be.

Unbeknown to them both, Sarina and Garr had both entered the big race. It was a tough race, up and over the hills behind the site and through the woods.

The evenings and the nights were dance times. People from fifty different cultures, and varying in a dozen shades, added their individuality to a swaying, hopping, and spinning experience. Yes, that demon alcohol was around, and many other relaxation aids, but if you wanted to see the night through, it was a matter of slowly, slowly.

Two days turned to four, and, Garr, together with the others, established themselves by one means or another. Folks who had not known either Knap or Garr, now recognized them and the issues they had been discussing at every opportunity were now talked of often amongst the crowd.

It was decided that at the next occasion when a large crowd was available, they needed to bring the issues to a head by discussing their ideas to a mass, thereby bringing forth more open appraisal or indeed argument.

The approach was agreed by Garr's party. As most of the people seemed generally in favour of change, there needed to be a focal point around which all could gather. An easy starting point in which the hill folk could place some kind of allegiance would be the election of a council with councillors from all areas.

They had realised the impossibility of holding an initial election, and so settled on the idea of voluntary councillors, if, of course, it was acceptable to the crowd but how much power should these councillors have? They decided that councillors should be allowed to generate assistance, in the form of food or wood, from those they represented, but nothing could be coerced.

From the discussions they had, they knew the extremes of distance that folks had travelled to the Gathering, and so a master map was created covering the area, which spread far to the north, south, east, and west. They entered the geographical features they knew while gathering additional information from others they spoke too. For council districts, they used natural boundaries such as rivers, mountain ranges, and landmarks, as well as large communities.

They did their best to locate the centre of the whole area as a place for major meetings. Then they decided that a number of meeting places should be selected, in order to fairly ensure that no-one was disadvantaged by the distance they had to travel.

It was a simple formula, as it needed to be. All that was needed now was the opportunity to discuss the proposals openly, and for the people to agree and give real support rather than lip service. This was the hardest part and it required a leap of optimism. While there seemed to be enthusiasm for such arrangements, were these just desires generated by the occasion? Once back into their normal routines, could people be relied upon to convert wishes and commitments into actions.

As they contemplated this, it was tempting to feel they had been naïve in promoting their ideas. Despite their progress so far, what if it would all prove meaningless and pointless. It was Clark and Volka that re-energised them. Garr was quick to follow their lead, and before too long, the earlier enthusiasm was again fully installed in the group.

Recharged, they made tall pointed hats from reeds so that they could be identified easily. They decided that Idor, Clark, and Garr should take centre stage, while the others should mingle throughout the crowd and encourage their attention if it was at all possible. They spoke to the groups of musicians, the organisers of the competitions and games, and the stall-holders adjacent the central stone circle. To all of them, they explained their intentions that today, come early evening, they would try to bring the people together. Once again, they began to feel nervous, yet excited, for overall there was a desire for change amongst the people.

There was no more they could do, and, anyway, there was an archery competition to attend.

Yegor, Idor, and Garr checked their bows and then selected the best of strings and straightest of arrows. The competition would be tough, for everyone was a hunter; their existence relied upon their skill to bring home the meat and, occasionally, to stay alive.

There were two elements to the competition. Firstly, a straight knock out, one against one, using a fixed target, consisting of a brown outer ring, a white inner ring, and a red bull's eye. Each competitor had three shots. Secondly, the final ten would play off on a points basis, using a smaller swinging target. Each of the final ten were allowed any number of arrows until the target stopped swinging. This tested accuracy, judgement, and speed. The winner obtained a status of almost godlike proportion.

There were other competitions that had been carried out during the Gathering, entailing spears and axe throwing, which required great skill, but none had a status equal to archery.

Garr had done well in the past, normally reaching the final group, but, as yet, she had never been the victor. She had progressed slowly higher within those final ten over the last few years, finishing somewhere within the top four. It felt like her time had come, and privately she was expecting, or was it hoping, to wear the crown of glory.

Folk of all types, ages, and sex took their turn. Some were fully prepared, others entered for the mere fun of the occasion. Their numbers were reduced quickly, layer after layer dismissed back into reality, illusions destroyed and dreams shattered.

Slowly the general array of recognized archers began to near the final ten. Each year saw old champions dismissed and new contenders arrive. Each one had a band of dedicated supporters shouting aloud their encouragement and jeering at the judgements which eliminated their heroes.

At this stage, it was a noisy event and indeed a noisy gathering. As the intensity increased, the sounds changed to oohs and aahs, intermingled with the dead silence of concentration followed by great sighs.

Folks re-arranged themselves for better viewing, sitting on shoulders and standing on casks or wagons. The fine details of the competition were discussed by onlookers as the leather pouches of alcohol were passed from one to the other until their ownership was unknown and unimportant. The excitement was exhausting and exhilarating.

There had been some disputes, some serious arguments; one involving prejudice against the warriors because they were outsiders. Thankfully, the crowd was just and the offenders were sent from the scene in clear disgrace.

The three friends were all through to the final ten. They saluted each other. From here on, they were simply competitors.

Yegor and Idor used arrow quivers, which fitted their lifestyle, while Garr preferred pre placed arrows lined before her in competition. Some with large bows knelt, resting the extended tail of their bows upon the ground; no competitors using crossbows had reached the final ten.

Nerves were beginning to show as the ten shook hands. The moment was nigh and all keenly knew that any of them could fall at this stage. A puff of unexpected wind, a second's lack of concentration, a missed final adjustment or a wrongly taken breath; all of this could mean one point less. In the past, the competition had often been won by that one point. It could mean the difference between elation and depression, between the championship and nothing.

The stakes were very high and the pressure immense.

Nic and Sarina, with the boys on their shoulders, were there together with all their friends. Nic had known that if he was to see Garr, this is where it would happen. Even when they were younger, he had envied her skill with the bow; she had always been a natural. Over the years, the envy had turned into something more adult. Now, the amount of pleasure, pride, and warmth that pulsed through him as he watched his sister was enormous.

Above all others, his voice could be heard, which was not his natural way at all. He also knew, now with his own life and family well established, the sacrifice that Garr had made in allowing him the time to be with Sarina. She had given him the time to grow into a man without being able to revert or hide within the sorrows of the past.

As soon as Nic saw Garr, his life had flashed back to those earlier years together, the good and the bad ones, and he hungered to take her within his arms and display his brotherly love and devotion. He wanted and needed his own family to enjoy his pleasure and share in the rewards that came from that feeling of closeness. No, he had never allowed her to be far away from his thoughts. His children knew of her and the adventures that he and his sister had shared in their childhood. As they had grown older, they had met Garr at the Gathering for but a few days.

Now she stood before them as an archer of repute at the centre of this spectacle, which everybody they knew held in the highest esteem.

Standing upon an open cart, the organiser raised both arms to call for hush.

"The skill of our archers improves year upon year. It has been decided that an additional layer is to be added to the competition. The four highest scorers will be called upon this year and for years henceforth to complete a final further round of three arrows only, upon the fixed target, taking it in turn with a single arrow. Do we all agree?"

The crowd in rapturous response indicated clearly that the more competition they could view, the better they liked it.

"I think that was a roar of agreement, my friends. So let the battle commence and the champion be found."

It was an uplifting start, and the chattering of expectation moved across the crowd.

It was strange that here, before the competition, this enormous group of fiercely independent people who normally spent most of their existence in a solitary manner, hunting and gathering, now appeared as one.

The arrows flew.

The tension continued to mount.

The target swung again and again, creaking and squeaking, and then stopping with a decisive click each time the momentum ceased.

A young lad of around seventeen was amazingly fast, his aide having to replace his supply of arrows twice. He managed to shoot off thirty-two arrows before confronted by the inevitable click, but his arrows could have been truer. Twenty on target, but far too many within the outer ring—twelve. Six were declared within the inner ring, but only two on the bull's eye. His total score was one hundred and forty.

Capable scribes marked down the results.

He raised his hands in victory, a little prematurely, Garr thought.

Yegor had drawn to shoot second. It was a disadvantage to be early to fire.

"He is much good archer, Garr," Idor said, "very quickly, very true. He and me, both maybe win. One time, Yegor. One time, me. You watch."

Idor's words were true. Yegor stared hard at the target for a second, then making the younger lad appear a novice, he began to let fly. The aide reloading Yegor's arrows needed further assistance to match his speed.

Thud, thud, thud was heard by an amazed audience, as arrow after arrow found its mark upon the swing target. The magic was finally stopped by the dreaded click. Yegor had discharged forty-one arrows; thirty-five had hit the target, with nine on bull's eye. It was, by any standard, a magnificent display. Yegor was obviously pleased and relieved.

There was no distinction noticed between race, tribe or creed; this was truly about archers of distinction alone.

He returned to stand with Idor and Garr, glowing with satisfaction. They shook his hand enthusiastically in congratulation.

The tension was mounting, and, within both Garr and Idor, unspoken doubts began to appear. Three-hundred and fifty was an enormous score, and, at this moment, it felt unbeatable.

Archer after archer stood before the creaky and squeaking target, apprehensively preparing for their best.

Garr had been drawn seventh to shoot and Idor last. The time passed slowly and, within their heads, only the intrusive roar of the crowd enabled them to remain in the reality of the competition.

The scores and standard of skill was exceptional: 345, 295, 320, and then 345 again. It was Garr's time to be tested. Her two comrades patted her on the shoulder. She took possibly the largest breath she had ever taken, straightened herself, and stepped forward.

From within the crowd, the roar of Nic was heard above all others, and, for a second, she glanced in that direction; she couldn't see her brother, but she knew it was him. As her head swivelled back towards her task, she reflected briefly upon a child waving vigorously, sat upon somebody's shoulders, and knew that it must be Jac or Ban.

The task leaped back to the fore of her mind, and she studied the target like never before.

It was her enemy. She hated it. It must die so she could survive to share her life with those she loved. The feeling grew as she lined her arrows before her, each precisely placed.

"Are you ready, Garr?"

She nodded her readiness.

The target was swung. She never heard the creaking and squeaking, the roars, or whooping. She entered a silent world of concentration.

Fast as she was, the speed of Yegor was not the objective and placed no pressure upon her. The arrows flew, fast and steady. Concentrating upon the movement of the imaginary breast and the escaping enemy, she sent her arrows repeatedly onto the target, with each shot met by the unheard roar from the excited crowd.

The target began to slow and she instinctively adjusted.

Thirty arrows had been released. She knew the flight of most had been true. She slowed now instead of speeding, this was the time to find the eye. Each leaping beast within her mind was taken to the ground before the click of stillness broke her concentration.

The roaring crowd broke through. She returned to earth and sighed, her weary bow in hand at her side.

Before her remained four arrows. She had managed thirty eight; more than she had expected.

Judgements were being made at the motionless target, and both her and the crowd waited in expectation.

Scores were being scribed. Then the boards were held aloft.

"Outer, nineteen … inner, six … and bulls, ten." It was magnificent: 355.

Garr leapt high above the ground and whooped herself hoarse.

The crowd roared yet again in appreciation as Idor and Yegor rushed forward with genuine glee at their friend's fine display. As all three embraced in celebration, Garr relaxed fully for the first time. They walked together to the side-lines as competitor number eight took position.

Again, the crowd braced itself and prepared to be entertained.

By the time Idor was called, a tense situation had developed.

Garr still held the lead score, followed by Yegor and Leron, a hill man, both scoring 350. Idor would have to excel and achieve a score of at least 350 to be standing there for the final shoot off.

Unusually, his discomfort could be seen. Although a powerful man within his community, he had humility but he, like anyone, wanted success and victory.

He relaxed and nodded his readiness. The squeaking began simultaneously with the flight of arrows.

Garr and Yegor watch on in suspended pain mixed with good will.

If it was possible, his release rate appeared a little faster than Yegor's. This was perhaps the wrong tactic. He had already said that Yegor was the fastest archer he had ever seen and was renowned amongst his people.

From the side-lines, time passed slowly—very slowly.

His arm pumping quickly from quiver to bow, he managed to copy Garr's slowing as the target reduced its speed and he made the final effort.

It was once again a brilliant display of archery, and Garr was proud of him. Within the crowd, Sala also glowed a little with pride as that tall majestic man completed his task.

In reality, he wasn't happy with his effort. He knew he had started too quickly and secretly cursed his haste.

Garr had moved beside him, while they awaited the final scores.

350 was good enough, not for his self-esteem, but it allowed him another opportunity; the crown could still be his.

The targets were exchanged.

The four finalists were called forward.

The new rules were explained again. Each was to fire a single shot three times, in turn, with no time limit. In the case of a draw, the game would be replayed until the victor was found. The target had been moved further away by ten metres; it really tested accuracy.

They shook hands in mutual appreciation. All knowing that the crown could be worn by any of them. The order of firing was decided.

Two nomad warriors, a tall athletic blond woman, and a dark-skinned hill man toed the line as requested. It was electric and the crowd understood the excellence that was before them.

At the centre of a hushed gathering, Garr took her shot.

It felt right.

The eyes and heads of the crowd followed the flight of the arrow as one. It found its mark; a bull's eye. Garr, fists clenched, as she leapt with joy.

Yegor stepped forward, stared at his target, and let fly. They all stood to watch its flight, then held their breaths as the arrow dropped slightly, before thudding home into the red of the bull's eye once more.

Yegor upstaged Garr's delight by jumping forward with arms held high.

"Ya, ya. Tis good. Yoll, yoll!" He danced a small jig in a circle of pleasure.

Once the mutter of the crowd had died away, Leron stepped forward for his attempt, adjusted carefully his ancient pair of glasses, and stood in deep concentration. His black skin showed the reflection of the lowering sun upon his wet brow. He raised his bow and took a steady aim, pulling the string back into a deep vee, and released his arrow. Heads arced with the flight, and cheers burst from the crowd as the thudding shot plunged once again into the red of the bull's eye.

He stood proudly, with his bow and arm high in salute to his appreciative audience.

His fellow competitors took his hand in respect and congratulations.

With three direct hits upon the bull's eye, Idor was under immense pressure. His body disguised his concern, but his eyes told a different story, and both Garr and Yegor could see it.

He followed the procedure. The crowd held their breaths once more. He raised his bow and took aim. As soon as he released, he knew. The smallest degree of hesitation was enough. He turned away awaiting confirmation of disappointment.

It landed within the outer of the target—brown.

He stared across the empty range, believing and not believing the result.

From where Sala stood, she could feel his despair, and from where Garr stood, looking across at this man, she could see it also.

She mustn't rush to him; it would be humiliation for sure.

The shooting of the second arrows were as tense. Garr, brown; Yegor, another bull's eye; Leron, a further bull's eye, and Idor scored white. Now with Yegor and Leron beginning to pull ahead with two bull's eyes each, it was impossible for anybody to relax.

As the third and final round began, a pin could have been heard if dropped.

They stepped forward in order. Leron let fly; it looked good yet appeared to dip at the last moment, plunging between red and white. The judges now debated, and, much to Leron's disappointment, he was judged to be within white.

Garr, who couldn't now win, still wanted another bull's eye added to her score. She aimed then stopped and readjusted. She aimed yet again and let fly her arrow. The seconds felt like minutes, followed by the thud of the arrow falling into the white inner ring. She jumped in disappointment and then took Leron's hand.

Idor was next, and, realizing it was impossible for him to win, let go his arrow at speed. It flew well and straight, and, to his surprise, thudded into dead centre—red.

To win, Yegor needed red; nothing else would do. If he scored in the outer ring, he would come second.

This, the final shot, was really down to extreme skill and nerve.

Folks within the crowd adjusted their positions. This was not the time to miss the flight or thud of the arrow.

The tension was exhausting.

Yegor took in a good, deep breath and steadied himself. He tossed his head to send his hair backwards. He stretched his fingers and closed them. He stepped forward, the crowd mumbled and were then hushed. Time stood still. He aimed, slowly drawing back his arrow of intent, and sent his best effort forward.

The heads of the crowd arched in unison.

The thud resounded around the crowd.

It went straight to the very heart of the bull's eye—perfection.

As realisation of the achievement settled on the crowd, a great roar erupted from the crowd. Yegor was the champion; he had achieved the impossible for himself, for the warriors, and for the future wellbeing of all.

Without consideration for who or what he was, he was raised upon shoulders and disappeared from the view of Garr, Leron, and Idor.

They would now all be welcome amongst hill folk anywhere. They would forever be icons.

Suddenly, two small, warm hands appeared around Garr and Idor and squeezed them close.

"Hi, Sal. We didn't do too badly, did we?"

The opportunity for a meeting with the people had vanished with the excitement of the competition.

Yegor was carried around and around the Big Gathering site. Wherever they stopped, he was offered food, drink, and gifts. Young women collected in small bands of adulation and followed the group, discussing his amazing virtues and looks. It was obvious that most had spent time dressing in their party finery and attending to their hair with flowers and bows.

Sala and the others rushed around in an attempt to adjust the arrangements for the proposed meeting; tomorrow would be their day.

Garr had excused herself and gone to find her brother. Nic had done likewise, but the swirling of the crowds as they dispersed confused the situation. Both Nic and Garr struggled hopelessly through the moving mass.

Idor found the defeat more difficult to accept, although he experienced great pride in that Yegor, one of his own, was now the champion. This alone would forge lasting bonds between the peoples. Garr took a more resolute view, and within her soul was determined that at the next Big Gathering, it would be her moment of victory.

She would retrain and retrain, practise and practise; she now expected nothing less than perfection from herself, and she knew that she, Garr, the woman from the mountains, could achieve this.

Sarina, together with her friends, had moved with the crowd back towards their campsite. Nic had decided with her that he should continue to search for Garr.

It was by good fortune that they spied one another through one of those strange openings that suddenly appear within a crowded area. Like magic, Nic stood at one end of the clearing and Garr at the other. The sun was throwing the last of its rays upon the scene. Ignoring the hubbub of the crowd, they walked into each other's embrace, enjoying a pleasure that was well overdue. They held on tightly, allowing the moment to be absorbed, allowing memories, warmth, and mutual love to flood their minds.

The moment having passed, they began to speak of everything and anything, their chatter intermingling and overlapping. Nic had an easy arm around Garr's shoulders, feeling the man of the family; she felt supported by her brother and small, maybe even childlike, for a moment.

Nic explained the terrible story of the boys' disappearance, the battle with the warrior band, and how his small village had grown and developed.

She told him of her life upon her mountain and her cave, her plans regarding the formation of councils, and, of course, stories about Monster, Idor and Sal.

Indeed, where was Monster? She was suddenly concerned that she hadn't seen him for quite a while.

"Nic, I must check on him. He's the most magnificent creature you've ever seen. Look, tomorrow afternoon I and my colleagues must speak to the Gathering without failure or the moment will be gone. Where is your campsite?"

"Firstly, Garr, you forget I've seen Monster when he was very young, he was some kind of special dog even then. As for our campsite, dear sister, it's to the far south of the site backing onto the forest. All the tents have red banners upon them, you won't miss us."

"Okay, may I bring my friends and Monster to your camp this evening—we've still got some food. Let's spend tonight together, us and our friends. That would be so wonderful."

"It sounds perfect, Garr."

They embraced again and parted, both walking away from each other with lightness in their step.

Garr, still enduring congratulations as she walked through the thinning crowd, made her way back to her own campsite, with the glimmer of fires and torches now marking her way. She was met by further embraces as she entered her own camp and, to her relief, a bounding Monster, leaping and jumping with pleasure at her appearance.

The evening went well, with Sarina, Garr, Sala, and the boys naturally bonding together. There was nearly an incident when Idor, Yegor, and Volka, strolling leisurely behind Garr and the others, caused some dismay to Brian and his sons. Not realising they were part of Garr's group, he stood to prevent their entrance to the campsite. It was a tense and difficult moment.

The situation calmed quickly once the relationship was explained, but it left an atmosphere for some time, regardless of the efforts of Idor and his brothers to lay their hosts' fears to rest. Brian relaxed a little and attempted to explain and apologise for his response by telling them the story of the attack upon their village by the nomad warriors. He also explained that until this point he had never understood the differences between the nomadic warrior tribes. In response, Volka told an interested Brian about the varied tribes, the different places they came from, and their different cultures and beliefs, which led them into their varied ways of life.

It was without doubt a most difficult task they were all set upon. These were people who were traditionally enemies and who did not understand one another's ways. The different groups had for years deliberately avoided contact with one another and stubbornly did not want to understand. These were hard people who were now here attempting the impossible. It required calling on the very best of themselves and placing their doubts into the background.

Garr and Knap saw them all raising and passing the dreaded leather pouches. It was a cleft stick; pleasure at their bonding, fear of drunkenness due to tomorrow's mission.

As Clark and his group joined the other men, Nic took Garr's hand and led her to the side of the site where they sat close and enjoyed chatter of their past adventures.

Garr explained her mission in more detail and Nic was keen to support his sister in whatever way her heart desired. She asked Nic if he would volunteer to be the councillor for the area around Prallian and explained the boundaries. He corrected some of her information and said that he should first speak with Sarina and the rest of his group. Garr was secretly pleased with his response, as it showed the respect for others that she would have wanted from her brother and a man taking on such a difficult task.

The evening ended with avowals of brotherhood, goodwill, and promises of meeting regularly. Garr and Knap, in particular, were pleased by everything that had occurred.

Such an extended family made up of people with differing lifestyles was a rare thing. Possibly it was merely an exception, or maybe it simply showed them that the future could be like this if all pulled together and undertook the compromises needed to achieve something for the common good.

That cold night, all slept well, as the day had been special and busy by any measure. Just a little nervousness crept into the thoughts of Garr as she lay thinking through their plans and intentions.

Morning was bright and blue, with only a light frost lying upon the northern slopes. There was an ease within the camp; all joined in the necessary tidying, and, before too long, the fire crackled at the centre of an organised campsite. Knap, Clark, Idor, and Garr talked of how to handle the talks and, between them, they decided that Yegor should also climb upon the cart with an introductory few words. He was the archery champion after all, recognisable to everyone, and his status would certainly hush the crowd and hold their attention. Although uncomfortable about it, Yegor agreed and was schooled by Knap for some time in how and what to say.

By midday, there was a substantial crowd gathered around the central area, so those not required upon the cart, which was to be their stage, were sent amongst the crowd to inform folk of the talk to take place.

People moved towards the stone circle, and it did not take too long before the whole of the area was full of an expectant crowd keen to discover what on earth these people wanted to express and why.

None were used to public speaking or indeed listening to it; everything was of an unusual nature. There was fear and caution, mixed uncomfortably with intrigue.

The five climbed upon the levelled cart, somewhat unnoticed. A horn was blown.

It was blown three or four more times, it's deep tone spreading and rumbling across the site and the hills beyond, again drawing folks' attention.

More from all around now wandered towards the centre while low chatter became even lower. Yegor raised his arms and, as if in response to God, the crowd become quiet, all their expectant eyes focused on him.

"Hill folk and honoured guests like myself, Yegor—who is now your champion and always your friend."

He stared around slowly at the whole gathering and, as he did so, he began to clap the crowd. They responded and returned the applause. It rose to a great crescendo, and, at that moment, Yegor confidently raised his arms once more, turning from one side to the other. The great crowd hushed and returned to silence.

"Hill folk, this is Garr, one of your own—a great archer. She lives to the north of here and wishes to talk to you about a more secure land and a better peace across our mixed peoples."

"Greetings, brothers and sisters. Here standing next to me are my friends and, indeed, your friends. This is Clark, an important man from Dartell, three of his fellows have come to the Gathering with him. They are councillors of that great township.

"This is Idor, a prince of his tribe here at the Big Gathering with his two brothers. He is a nomad warrior. Some nomad warriors cause trouble for all of us, but not all nomad warriors are guilty of this."

There was a low moaning and mumble that spread through the crowd, creating a moment of tension.

Garr push on, through the tension with her words and regained their attention, displaying her natural leadership and steely personality.

"They attack us while we sleep, steal goods and crops, our children and our women. We hill folk have no defence, and neither do the settlers in little communities and even the shufflers in great townships like Dartell, with their guards and archers.

"This is Knap, a hill man like most of us here. Many of you will know him, for he is renowned for his wisdom."

Garr stopped and took her breath. The crowd was listening and ready for her next words.

"My friends and I believe it is time that all the peoples that live across our land should try to join together and form a council. Every area should have or choose somebody to lead them in that area. When those leaders meet at the council, they can agree how we should defend ourselves and how we could help one another.

"If a rule or indeed a great law was needed in our land, they, with our help and opinions, could agree to that law."

Much to Garr's surprise, great cheers and clapping rose from the crowd, then silenced.

"If a man or women should be chosen as leader, we must help them, as our time is used mostly to hunt or to gather firewood. These councillors would have to spend time talking to their neighbours and would need to reach the council meetings all over this land.

"If, like my friends here upon this cart—Clark, Knap, Idor and, of course, Yegor—you all agree that this should be done, then raise your hands to show it is agreed."

It looked like the majority were in favour. It certainly sounded that way.

"Now, would those against the idea of a council raise their hands?"

Those hands were sparse. Indeed, it was a clear victory. Upon the cart, they all agreed that the crowd was in favour.

"We agree, nearly all of us, we agree there should be a council."

Garr started to clap the crowd again, and all responded before the sound gently died away, and they stood and awaited more words.

"Arranging our council will take some time. My friends and I will travel and work hard for this. If you think you could be a leader for the area where you live, come forward now, look at the maps we have drawn and help us correct them. Add the rivers, mountains, and other features across our land because they will form the borders of each area."

The harmony was broken for a moment by doubters.

"Stupid idea! It will never, never work."

"Shut it, you oaf," responded another and so it raged for a while, with each shout contradicting another as the anger rose.

"Please, please, everyone must be able to say what they want," Garr shouted over the growing din. "Respect from all, to all. We hill folk always disagree. That is why we need a council."

Garr seemed to be losing the fight to restore order and interest.

Yegor took the initiative and stood forward, holding his arms aloft in a subduing gesture. Knap stood forward also, shoulder to shoulder with him. The crowd began to quieten once again. Garr continued.

"We will travel this land and explain these ideas we agreed upon. We will help this wondrous plan to become a reality to north, south, east, and west. All councillors and helpers will wear yellow ribbons on their left arms so you can recognise them—you will see us amongst you."

Clark and Idor now stood forward and clapped and cheered at the crowd, while the others dismounted the cart. Garr looked back up at Clark.

"Clark, ask any leaders to come forward. We need to speak to as many as possible. Knap, that was a good idea about the ribbons."

The five leaders all tied the yellow ribbons upon each other's arms. It looked good and quite official.

"Knap, I'm sorry," said Garr to her friend. "The talk didn't really go as we agreed. It's not so easy when you're standing on top of that cart is it?"

"No, it's not. I was pleased you did it. What about Yegor, wasn't he just a natural? He loved it, and, boy, don't they love him. Anyway, let's talk to these people, shall we?"

"You go on, Knap, I'm a little hoarse after all that shouting. I'm going to find Nic and Sarina, and get Nic to help us. He could be our first leader or councillor, I think, if I twist his arm hard enough."

It was a busy afternoon and evening. There was a lot of interest and a lot of questions, and there was going to be a massive amount of work to be undertaken. Every time they spoke of the council, more issues and problems arose from their discussions; from here onwards it was going to grow or fall.

The leaders' lives had begun to change forever, maybe never to return to normal. Something was really happening here amongst these few people.

Clark and his team were brilliant at the organising, together with Mara, who managed to support every activity that the groups generated, in-between cooking wonderful pots of stew, together with Sala, and keeping the fire flaming.

Stony, Brian, Maggie, and the rest of their group supported the idea of Nic as the councillor and were prepared to spread the news and the idea of the central council, while seeking the approval of folks within their area. That would be a great start; Nic already wore his yellow ribbons with obvious pride.

As they all sat exhausted around the fire that night, slowly allowing the buzz of the day to drift away, Garr was unable to speak. Her now deep and gravelly voice was a perfect vehicle for jest, and they all exploited it to the fullest.

As she and Sala snuggled down to sleep, Sala whispered to check she was awake.

"Garr, I spoke to Dad today about staying with you. He didn't say much. He only said that I should take care and only listen for a happy heart. That's good advice I thought. Has he spoken to you at all?"

"Sala, he can see we are happy living together. As I said on that cart; he's a wise man. He really is. Just make sure your mum's okay. She'll miss you, but Knap will arrange for Mara to stay at your brothers when he's away from home. She'll be okay, she's sound. Sorry, Sal, just can't talk anymore. Speak in the morning, you sleep well. What a great Gathering it's been."

The following day, the Big Gathering site began to clear, as folk reset their minds to the more mundane matters of life. There were endless farewells. All had many new friends to remember, as well as something important to think and talk about. For the first time ever, their champion was an outsider—a nomad warrior. Warriors would never be looked upon as they once were but only a week ago.

The homeward journey was always going to be longer, harder, and slower.

As with any group, the late nights, the drink, and the music still lingered in the souls of Garr and her group, pulling their shoulders down and reducing their chatter.

Even Monster appeared to trudge with indifference, his load seemingly twice as heavy as before and, indeed, it probably was.

The only ones not suffering seemed to be Idor and his brothers. They still managed a lightness of step and a straightness of back, regardless of their over indulgences throughout the Gathering.

All had played a magnificent part. They had achieved enormous leaps forward into a brave and new tomorrow.

But that was indeed, only a beginning.

Sometime later.

The days had turned decidedly shorter now and those frosty mornings were a regular event mixed with icy ones. For it to be so very cold throughout the night was a little unusual for the time of year, and that was a worrying sign.

Garr's cave home generally maintained a reasonable temperature, even when the outside world was frozen over. She normally prepared for extremes, well at least as far as she could do. Reality always was a problem once she left the cave to hunt and check traps.

Green leaves were caught unsuspectingly by the sudden cold, and late wild flowers had to hurry their process towards winter slumber. Late fruit and nuts were lost, and, for those ill-prepared, there was a hard and cold winter ahead.

A storm of storms had sent torrents of water upon the landscape, not letting up for a second in three days and nights. It had encompassed every type of converted water from hail to snow to ice.

A dark and turgid sky greeted them each morning, and each night the view across the valley was nothing but the darkest of grey nothingness, in which even the torrents from the sky captured no silvery reflection, as the moon and stars had disappeared from view.

Each morning, for nearly a whole week, the sky and landscape was now full of thick, snowy, dark and heavy clouds. On two mornings, as they scurried about the cave, wrapped in furs to rebuild the fire or relieve themselves, they noticed that even the stream within Garr's cave was embraced by a covering of loose ice. Garr had never seen this before. The cave entrance was well above ground level but once deep inside the cave, an ambient temperature existed, but the icy water was a contradiction to that fact.

Now there was a feeling that one was very alone, sitting upon the top of the world and floating with nothing and nobody below.

Within Garr's valley, towards Dartell, there appeared a great lake. Nobody had ever seen such before, or the endless cascading waterfalls, some of which fell at either side of Garr's cave entrance. Unfortunately, they turned inwards towards her downward track and enjoyed the jumping and swirling in which they engaged.

Descending became impossible for some time, much to the annoyance of Monster.

Garr and Sala spent their time in repairing and organising. They hung skins to reduce the size of the sleep area, to control any downward draughts, and across the entrance to prevent the biting wind which occasionally would visit them uninvited.

The skins that covered the entrance had been worked on over the last three years; it was just a matter of unrolling the poles so that, with a little force, they fitted tightly from floor to rocky roof. Across the centre was an overlapping join, the outside flap preventing the wind coming within. The flap could be held open, for a moment forming a diamond shaped window or entrance, whenever necessary.

Garr's river was a torrent, and the fish within her dammed pool had vacated with the flood waters and were gone upon their adventures.

It was also through these times that Garr's forethought had won through. Her stores of just about everything sustained them well.

When not busy, they sat close to the fire, and, fitted out in skins and fur, they were warm enough. One of them regularly walked across to the cave entrance to assess whether a waterfall or track existed. This called for bravery each time. You had to remove your warm clothes, before rushing back to the warmth of the fire, quickly drying off, and getting back into further skins and warmth.

The dramatic downward turn in the weather had caused all their inspired plans to falter. Inside the relative comfort of

Dartell and high within the ancient village of Prallian, they all sat awaiting a change in the weather.

Within the encampment below Garr's cave and right across the world of hill folk, there was nothing that could be carried forward as regards the planned council, apart from even further planning and thinking, going through again and again those original plans to make adjustments and improvements.

Idor had not had the opportunity to visit or assist Sala and Garr for over a week now.

The key of time turned and, once again, blue skies were there to greet them one morning. Elation and simple relief erupted over the hills and plains, as folk once again entered the wider world to salvage, repair, and make good, while looking with amazement at the changed environment that now surrounded them. Garr knew that such weather would have caused many premature deaths amongst people across the valley. As usual, youngsters and the older folk suffered most. For those ill-prepared, there was no way they could make it through such a difficult period. There was a virtue in such circumstances which nobody really spoke of—the clearing of the infirm or those least able to contribute. It was an unfortunate reality of the life they lived; survival of the fittest strengthened those who lived on.

The arrival of better weather also brought Idor to Garr's cave entrance. He, together with his tribe, had endured. As formally nomadic people, they had tried and tested solutions to the extremes their ancestors lived through.

"Oh, Idor, how very wonderful to see you at last. Did you have many problems?"

Idor stepped inside the cave, a broad smile
face, and without a word gathered both Sala ¿
kissing them gently, and they him. It felt that
apart for years.

With no words spoken, he started to remove the skins and
furs that covered these two women. They stood still, drawn
immediately within his power. When they were both naked,
he told them both to stand still. He looked at them, their
young bodies suntanned and athletic. He touched them gently
and walked around them. He made them both stand astride,
his enthusiasm rising within him. He circled them again,
rediscovering their privacy while one hand softly and slowly
draped around their bodies.

He was now also naked.

He lead them both to the bedding area and placed them to
kneel; with a hand to either side of them, he pulled them close
to each other and, with no further foreplay, indulged himself
within them, thrusting quick and hard, alternating from one to
the other.

Physically, the women stayed passive, their butts protruding
proudly. Captured by his touch, his presence, and his thrusting,
they breathed deeply, uttering grunts and other sounds of
pleasure.

Their bodies grew tenser; Sala squealed her pleasure. There
was no slowing of their joy. All their tensions and ecstasy was
released again and again, before he finally began to slow his
thrusting.

It was like he couldn't stop, like he needed to be forever
within the warmth of those two bodies.

When completely drained and exhausted, the three lay under
the bedding, wrapped within one another's comfort, damp with
sweat and sex, they slept happy and satisfied.

Eventually waking, still wrapped within Idor's arms, smiles spread across their faces. He cuddled them close.

"Have we any food, Garr? We've many plans to make. Look, I have had time to think of many things. Today before me here, I organise present for you and Sala."

They all smiled, a different smile this time.

"A present. Idor, what could that be?"

"You dress, come to me camp, see present, ya."

Garr and Sala cleaned themselves in the still icy water and dressed. They had only thought so far of checking traps prior to Idor's appearance, a job that was badly in need of doing, but curiosity drove them, and, within a further fifteen minutes, the three of them plus an excited Monster were making their way down the now very rocky and slippery track, which still had water cascading and ice underfoot.

As they entered Idor's soggy encampment and moved between the tents on the lowered walkways, both warriors and their women folk nodded respectfully. The odd children looked on with bewilderment. Yegor and Volka stepped towards them, greeting them with affection and walked with them to a central area. There stood a small, crude yet neat cart and, before it, a good looking horse, wide at the hoof and broad at the beam. Coloured in white and brown patches, he tossed his tangled mane and stamped upon the spongy ground, causing splashes that reached them all.

"Idor, is this really for us?" Sala exclaimed. "It's beautiful and wonderful."

"Really, really wonderful," Garr agreed. "I've never received such a gift."

They walked forward, running their hands over the excellent woodwork and stroking the horse.

"Has he a name, Idor?"

"Keppa. He strong and friendly, a good horse. He will serve you well upon your journeys around our land. This is a good present, ya? We make in tent while big rains here."

"Oh yes, Idor, very much yes", Garr replied. "We are humbled by your gift and effort."

"We love you and your family for this gift, Idor," agreed Sala.

The women hadn't realised that while they were talking, many of the tribe had gathered around and, at seeing their pleasure, clapped and whooped.

"The gift is for your friendship to our people without favour. Tis for the honour to Yegor the champion and also you continue the big plans for council. You must visit Dartell and many places across land. This gift is from the tribe people, they know we have chosen to be together and are happy for us all. You, Sala and Garr, are now leaders amongst these people for you stand with me. You are happy about this?"

They were lost for the words with which to answer and scared that so much had happened within Idor's camp whilst the storms had raged. It was hard to absorb all that was happening and to be sure it was as they wanted, either individually or as one.

Nonetheless, they answered favourably and with smiles of happiness, while the inward doubts they both felt were concealed.

In the time that followed, Garr, with Sala's help, repaired her fishpond and began to restock the depleted stores. On her own, she revisited all her traps and harvesting places whilst Sala undertook the task of learning how to drive Keppa and build a strong and worthy relationship with him.

Sala took some time to both practise further with the cart and to visit Knap and Mara, checking their wellbeing and arrangements as regards the plans to circulate among those who had showed keen interest in creating the council. Luckily, Idor had insisted that Volka travel with her. As it happened, he was her saviour many times. The saturated ground didn't mix well with a little cart, and, despite Keppa's endless heroic efforts, the cart would have been lost to the swampy ground through which they travelled.

To her surprise, Garr enjoyed the short time on her own. It was like touching base once again, and besides that, she found that having Idor solely to herself was different; no, it was wonderful.

Of course, once Sala had returned from that arduous journey fraught with problems, Garr was again so pleased to see her. She was at a loss to understand her earlier feelings.

Emotions are the strangest of experiences.

The In-Between Years

Time became their enemy, and endeavour their master.

All their lives were so involved with journeying far and wide—endless meetings and hurried liaisons—it was almost impossible to remember the simple days of eking a living from the land and awakening to admire the view across the valley.

The little cart was serving them well and became a recognisable symbol for all the peoples of Garr. It was often greeted with great enthusiasm along many a track and when approaching town, village, or smallholding.

Days, months, and years evaporated. Their famous little cart needed repair many a time. People died, and occasionally a child was born. The effort showed upon all those committed to the cause; even Monster began to show some grey hair.

Knap also maintained his commitment, and his wisdom was respected in all cultures. Eventually, beginning to feel drained, together with the effects of age, he spoke of less involvement, wanting to spend more time with Mara, who had begun to show signs of illness. He also wished to see more of his grandchildren and Sala, when her child was born in three months.

Sala and Volka, through the time on the road together, had developed a close relationship, but it wasn't going to be sufficient when the child was born, and Garr once again could see great changes affecting all their lives, let alone some difficulties between Idor and his brother, Volka.

As for Garr and Sala's journey together, it was going to be changed forever, and, even though promises and commitments had been undertaken, they could see the impossibilities within the future.

They both spent endless nights thinking through the process of disengaging themselves from peace talks, creating new rules, and passing judgements on issues of life and death, But life itself tends to be the leader ultimately. The days of believing they were in charge of destiny were far behind them now; they were but servants or slaves to their mission.

Idor had supported Garr and Sala without fail over the years. He had accepted the changing relationship eventually, although, at the time, Volka nearly died at his hand. The tribe also had disapproved of the insult to their leader and they too would have put an end to his brother's life if Idor had not adjusted his heart.

With great courage, Idor forgave Volka before the tribe and once again took him as his brother.

Ideas and cultures mixed and people dealt with it, grew, and moved on.

Although Sala and Garr still spent much of their time together when Garr was at her mountain, it was Idor who consistently stepped forward to support her, occasionally travelling with her to far off places or sending a warrior or two for the protection of his princess. They grew closer and closer, emotionally, spiritually, and mentally. When reunited, the warmth of one another's arms and the kisses of such gentleness and caring became essential to their very existence.

Eventually, as one would hope, Garr became pregnant, and, although Idor's children already populated the tribe, this birth was to be something very special to him. Now, both he and his brother would become parents again, creating yet another layer of responsibility.

With the passing of time, all had become wiser to the ways of their world. They increasingly knew how to manipulate situations, where the lines had to be drawn, and when to be publicly hard or soft. Garr was growing at a faster rate than the others in both wisdom and stature.

Their lives, like the wind, blew past, gone to a place which nobody could find or hold on to.

Idor knew that when his and Garr's child was born, he would announce it to the world with a great celebration, inviting all the dignitaries of the land. It was an occasion which marked the success of both their efforts and the efforts of many folk across a wide area. The common effort to form the council had generated more than had been planned or expected, and, somehow, Garr and Idor's child represented that success; it was a living symbol of the unity of different people around which to gather.

A Land is Born

Garr stood, while the others around the table remained seated and ceased their chatter.

"There is some news to pass on to you all. It's not good news—it's very bad news. Some of you may have already heard the talk. A large, troublesome tribe has entered our land. They've probably been here before and experienced no opposition. No doubt they thought that we were easy targets to abuse one by one, as in the past. Well, now they are very wrong. We are united—we have bonded together."

Garr took a breath and looked around the table at the serious faces. She could see the hesitation and feel the sudden worry.

"These people have attacked Nimella to the southeast of our land. I gather that there are many dead and much destruction. They did light the warning towers but too late for any assistance to reach them. So, we have two problems to deal with. Our system failed us on the first really serious issue. And how do we deal with these crazy dogs?"

She paused again for effect. She knew where this discussion must end; it wasn't difficult to imagine. She also knew now from experience that some would resist the obvious and needed to be driven past the obstacles in their minds.

"So we must immediately send a party to the enemy with a warning. As they have completed their first attack, there will be time before it occurs again. We will estimate this and anticipate the time of a possible second attack. This will allow us to call upon the people to gather, so we are able to reject these monsters as soon as the final day of our warning notice expires. Who at this council wishes to speak?"

Leron rose and Garr slid the speaking stone before him as she sat down.

"I offer myself to lead the delegation to these warriors. I for one agree with all you said, Garr. There is but one other issue here, and that is there will be assistance needed in Nimella. I suggest that a further party is organised—one capable and prepared to assist our brothers and sisters to repair their lives and township."

Leron slid the stone back towards Garr. She looked around the table again and noticed Clark ready to speak. The stone was passed over, and Clark rose to address the council members.

"Brothers and sisters, making rules and generating ideas is easy—asking folk to fight and maybe die is not. Small skirmishes have been dealt with before, but this would not be like those. I also agree with what Garr has said. We must be as one until this threat is dealt with. I will pledge two hundred of our warriors and guards from Dartell and a hundred more workmen to assist the folks of Nimella. On top of this, time allowing, I will organise any of our brothers from hill, tribe, and village within our region to come to the aid of this land of ours with no name."

He sat down. A mumble went around the table. Neon raised a hand and received the stone of consent.

"I agree with the plan outlined around this table. I cannot promise the numbers brother Clark can, but a good number it will be; I promise. I believe we should only call upon those from the southeast of our land, as time is of the essence here. This is not an issue for those of the north or west".

"Our land of no name gives us no banner to fight beneath. We have spoken of this many times, with no conclusions. Let us now, in this time of great difficulty, give our land a name. I have thought of one that may be acceptable to us all.

"Dartell has given generously and supported this council well—without Dartell we would not have been so well organised. Garr is recognised throughout our land, and she and her friends started this great journey. I suggest Garrtellia."

Neon sat knowing his words would cause muttering around the table. Garr sat forward feeling awkward, with head in hands, and looked down the table at Clark. He obviously liked the idea. Garr found herself shaking her head, not being able to take this suggestion on board.

The mutterings sounded positive. Clark raised his hand once again, before taking hold of the stone of consent and standing.

"Councillors, I heard the mutterings of consent and agreement. Garr is embarrassed, I know her well as maybe you do. She is a woman of great strength and resolve, yet gentleness, of truth yet diplomacy, love and honour. She is thinking that the beginning of our land was created by many hands and voices, not hers alone. But she is still the fist that drives us all forward. She is our unspoken leader, our queen. I second the name. It's a good name Neon, and it has a good sound, a good feeling. I call for a vote on this right here and now. All in favour raise a hand."

Hands were raised, and the vote was taken. It was carried with the support of all except Garr, hence the name of Garrtellia was born while Garr sat with her head once again within her hands, feeling awkward and uncomfortable at the council table. Her own vote this day was of no consequence, yet her personality and leadership obviously embraced them all. She felt that she should run from the room, such was her feeling of embarrassment.

Clark held onto the stone of consent he now had.

"So, to war it may be for Garrtellia."

Now Clark raised his mug, the others also rose with their mugs held high, and all paused awaiting Garr. Slowly she relented and rose with the others. She held forth her own tankard and spoke loud and clear.

"Never to be broken, never to be parted, as one forever. I give you the birth of our great child, Garrtellia."

There was a great clash of tankard against tankard. Smiles spread around the table. At last, after so much time, they really were one.

"Possibly a break and food is needed, allowing us all to celebrate for a moment and consider what we can offer our cause. If all are in agreement, I will begin to draft our notice to these foolish warriors who just might be smart enough to accept its terms."

A Notice of Warning.

We, the peoples of Garrtellia give you notice that if your tribe has not left our land within four days, you the warriors of your tribe, together with your families, will be slaughtered without mercy or compassion.

You have three full suns before our wrath will be upon you. If you attack or plunder or harm anymore of our people in that time, our wrath will be upon you.

Your prisoners will be returned without further harm upon the day of the first sun.

If you return to our land you will be slaughtered.

This notice is not negotiable. We will not discuss this warning further.

The People of Garrtellia

Clark read the draft notice to the council. He felt it was direct, absolute, and harsh. What else should it be? This wasn't a time for softness or for politics. Garr sat and read it carefully, as did all the other councillors. They couldn't fault it, although all were obviously nervous about their decision.

Somebody questioned if they would be able to read the notice once delivered. Idor suggested that he write it in as many languages as he understood, just in case. It was agreed. A number of notices were inscribed upon parchment, rolled, and dispatched with Leron and his small party.

Messengers had already been dispatched around the south-eastern regions of the land to advise the people there of the requirements for men and supplies. Councillors had been allocated tasks. The council had agreed to move nearer the area of action. Tensions grew. Fear grew.

Garr wished Sala was with her.

She paced around thinking about and double checking all that had been said, with Monster trotting closely at her side.

Meanwhile, Idor was at the centre of a group discussing tactics and the layout of the ground around the area where the enemy was known to be located.

Within five days of the meeting, the council was reconvened at an excellent location to the northwest of Nimella. The position allowed rapid access to both Nimella, which was of a similar size to Dartell, and the site where the enemy stood.

Leron and his party had travelled ahead on horse to fulfil their mission of delivering the ultimatum to the warlike nomadic tribe.

Delivering the message was not straight forward. To ride into this camp of iniquity under a banner of truce was not wise. It was decided by Leron that they should capture some of their people and then send them back after small intervals, each delivering the same warning from Garrtellia. Thus an ambush was constructed.

The small group had lain upon a hilltop observing the encampment. It was large, with six hundred to a thousand tents before them. Leron had been given Garr's treasured binoculars to aid his task. He viewed sights he didn't wish to see; captives from Nimella hung and strung up like meat, beaten, and abused; women stripped of all their dignity in groups to one side of the encampment, again tied either by both hands, or hands and feet, and attached to stout stakes. Around the camp fires, the tribe's people ate or talked with apparently not a care in the world.

His blood boiled and his hatred grew intensely within him.

They selected two positions that appeared best for their purpose. The group split to undertake their mission. The track around which they hid was not the main entrance to and from the campsite. This made good sense to Leron; it was used by lesser members of the tribe and was a kind of back route. Luckily the track weaved through convenient areas of dense cover.

With one group to either side of the track and lookouts positioned to warn of others that were approaching the ambush spot, all was set.

A group of women passed by, talking incessantly, possibly going to gather materials needed within camp. They let them pass.

For a long time nobody used the pathway, and Leron was beginning to think he had made a bad decision.

Then came the perfect opportunity; a group of young warriors, not yet full blooded, were idling around and passing the time of day.

The signal was given, and they fiercely erupted from both sides of the track upon the three unsuspecting young warriors, who were totally bewildered and in obvious fear for their lives. They twisted and turned in an attempt to avoid capture; one was so scared that he urinated on himself. Another, with more spunk, jumped free at one stage and was ready to fight, until a heavy blow around the head put him to ground.

As quickly as possible, they were tied and gagged and dragged back into the dense cover whilst the group kept one eye on the lookouts for warnings of trouble.

Each captive was beaten into silence and made to pay attention to the words spoken to them. They were given a scroll, which had upon it the warning from the council of Garrtellia written in five languages.

Leron had it in his mind that it was necessary to place the fear of fears into these messengers, and, for the good of Garrtellia, he would do that.

They pulled one from the ground, would he be the first to deliver the message? No, he wouldn't, but his blood would be spread upon the others; they were to be the messengers.

Leron turned quickly, his shining and sharp-edged knife cutting deeply into the young man's throat and across his jugular vein, whose eyes remain fixed in an expression of disbelief as the blood flowed from his body.

Leron grabbed the dying lad's hair and dragged him forward so his blood ran and squirted over his two friends. He held him there for a second or two, until his legs began to fold, and, with no compassion, pushed him harshly aside.

The two blood stained colleagues were now stood up and, while they shook violently, their bonds were cut and one was sent upon his way with a scroll.

Taking the other captive with them, the group began to make their way through the wooded area as quickly as possible until they reached another track which lead independently into the encampment and let him go. Timing here was everything because if they took too long with their plan, they risked being hunted down and captured themselves.

They wanted both of their messengers to have to walk or run through the camp, towards the centre where the tribal leaders were gathered. This would clearly demonstrate to their enemies that something awesome and threatening was upon them.

Leron felt confident that the plan would achieve its aim. They didn't wait to find that out, but made their way via a pre-planned route towards the place where the council of Garrtellia had relocated.

As their messages were being delivered to horrified faces, the soldiers and servants of Garrtellia were making their way towards the troubled region. The news of the newly completed union, their land having a name, brought joy to almost all. They travelled under a new and spiritual banner as a unified people with one cause to serve.

As the music of marching soldiers spread across the southeast of Garrtellia, the nomadic tribe of warriors called the Kahn considered their options. Unfortunately, due to history, they were not convinced. They were a little unsettled and a little nervous. But, as yet, they didn't know who their enemy was, where it was, and with what might it dared to threaten the fearless warriors of the Kahn.

Garr was troubled now by the whole affair. She had paced and thought, she'd sat with buried head in hands and thought. She hadn't as yet spoken to anybody else.

She wanted to avoid further bloodshed if possible; her anger and hatred had diminished somewhat. To have more blood of her own people spilled and wasted upon the ground should be avoided, if possible. She spoke to the councillor of the region about the geography of the land. She conjured a plan and presented it to the council members.

"Councillors, I am troubled. I can only see more of Garrtellian blood spilt upon this ground. There has been enough bloodshed in and around Nimella so far, but, as yet, not by our hand.

"I believe that more blood is not the point here. I also believe that to display strength and create some fear in the delivery of justice may provide the solution we seek."

"There will be much work called for in rebuilding Nimella."

"I want you to consider this. When our people are gathered, we spread them around the top of the hills surrounding the Kahn tribe. Our numbers would surely convince them of our power and the futility of resistance. If, in those circumstances, they surrendered, they could be forced to follow the lowland valleys away from our land forever, with no more death of our people. We could follow them until clear of our land.

"If, alternatively, they were foolish enough to desire further conflict, we would be in the perfect position with our archers at hand to fulfil our initial plan of annihilation, which I do not believe is the correct way forward if we are to promote justice amongst our people and amongst others.

"It is with considerable regret that I suggest we should request Leron to enforce our intent by the slaughter of a few, thereby showing our resolve to match their cowardly and ghastly behaviour.

"It is a clear option. We the council, have the power to decide the way forward, not only here today but for the future of our land and the way we aspire to be.

"Are we simply going to be a larger, more bloodthirsty tribe, or are we attempting to lead in a new way, a fairer way, and be a land, a kingdom. What say you?"

Garr sat and, as usual, took a deep breath and waited for the deliberation to begin.

Nic, Garr's brother, and Clark stood and clapped her words. But others needed time.

Leron considered this change of tactics; it blended with the actions he had already taken with the messengers. Garr had approved, that was what mattered. And, Garr's words of common sense echoed through his thoughts, and he chose to support her plan and respect her words and authority, although it meant he must take further abhorrent actions.

172

Small parties of Garrtellian warriors took up positions around the Kahn encampment. Lookouts were positioned upon the hills and, where possible, supplied with binoculars.

Whilst the main plan was put into action, Leron began to carry out his new orders. Stragglers from the Kahn encampment were collected and small raiding groups were taken prisoner. They were slaughtered and their body parts sent within the camp of the Kahn upon horseback. Thirty blood stained horses carried the dangling body parts, with each horse smeared with clay intermingled with intestines. As they cantered amongst the Kahn, the horses delivered a message which was impossible to ignore or misunderstand.

The main part of Garr's army was still to arrive at the scene, and those from the immediate areas that had arrived in great numbers had been quickly dispatched to strategic posts. The council gathering itself stood at risk of attack without adequate defence. This, if any, was the time of danger, for if the Kahn were to resist their warning, it would be now, before they were ready for battle, that the enemy would strike, and it would be the council that would be
destroyed instead.

It was further decided that a high-ranking warrior of the Kahn should be captured, from whom information could be obtained.

Every decision taken was as new; even with their experience, neither Idor nor Clark had ever needed to deal with such a sensitive and large operation.

There were negative mumbles from those of talk and no action. Clark, seeing the problem, employed them with assignments and responsibilities, so disabling their negativity and keeping the council as one.

A messenger arrived from Idor's camp; it bore bad tidings. Mara had fallen seriously ill. She had others at hand to attend her, but Knap had no indecision. He took Garr close and kissed her as a daughter. Garr could see how weary he was and how much pain it caused him to not be by her side. In this moment, he must go to be with his woman.

"I should be there with Mara also, Knap, but it is impossible. Travel safe, my great friend. My spirit will be with you both." With that, Knap left upon horseback, accompanied by two warriors, his heart full of pain and worry.

Garr felt alone. She regarded Knap and Mara as substitute parents, and not having Knap's caring presence and wisdom was a blow to her confidence and stability.

The prisoners of Nimella were returned and met at the boundary of the Kahn encampment, but something felt wrong. Within the camp, there appeared little activity; it was reported to the council and the plan announced.

The army of Garrtellia was now arriving in great numbers. As warriors arrived, they were dispatched to the hills around the Kahn encampment.

Leron had taken a Kahn warrior of importance who had to endure pain and suffering in exchange for information; ultimately, his death was slow and undignified, with little gain.

Upon the day of the third sun, all were assembled. Garr gave the order that all the warriors surrounding the Kahn should move as one at sunrise to the crest of the hills upon which they were positioned, demonstrating their numbers and power. Before sunrise, great fires were lit, encircling the Kahn in a horseshoe, leaving only the far south-eastern end open and clearly showing the Kahn their only route of escape.

The message of the great fires was spread amongst the Kahn, and all stood and stared upwards to the encirclement. As the sun rose, the warriors of Garrtellia moved like one as instructed to line the crest of the surrounding hills.

It was an awesome sight, and all that stood on the edge of battle felt its fearful power.

A further refinement had been agreed by the council. A party of nine hardy warriors was selected to accompany Garr into the Kahn camp. She had insisted she be there, and, although there was much dismay and dispute about her decision, she had her way. They would give the Kahn people two hours to be on the way from the land, not a moment longer.

As the small party mounted, Idor came to Garr's side.

"You may now be a great leader, Garr, but you are my woman and you secretly carry our child. I will ride by your side."

She felt a warm glow flush through her. It was true that she still looked the perfect athlete; there was no sign that she carried a child and only the closest new of her condition.

"No, Idor, you should stay."

"No, Garr, I will not, woman. Shall you and I fight here amongst this council?"

He rode beside her.

As they entered the encampment, Kahn warriors stepped forward, facing the loaded bows. Garr called the party to a stop and they stared at the humiliated Kahn until their weapons were laid upon the ground. They rode on to the centre and stood in front of the Kahn elders. Leron spoke the message to them.

"You have two hours only to start moving your people, or you will all, each one, die this day."

"Who are you that speaks and who is this Garr and who is Idor?"

Garr said nothing. She sat amongst her protectors. Leron repeated his message, and, in turn, the Garrtellian warriors turned slowly and began to retreat from the camp.

For one of the elders, it was too much, and he foolishly raised his axe, possibly to shake it in anger, possibly to throw. Three arrows pierced his skin within the blink of an eye, and he fell backwards from where he stood, twitched but once, and lay still.

The tension was immense; bows were drawn to a maximum, ready for release. The horses jigged and neighed as warrior after warrior drew his weapon for action and womenfolk pushed forward with shaking fists and cursing tongues.

Suddenly and unexpectedly from the hillsides, there was a great sound—a threatening howl that floated across the encampment and then faded into silence, followed by another roar that left a mumbling fear to settle over the Kahn.

It had the desired effect. A Kahn elder, or was it the leader, stepped forward with raised arms to hush and still his people. Reluctantly, they submitted with defiant cursing, slowly laying down their weapons yet again.

"Two hour, we be gone. Tell your Garr, we have respect. We will not return, but in peace." He turned away and gave instructions, which his people immediately started to follow.

The Garrtellians retreated slowly, maintaining their readiness, and then joined their army upon the hilltops to sit, wait, and watch the Kahn dismantle their encampment and slowly drift in a long ragged column, vanishing into other lands to the southeast of Garrtellia.

It was a further two days before all the small parties of Garr's people returned to the council to report that the Kahn had vacated the land.

An exhausted council adjourned so its members could return to loved ones of their own and the mundane matters of life. For Garr and Idor, it was time to turn their attention to the birth of their child.

Garr was feeling drained by the time she entered her own territory, but it was right that she called in to see Knap en route. Mara had deteriorated and lay weakly, hardly saying a word; it didn't look good.

In attendance were their sons and Sala with a babe in her arms who Volka was yet to meet.

For Sala and Garr, it was a difficult situation. They were filled with both joy at seeing one another and sorrow at the illness of Mara, Sala's mother.

Added to this heavy load, for all of them, was the recent years of commitment and the heavy load of responsibility that came from the conflict with the Kahn people.

Knap was inconsolable, filled with guilt and sorrow that he hadn't been at Mara's side the whole time. His only consolation was Sala's child, a bright and active boy with thick, dark black hair. As a signal of respect, he was to be named Idor.

Indeed it was the only time Mara had roused from her bed, and the tiny child had generated a soft smile of approval upon her face, whereupon Sala laid the child cradled against her mother.

They all felt so inadequate, practically and emotionally. The cost of their endeavours with Garrtellia now seemed both far too heavy and self-indulgent.

In moments when faces were dry, they resolved to change their ways and rethink their objectives. Deep down, all knew it was their hearts speaking and that it was impossible to go back to the mornings of staring across the valley, the days amongst the trees and grassland, and the nights in endless joy with a sky full of the glory of a million stars.

Knap, holding Mara's hand, watched his wonderful companion of a lifetime slip into another world and knew in that moment that he would never be the same person again.

Sala, Garr, and Knap's family saw within his face that moment of irreversible change; the moment when something spiritually drifted away from him.

Children, Drought, Famine, and Doubts

Volka, Sala, and the young Idor stayed on with Knap to see him through his grieving.

Garr returned once again to her mountain where Idor had organised her comforts before returning to his tribe with Yegor and other warriors. He sent womenfolk to attend to her needs.

Over the years that had passed by, Idor's tribe had developed their encampment to include permanent structures. Mainly they were built under the lower rock faces, where it was possible to also use the cover and protection that the mountain could provide. Some of his people still indulged in the nomadic life but returned to the settlement that now existed.

The birth of Garr's daughter Luana didn't happen easily.

As it often is with these occasions, there was great pain, while Idor and his tribe, together with Sala, Volka and Knap, paced endlessly and the tribe's women employed all their birthing skills and experience.

It was good fortune that Garr was a fit person or she may have fatally parted company with her splendid and beautiful daughter, Luana.

All were full of joy when the ordeal was over; tears of pleasure and relief spread from hillside cave to lower settlement and across the valleys and planes of the land.

Knap, now looking a good deal older, thanks to his stooped back and gaunt face, took Garr's hand at the bedside, telling her how proud and pleased Mara would have been. Tears and dampened faces surrounded the occasion.

Sala and Volka introduced little Idor to Luana, and Yegor, not being able to hold back any further, burst into the birthing area full of rapturous congratulations and emotion.

Idor, well, his pleasure was indescribable.

Remembering his pledge, he began immediately organising the celebrations in-between strutting up and down with his daughter in his arms, kissing her tenderly, and telling her stories of great battles and how her mother had stood before the great tribe of the mighty Kahn and won the greatest ever victory without a war.

He never mentioned in his version of the story that the Khan had broken their word sometime later and had sent small raiding parties once again into Garrtellia to plunder and rape all before them.

He also never mentioned how the Garrtellian warriors had captured Mungar, their leader, and set him before Garr and the main council for trial and execution. Mungar had stood there before them unchained, free to explain his and his people's actions—how he had lied and mocked their notion of justice and possession of land that was there for all. He had spat at Garr and the councillors before him, and Garr had decided there was no option but death for Mungar and his brothers. Their bodies had been hung from trees along the border of Garrtellia to rot slowly before all that decided to challenge the sovereignty of Garrtellia and disrespect their laws and the leaders of this free and just land.

Now was not the time for stories such as these, but for fairy tales. His new daughter was his treasure. She would learn, unfortunately, the trials and tribulations involved with love and war in due course, and that thought saddened him enough to dampen his eyes.

Luana and young Idor grew fast, hardly ever apart. From day one they had bonded happily, and, without presumption, they acted and were treated like royalty wherever they travelled.

By the time they were both four, brothers and sisters had joined them.

Although Idor and Garr, Sala and Volka, still travelled to council meetings, it was less often than before. Occasionally, they meet up with Clark and his family, simply as old friends. He had always been a strong supporter of the council and, of course, Garr.

On other occasions, they all spent time in Prallian with Nic and Sarina, Jac and Ban, now young men in their own right.

With input from all, Garrtellia had grown into a relatively safe land. It was land with some justice and fairness, with time to educate the young ones and care more for the elderly. Furthermore, it was a land where the production of invaluable items was beginning, where horse and cart travel had become common, and where farming was spread amongst all.

With the guidance of Clark and his council, coinage was created and used throughout the land; this with a triannual Grand Festival of Garrtellia.

Yegor, Idor, and Garr still competed at the Big Gathering, with Yegor remaining the champion for many years.

Knap regained some of his old sparkle, and, although still looking a good deal older than he did once upon a time or indeed should, his wisdom was still called upon from time to time.

Idor, the most devoted of leaders and fathers, had also aged beyond his years and was now a little bent at the back. His thick blond hair was a little thinner, and the wrinkles upon his still proud face had multiplied and deepened.

It was for some unknown reason that only Garr and Sala remained unaffected by time, regardless of their families, responsibilities, and devotions.

With all kingdoms, there comes a time when they take their success for granted. In Garrtellia's case, it wasn't so much complacency, as the fact that they had grown to forget the ability of life and the world to surprise and overturn the best laid plans.

Maintaining is a different skill to creating and generally lesser or different minds were set to that task.

A brutally cold winter had passed, in which deep ice and frost lay over the land like never before, and all awaited the reward of spring and a good summer. But the spring was short and the summer was as mercilessly hot as the winter had been cold. Temperatures crept forever upwards, levelling around the hundred and forties; this had never been experienced in the memories of most.

Food stores were low, as there had not recently been cause to stockpile them to the degree now needed.

Game perished with the lack of grass, and harvests of all types were minimal. Rivers dried up and fish disappeared. Wildfires spread across the land, and the far off regions and neighbouring kingdoms called upon the council of Garrtellia for assistance. It wasn't possible to assist others; it was difficult enough to assist those within Garrtellia.

Emergency councils were called for and set up in all regions, and survival plans discussed.

A census was taken across the land, and allocations and distribution plans were drawn up. It was a massive undertaking, truly testing the skills of the council and the people of Garrtellia.

Some of those well placed resisted the plans, and tensions grew between, families, friends, and neighbours alike.

Two great townships to the north, Toulou and Monta, split away from the union, prepared to fight their brothers rather than concede or share any good fortune they might possess. Delegation after delegation was sent to make the case for Garrtellia, but hunger drove the places away from unity.

In a moment of particular despair, Dartell decided to also break with the union, but luckily, under Clark's sturdy guidance and his endless effort, the decision was overturned and those responsible removed from the council.

Toulou and Monta had inadvertently sown the seeds of their own destruction. So pre-occupied were they in defending their borders to the south from an imagined attack from Garrtellia, they became vulnerable to an invasion from the north. There, nomadic tribes were of the worst of cultures but had ironically bonded together, following the examples set before them. They raided regularly to start with, testing and weakening the two cities, and then sent a full and disciplined force against Monta.

After a four day battle, the township was routed and plundered with massive loss of life. Those managing to escape the slaughter ran to Toulou for help and protection, only to be turned away at the outer walls and left to their own devices.

Some, not believing their rejection, stood to question or beg, only to be shot down were they stood.

Toulou, in their desperation, turned once again to Garrtellia for aid and protection.

The loyal General Leron was sent to resolve the issue. He took with him a numerically inadequate force, but a force of his own selection formed from the experience of many small conflicts with which he had dealt over the years.

Within the township, he sat with the local council and told them of his conditions, enabling them to return under the protection of Garrtellia.

In disbelief, they stood and shouted, waving their arms and cursing. Leron sat with confidence before them and repeated his terms. This was not the time for foolish generosity and he, above all of Garr's faithful generals, was not the man to consider such sentiment after their traitorous and cowardly actions.

Enough was enough and his plan was enacted. The current council was disbanded. Objection disappeared and a new council was formed partly from Toulou and partly from the loyal people of the rest of Garrtellia.

Garr would not have approved his actions openly, but in difficult situations she knew Leron to be the right man. Now a man in his late fifties and older than most around him, who badly needed his glasses for archery, he was a man of black and white and in these days he was done with diplomacy. What remained was a dedication to the needs of Garr and Garrtellia.

When he rode towards Monta at the head a large army strengthened by people of Toulou, the banner of Garrtellia flew above them. Among the warrior horde waiting for them in Monta were people of the Kahn. Memories were long; the Kahn remembered the harshness of Leron,

the firmness of Garr's leadership, and the accuracy of Garrtellian arrows.

Why fight when you had already taken all that was available? The Kahn licked their wounds of old, deserted Monta, and moving onto new and weaker targets, leaving but two tribes in Monta who had not faced a Garrtellian army before and were, therefore, foolishly overconfident in their ability to withstand and win the oncoming conflict.

Leron followed long established tactics.

Around the township, he lit large fires at night and didn't allow his numbers to be seen. He repeated this for three days, adding further fires each day, never once allowing his men to be seen by the tribes within Monta, whose fears of certain destruction rose. The plan caused tensions and disarray to spread between Garrtellia's enemies. Arguments raged over water, women, and food, and they buried their fears in alcohol.

On the night of the third day, all the fires were extinguished simultaneously. Then, at sunrise on the fourth day, when Leron lead his army to Monta, he found a sleepy, disorganised horde who were already beaten. The only obstacle was the gates of Monta against which a great fire was lit. Once through, his men, mainly on horseback, hacked freely to left and right.

By Leron's side rode Nic and Brian, with his sons; their deadly responses in battle were now well honed.

For those that stayed and fought it was a worthless and pointless spilling of blood. Mutilated and crawling within with the gutters of Monta, the dazed nomads had lost well before the bloodletting had begun. Nonetheless, Leron ordered his men to complete the job; any that were prepared to stand before the Garrtellian soldiers were to be cut down.

Throughout the following days, the bodies were cleared from inside the township and piled high outside the walls. Any remaining councillors were rounded up and met their own fate before being laid atop their enemies.

Hungry and tired, Leron and his men rode away from Monta, leaving the remaining people of the township to their own fate.

They could now rebuild their township or disperse across the land; Leron didn't care if that was their choice. Alternatively, they could go upon their knees before Garr and the main council and try to redeem their desertion.

This wasn't Leron's responsibility. His task was complete and, although he understood the measure of his worth and purpose to the Garrtellians, he trusted in Garr's wisdom to resolve the ultimate troubles of the northern regions—their pain and their hunger.

Leron, like Brian and Garr's faithful brother, Nic, was finished with battle. None of them wanted to go there again. They, like so many, had travelled the journey from simple hill folk, nomads or townsmen, to councillors and soldiers of a great land and were there of necessity. But it was time for the task to be handed forward; yes, with pride, but from tired hands and hearts.

Garr had decided to hold council at her mountain location. An endless flow of problems entered her home each day. From one grew another and from the other grew more.

She learnt to delegate more and more, her closest adding sound advice and good council.

It was time for Garr to consider her position thoroughly. She needed and wanted more time with her family and her loved ones. She needed to be seen by the people of Garrtellia, to maintain the union of all, and she was needed by the main council, who saw her as she didn't see herself; as their natural and only leader—as a queen.

She knew her position had grown unduly, mainly down to her sex and outstanding colouring, she stood apart; she was still the only woman at the main council.

It was a strange conclusion to arrive at. She knew within herself that she still had something to contribute, but she thought it no

186

more than others in reality. Therefore, her image and presence could be her only outstanding feature. Regardless of what she thought, people had pushed her to the fore and gathered around her alone for a long time. It was her they all looked towards, her they all relied upon, and her they feared and loved.

She felt she couldn't speak of her inner thoughts to anybody, even Idor.

If she displayed doubt or weakness, it would inevitably spread, and others would step forward with different intensions that she had fought against from the beginning. Greed and power were dangerous tools in any hands.

She resolved to change the balance of her own life.

She would accept the mantle; she could see no option in this matter. However, she would slowly reorganise the structure, creating more responsibility for others, encouraging the support and participation of more womenfolk, and ensuring that the succession of her position was easy and pre-determined. The survival and success of Garrtellia must be guaranteed.

"Councillors, we have major problems to discuss here today, as well as a thousand smaller issues. Firstly, let me tell you that the traitorous actions of our old brothers in the north have been dealt with. The enemies of Garrtellia have been rejected. We have yet to decide whether the peoples of Monta and Toulou will remain part of Garrtellia. Much of that decision remains in their own hands.

"Secondly, with great sorrow I must tell you that the council of Dartell has yet again withdrawn from assisting our efforts against drought across our land. Clark has failed to turn their opinion, and I know not of his fate. This makes my heart so heavy, it is hard to speak of it—and I know it will weigh upon yours also."

Fearful looks travelled around the table, for all were aware of the implications; troubles to the north had been followed by troubles to the east. Was the land to dissolve at the first real test and by the hands of one of Garrtellia's strongest supporters?

While the councillors mumbled, Garr thought of her recent resolve to change things and smiled to herself cynically.

"Please, my friends, if I may continue. The time to debate these matters is when sound and reliable information is available to us.

"On the issue of the northern townships, we need to express our gratitude yet again to Leron. To summarise his report to me, the nomadic tribes have been dispatched from our land. The peoples of Monta and Toulou must decide their own fates. Leron and our army removed the traitorous councillors from office and left those townships to discuss their situation. If they elect to approach this council, we should be ready with the answers, terms, and conditions we would lay upon them if they wish to stay within the union of our land.

"As regards Dartell, I have already sent a small delegation from this council together with warriors to discuss their defection and to see if there is any room for movement between us. As all of us here know, it is very much in both parties' interests to resolve this matter quietly and peacefully.

"Do you the council for Garrtellia approve this action?"

To a man, Garr's action was approved. Garr remained standing, her hand firmly holding the stone.

"Thank you. While I still hold the stone of consent at this table, there is a further issue I wish to raise. This is not one that you would be expecting.

"I am but a councillor as you my brothers are—"

At those words, there was an eruption of objections. Garr raised her voice a little.

"Please, I hold the stone." They quietened and Garr was able to continue.

"And yet I feel a heavier load upon my shoulders. I have your guidance with this land of ours. I, as you are aware, also have the wise council of my loved ones, and, indeed, so do we all. I speak of Knap, Idor, Volka, Sala, and Clark of Dartell, whose fate is yet unknown, and many others. I believe our advisers should be recognised.

"They work tirelessly, with no privileges by right, with no stores provided for them as we the councillors have. For example, Leron has often led our armies for us, yes for us. Clark is not a councillor of Dartell, and yet he has worked endlessly to lay out our drought and famine plans and to create the organisation of our coinage. This land owes them more than respect in words. It owes due care to them and their families.

"I believe that areas of responsibility should be created for each of us council members because we need to create a system that is sustainable beyond ourselves. We need to prepare for a time when neither you nor I are on this council by creating a stable and efficient system.

"I'm aware as you are that Luigi has a long, long list which we should work through over the next few days, but, my friends, at each and every meeting we fail to complete that list. Therefore, for our people, our land and our lives, I believe we need to rethink and then slowly re-organise.

"I personally wish to spend more time with my own family. I am a little older now than when we all first met, and sometimes I find myself a little tired."

Garr sat and looked around at those at the table and those beyond the councillors, pushing the stone towards the middle and waiting for somebody to grasp the stone and respond.

Whilst those serious issues were being discussed, archery was being practised on land adjacent to Idor's encampment with Yegor as the instructor.

Luana nudged young Idor, trying to ensure Yegor didn't notice.

"Bet I can get nearer that pole holding the banner."

"I bet you two arrows you can't. What about Yegy?"

"Leave him to me, Idor. Hide those arrows and watch and learn."

Young Idor did as Luana told him, as usual, and hid all the spare arrows in the bracken behind them as quickly as possible. Yegor was busy checking the target and talking away to himself.

"You two supposed to be listening," Yegor said to the children as he turned around. "Did you hear anything me say?"

"Yes, Yegor, you said we must hold our breaths when we release and in our hearts be the spirit of the arrow in flight. We do try, Uncle Yegy. We want to carry on, but we have no more arrows and I don't know where there are any more, do you Idor?"

"No, Luana. Boy, I'm tired, Uncle Yegy, but I heard everything you said, honest. If we had arrows, we could try it again."

"Aah! Okay, okay. You two stay right here, okay. You no move, ya."

With that, he turned around and ran off to collect more arrows.

"You first."

Luana took aim at the flagpole and let fly. It flew in a high arc above tents and families, missing the pole by a rabbit's ear. Idor then drew back his bow and waited for the breeze to drop before he sent his arrow towards the pole. They both stood watching its flight, two blue-eyed scallywags with thick and wild heads of hair, until the arrow dropped and thudded into the pole. Idor jumped for joy; full of self-satisfaction and the beating of Luana.

190

"That's a fine shot, Idy, but just you watch this one."

Luana let another arrow fly, and once again they stood and watched it find its mark.

"Luana, if I hit the mark this time, I must win, okay?"

"No, Id, it must be the best of three shots."

"You're just like your mother, Luana. You always want to make all the rules."

"And you, well, you're like Uncle Volka and let me have all my own way. Whose fault would that be?"

She said this with both arms resting upon Idor's shoulders, giving him a small kiss upon his cheek, which he quickly wiped with his sleeve.

"Uck! Pack it in, Lu, you know I don't like all that silly kissing stuff. Ucky, uck, uck."

They both laughed, holding tummies and exaggerating, before rolling around on the grass and tickling each other.

Fun over, Luana stretched and jumped up.

"Come on, one more go before Uncle Yegy gets back. It's the decider—you first."

"Going to beat you today, Lu. I just know it. Ooh, look over there. I think we're in trouble again."

Two of the tribe's women were looking over at them from the edge of the encampment, obviously pointing and talking about them. One of them shouted at them.

"Luana and Idor, here now. Now!"

"Quick shoot together and then we better run for it, Id."

They grabbed for their arrows and, with no time to waste, shot them towards the pole. As they did so, the two women started towards them.

They watched the two arrows for but a second, only to see them miss badly, and took to their toes and the woods.

"What about Uncle Yegy, Lu?"

"He'll be okay. Let's make a camp, shall we?"

"Ya, this is good," said Idor, and they both laughed and laughed once more as they wandered off without a care in the world.

They both enjoyed their lives, as kids should. Sometimes they travelled with Garr and Idor too far-off meetings. Other times they stayed with Sala and Volka, or Uncle Yegor would take care of them, endlessly and patiently teaching them all the skills of a nomadic person. He took them hunting, fishing, and trapping; he taught them when and how to harvest fruit, nuts, wild garlic, and asparagus.

On a couple of occasions, they had stayed with Uncle Nic and Aunt Sarina and had great fun with their bigger cousins, Jac and Ban, and other children of Prallian. There they learnt about growing potatoes, beans and corn, and living in a village house and community. They watched the village folk making cloths and tools, cheese and bread. Each of these educations were taken on board by these two very bright and privileged children.

They hated being separated, and they didn't like having to look after their small sisters and brothers. Books were okay; the pictures were good. But, strangely, they both hated that reading stuff.

When at home with Garr and Sala, they were generally good kids until the smell of the woods called them. Then, somehow or other, they'd slide away on another adventure, attacking an enemy or visiting one of their secret camps in the woods to return later than they should to a scolding, with Garr and Sala as mad at them as could be, while Volka and Idor would shrug their shoulders and blame Yegor, so the anger would be turned towards them or him.

Poor, wonderful Yegor would appear with a smile and take an onslaught relating to something of which he knew absolutely nothing.

He, in turn, would turn towards the children when the opportunity was available and wink at them with an "oh well" smile, then shake his finger at them as they crept from the scene.

Jac and Ban

Jac and Ban were now both eighteen—tall, straight, and good-looking young men. They were the apple of their mother's eye.

It had taken both of them many years to overcome the bad feelings related to their youthful capture. Luckily it was something they could share with their father, Nic, and their aunt, Garr.

Slowly, over the years, they had opened the door of those memories and, on occasions, shared the stories together. This process was good for all of them; it allowed them sometimes to throw away those bad memories forever and use the lessons learnt to good advantage.

Either sitting around a fire in the cold of winter in Prallian, the flames curling amongst the wood smoke, or sitting upon rocks in the spring sun watching birds and butterflies, they would talk together. One of the boys would suddenly start asking the questions and talking about those events of the past.

"Garr, when you were captured, were you always afraid? I was. I hated the night, being chained until morning, cold and always hungry. The days were okay once you were working and had learnt to bury your head in private thought."

"We were lucky really Garr because Jac and I were together". Ban continued. "There was a man called Garcia, or something like that. He was the worst of our fears—he liked boys, you know, young boys. It makes me feel sick to think of him. "He was slimy, creepy, with foul-looking teeth, and he stunk. He crept and lurked around late at night when most others were asleep, smiling his horrid smile, and tempting you to spend time with him for food.

"We both see him still in our nightmares. Sometimes, I'm still conscious of his dirty nails and hands, his foul breath, and then the sudden change of his mood, accompanied by hate in his eyes and a vicious look that meant you were about to be beaten and kicked or pissed on. Did you get all that, Garr?"

"I did, darling. So did your father. It lasts for years or maybe forever. I thought it would never end, never change, but it did for all of us. We've been the lucky ones. Some poor souls never escape, only by death. I am glad that I hear of such instances a good deal less these days."

Normally after such a chat, when those memories were emptied, a long silent period of thought would follow, only to be broken by the fun of the present.

"Come on, Jac, and you two, Ban and Nic. I'll race you to that big old tree."

Of course, somebody would run for it before the magic word "Go" was said, and others would tug at a jacket or robe. Everything was fair in such a game.

If the tree was ever reached, it was in total exhaustion punctuated by laughter and tongue-in-cheek accusations.

For Nic and Garr, these were wondrous occasions. Their joy in being together once again in a steady and regular relationship was an unexpected bonus in both their lives. Added to this was the children and being able to help and enjoy them.

Garr and Nic had been wise enough to share their own experiences with the two boys, as well as tell them how different life was these days and speak to them of the opportunities they had. To be a warrior, a fighting man or woman, was still expected of all, but the need had diminished immensely. Folks ate more regularly, they spoke more freely, and thought a little more beyond food, fire, sex, aggression and distrust.

Regardless of the occasional dramatic weather, which was a challenge for everybody, these were relatively good times.

Children and families had become more common, but in turn this created the problem of more people to care for and how to provide for their education as well as their survival.

To Jac and Ban, this was how it was in their lives. They understood, possibly better than Garr, how much privilege and respect being part of her family gave them in Prallian and wherever they travelled.

Many of Garr's idea's about community had been generated by the social structures in Prallian and Dartell; even the harsh rules they had applied for many decades had taught her the limits of liberty and the practical use of skills and energy, organisation and planning, and indeed retribution, which was the most difficult to learn and apply.

Jac and Ban had observed and absorbed all these things and now joined their father whenever called upon by the main council or Garr to do battle.

They were aware that, together with their cousins, they would one day be called upon to take major responsibilities within Gartellia.

The War with Dartell

Garr and the main council were rightly concerned. The first delegation sent to resolve the problems with Dartell returned empty-handed. Dismayed by their failure, they made their report to the council with much shrugging of shoulders and shaking of heads.

They had spoken with Dartell's leaders over a three day period, trying a different approach each day and pleading for some kind of gesture or concession they could return with. Instead, they were surprised and shocked by the intransigence of those they spoke too. Additionally, they were unable to discover the fate of Clark and others who were known to support his loyalty to Garrtellia.

Also, according to their report, a substantial crowd was permanently camped outside the walls of Dartell requesting food and assistance. It was an ominous situation with fear and confusion on both sides of the township wall.

"According to the earlier reports forwarded by Clark, Dartell had more than adequate supplies," said Garr, responding to the gloomy report. "I just can't understand why they should suddenly be so uncaring. Surely the new council know the situation. Did they not explain their position further and specify why they have withdrawn their support?

"They did freely allow us to look over their stores, but they repeatedly said that they must, above all, defend Dartell. They said they were sorry for their change of position. But when we asked where Clark was and if he could be made available, they repeatedly replied that we were there to deal with the council of Dartell and that was what we should do. The matter no longer concerned Clark and his followers.

"We even changed our tactics and personalised the situation, directly using your name, Garr. Reminding them that Clark was a close friend of yours, we said that you would be most disappointed not to be reassured of his wellbeing."

"And?"

"They changed tack and asked us to tell you, with the greatest of respect, that Clark and his colleagues were well and healthy, but that the change of council members was brought about by the people disapproving of the distribution of their stores of food. Evidently, the people demonstrated, demanding that the council stood down and that those native to Dartell should be placed first because they had worked for their stores to be full."

"I see, this is difficult. Many may starve because of this selfishness and it isn't the way forward for Garrtellia. We don't want a conflict. Our fighting people have had enough problems. Maybe if I go there in person I could change their opinion? What do you all think?"

There was much talk around and behind the table. The council understood the sentiments of Dartell, but in principle none could agree with their actions. If they did, what would happen in every other community, and what of the authority of the main council? Even the Dartellians' representative at the council had not been aware of their actions, and he was also in despair at the developing situation.

Knap eased himself to an upright position and hobbled to the table, requesting the stone of consent. Clearing his throat and straightening himself, he spoke.

"There are no choices for us to consider. Have they spoken to us before changing their policy? No. Did they discuss it with us or even with their own councillor? No. If they are a part of Garrtellia, then they must abide by our joint ways—ways that have been fairly and mutually agreed upon. We are not as people or as councillors made of stone. We are open to compromise, are we not?

"They greeted our delegation with superficial courtesy and respect, by the sound of it. But although there is no violence yet, I believe there will be, and, regrettably, probably must be.

"I also believe we should send a further delegation with some councillors, and possibly Leron or myself, and push at least for part provision of what Dartell owes us. Further to that, we can assure ourselves of Clark's wellbeing and the other members of the old council. If that was achieved, we would have begun to turn the matter around, slowly and peacefully."

Knap released the stone. Nodding in agreement with himself, he turned slowly and returned to his seat, aided by Idor in lowering himself.

Idor and Leron then both lent forward simultaneously to take the stone. Idor relented and Leron now spoke.

"I think Knap's words are wise, but Idor should lead not I. My reputation and name is only known for harshness and warfare, I'm seen only as a man of war, and this is not the time for my influence. It may come, we will see, but I hope not.

"I do think a small force should travel with the delegation, but, prior to all of this, I think we should do our best to readjust the allocations across the region. Nobody can be allowed to starve in our land."

There were nods of approval from all around the huge council bench.

The delegation was, in part, successful. An uncomfortable compromise was agreed upon, with one third of the original food allocation released. This, together with the re-organisation of food allocations across Garrtellia, allowed those in difficulties to survive.

But the endless heat was draining resources and patience.

The old councillors of Dartell were found to be restricted to their homes and not in the best of heath. Their release was negotiated, but Clark and Deck elected with their families to leave Dartell with the returning delegation and came away from the place of their birth with sorrow and pain in their hearts.

As they and the others rode from the township, there was many a guilty expression to be seen amongst the people as they shuffled along the narrow tracks. A few had the courage to approach and say their farewells and express their regrets, while others wanted to leave Dartell with them. These were sad and sorrowful times.

In time, both Clark and Deck resettled in Prallian, on the advice of Garr. Clark retained his position as an advisor to the main council.

Nobody in Garrtellia starved throughout that long, hot summer but as its heat drained away, it was rapidly replaced with winter. As one weather extreme gave way to another, all in the unhappy land were painfully aware that new hardships would once again show themselves.

Thankfully, although the winter started badly, it ended up being relatively short and mild, and the land still provided game enough. The herds of deer had become smaller and fewer, located within the thickest of forests; the carnivores were more active.

Rabbit and pheasant didn't seem affected in their numbers, but hunting them was long and hard work.

If a cow, horse, pig, or ox was slaughtered, nothing was wasted; arrangements between communities to alternate any such slaughtering were now commonplace.

By the spring of the following year, most communities had exhausted any supplies they had of corn, flour, and all preserved produce, their diet now consisting of meagre amounts of meat and fish, wild berries, vegetables, and nuts and fruits, if they could be found.

Across the land, it was only the larger townships that still had some supplies, and all eked out their valuable food stores as fairly as possible; all except Dartell.

Dartell, once the most loyal of settlements within Garrtellia, was becoming an enemy within, causing unrest in many quarters.

The council called an emergency meeting.

There was little preamble. The issue was pure and simple: "Do we take action against Dartell?"

The answer, with regret, was a resounding 'yes'.

Plans were drawn up and loyal commanders called upon.

Garr and the main council had never been happy with the position of Dartell, but under the circumstances they had up until now decided to let it be. They all had enough troubles, and they hoped against their better judgement that the error of Dartell's ways would be seen when the good and fair element amongst them would again take the lead. But that had not happened and the council's patience had now run out.

The council had decided, without Garr in attendance, to fulfil her suggestions and honour her requests regarding her and the other councillors' roles. But this only raised her status even further, and, although she sanctioned all major decisions, her absence from the council table led her into the position of a quasi-monarch ruling over her beloved Garrtellia.

After the council agreed to Garr's request to change her commitments and divide responsibilities among individual councillors, she regained a good deal of her old life thanks to the extra time she now had available.

Again she was able to occasionally hunt or even set her own traps, albeit with Luana and usually young Idor in toe. When Idor was away or staying with the tribe far below her now famous cave, she again found time to look across her beautiful valley towards the mountains and admire their snowy peaks.

With the children happy and asleep, and an older Monster snuggled to one side while a fire crackled happily at the other, she absorbed again the peace and tranquillity it afforded her.

Her nights were once again more peaceful and pleasurable, whether she was with Idor or Sala, Monster or the children. Each relationship gave her joy.

With time, the changes served her well and her old enthusiasm, which had become a little jaded, was slowly regained as the singular focus of her recent life was slowly abandoned.

Childbirth was a tiresome partner for leadership, but she and indeed Sala were privileged by the tireless support allocated to them in the form of the tribe's women. That, together with a continued warrior presence at the foot of the entrance track, allowed her to feel secure and relatively free from constant callers from all points of the compass.

Some years later.

The confrontation with Dartell was continually put off, even as its relationship with its old allies became almost non-existent.

Clark had led a number of meetings with their council. Thankfully, drought and hunger were no longer the problem, although the issue was never resolved satisfactorily. It had led to woeful disrespect towards the main council on the part of Dartell's rulers.

The main council's decision to go along with Dartell's paltry compromise some years ago had given them illusions of grandeur and importance. Now they continually challenged every decision from the main council or else totally ignored them. Dartell had even taken land from neighbouring villages, and lives had been lost.

Dignitaries from around the land heard tales and rumours and called for effective action against Dartell before unrest spread too far to be contained.

Garr sat at the head of the table. Around her sat the main councillors, together with ministers of the land.

Leron, General of Garrtellian Warriors, presented his plan.

An elite group would enter the township disguised as peasants and endeavour discretely to dispose of as many of the current council as possible. This was aimed at undermining both their confidence and leadership.

While that was happening, as was the way of war for Garrtellia, they would then surround slowly from far afield, capturing or destroying outlying posts which had been established by Dartell over recent years.

No warnings would be issued and no negotiation would be considered until the initial plan was fulfilled.

"It sounds like a good plan, Leron. Are there any comments from this table?"

Clark stood with the stone in hand.

"Garr, we should ensure that all the defensive tunnels are blocked or disabled somehow and that any encampments outside of the walls are moved on prior to serious action."

Leron looked towards Garr for permission to take the stone from Clark. She nodded her approval.

"Thanks for your words, Clark, as usual you speak wisely. The tunnels are covered in the plan, but I had overlooked those close to the Dartell outer walls. All I can suggest is that we move against them as quickly as possible prior to the siege becoming apparent. Whatever happens, we cannot compromise our position. If we attempt to warn them in any way prior to being ready, all could be lost."

Everybody at the table sat in silence and thought for a while. Casios took the stone.

"We should think on this further. Are we not rushing these decisions? Is there not much life at stake here?"

"I agree with Casios," said Cathlea, taking up the stone. "Dartell is a dangerous force. We should be cautious. Thought is required here."

Knap raised a crooked finger, and Garr nodded. There was no need for him to rise at the table any longer, nor indeed to hold the stone while he spoke.

"With great respect to all, but are we not giving too much credence to these Dartellians by believing in their power and importance? We have a whole land at our disposal, while they are but a township acting beyond itself disrespectfully. It appears to me that right and justice, not to mention patience, is really on our side.

"I suggest that we eliminate the leadership and disable the tunnels as suggested. Our warriors could be installed within the walls to ensure all three gates will be undefended, so our men can enter the township. All of this could be carried out in one evening with minimum disruption and loss of life."

From Garr's raised position, she walked back and forth in thought and looked around her council, all in similar contemplation. She was aware of their concerns.

"Leron, how many men can be ready tomorrow?"

"A thousand to fifteen hundred, Garr but—" Garr held out the palm of her hand.

"Leron, send forth two elite bands at the earliest possible moment, in fact, within the hour. One will infiltrate and dispose of the leadership as discussed, the other will disable the tunnels of Dartell. Set your first five hundred men in a line two kilometres from Dartell. Nobody must be allowed to pass over that line, nobody.

"Tomorrow we ride into this troublesome township. Leron, please leave now and make your arrangements. This council will stay here tonight, with no exceptions."

Mutterings flowed around the table. Casios leaned and took the stone.

"Garr, this is not correct. There has been no vote, no agreement, and insufficient discussion. I bow to you with respect of your leadership, but this should be agreed before it is ordered."

"Casios, normally what you say would be correct. Have you not noticed how Dartell has been able to move in opposition to our dictates prior to them being delivered to their council? Casios, this is war and I have decided that this is how it will be. Idor, please would you secure this area for me. This matter will be resolved within the next twenty four hours, peaceably if possible, but it will be resolved. And if dishonour is discovered around this table, beware. It will be dealt with by slow death alone." She paused for effect. "Shall we break and eat?"

As the members stretched their legs and partook in a little food, discussing the surprising and forceful position that Garr had taken, Idor and Volka stood looking up at the darkening sky and watched the golden edged clouds changing shape and colour while a lone bird fluttered from the tent tops and into the east.

Both of them had been privy to the likelihood of a traitor amongst them, and were not surprised by Garr's change of tactics. But they would have stood by her side in front of the council even if they had disagreed. She was family after all.

Garr sat and spoke to Knap.

His spine had curled over the last few years and he only now stood at around the same height as Luana, and his clothes now hung loosely on him. This together with his weathered and wrinkly skin gave him a wizened look. His poor fingers bent and curled, and the ill-fitting and scratched glasses perched upon the end of his extensive nose.

By the time they all settled once more around the great table, nearly an hour had passed. As they settled, a note was passed up to Garr; she took it and broke the seal. Leron was informing her that runners had been dispatched to notify the main force to gather and that already the initial force was moving towards Dartell to form the defensive circle. The two elite groups had been sent ahead by horse. Garr nodded in acknowledgement.

"Gentlemen, I assume you all understand the implications of my actions. Treachery is difficult to deal with, and I, as you, hope with all my heart that the precautions I have taken prove to be unwarranted.

"As we sit here, the plan is falling rapidly into place. By this time tomorrow afternoon, it will be fully underway, hopefully with minimal bloodshed.

"I have asked Clark and Idor to represent Garrtellia. They, with the assistance of Leron, will re-establish order. It remains to be seen whether Dartellians are truly loyal to this land or not."

A number around the table raised hands or leant forward to take the stone of consent. Garr raised her hand and the gathering fell silent.

There will be no further discussion at this table. The stakes are too high for all of us who are loyal to this land of ours."

Fists were banged upon the table, and a few councillors rose and walked away from the table in disgust, only to have their exit from the council area blocked by warriors.

The night was as black as black could be.

Not even a single star could be seen as the five hundred spread their line over the landscape outside of Dartell. Their mission was to block any movement to or from Dartell. As dawn broke, they could be seen stretching to the horizon.

Meanwhile, the elite groups had removed any guards without the walls outside without any problems and had then moved under the cover of darkness to the foot of the township walls, disabling one tunnel after another. Soon, each and every tunnel was blocked. It wasn't a total solution, but it was intended that as the main force moved into Dartell, the line of five hundred would move forward to repel any attempt to attack or escape via the tunnels.

Grappling hooks, wrapped in sheeting to silence them, were thrown over the walls, and the selected prime warriors crept silently into Dartell.

Each of the three groups then gathered within Dartell, intending to make their way to their designated hiding locations where they would await the appropriate time to attack their targets before moving towards the three gates.

The township slept and the track torches had been dowsed. All was pitch black, with not a sound to be heard apart from softly shuffling feet and the occasional clang, as the metal of a weapon touched a wall.

The southern group began to move forward into the darkness when, suddenly, light appeared to the left, then spread one flame by one flame until they were encircled with the light of numerous torches.

They froze, unable to see the enemy through the blinding glare that encircled them.

They heard the twang of a bow string released and, simultaneously, felt the pain as a shower of a hundred arrows tore into them. The unseen arrows of death continued until all lay dead, one upon the other.

Dead or dying, the elite warriors, twenty five brave men, lay with their blood running over each other. Slowly, for all of them, the lights dimmed and their souls flew to a higher land, to join their ancestors.

The other two groups fared better; yet not well.

From those, only thirty Garrtellian warriors evaded death, returning a fuselage of fire. The surviving warriors eventually grabbed at the arrows within their fallen brothers and fled into the darkness of Dartellian tracks and buildings.

They sent two flaming arrows high into the night sky as the agreed warning of problems.

The guardians ordered Dartell to be fully lit once again and searched the streets, tracks, and buildings for their enemies. The guardians beat their leather chest plates as they spread throughout the township, awakening the population. They broke down doors and dragged their own people, adults and children, into the tracks and streets while their homes were searched and ransacked.

It was a good and a bad policy because the fear of the hunters, the hunted, and the common folk soon turned to anger.

The surviving elite warriors knew their task and, by one means or another, made their way to the roofs or wall tops, lying low, crouching, and creeping like shadows slowly towards the Western Gate while the town fell into turmoil and disruption. Small conflicts were breaking out amongst the folk and guardians upon the streets, distracting the latter from their pursuit.

Leron, having seen the warning arrows high above the township, understood that all was not well and began to reconfigure the plans of battle.

He knew well that if possible, his elite warriors would reach the main gate on the western edge of the township, bypassing the capture of councillors and the two minor gates.

He ordered his line of five hundred to regather. He hastily had great wooden sledges constructed, which were loaded with brushwood and heavier timbers, tar and oil, and trussed firmly together. He lit them and sent them forward towards the Western Gate, which was not fully protected, as the capture of the Garrtellian invaders preoccupied Dartell's guardians. Nonetheless, the horses and men undertaking the task were pelted continuously with arrows and many fell in fulfilling the task.

As one burning sledge raced towards the great gate and then swerved to deposit its flaming load against the gate, it turned and jumped unexpectedly, flying high into the air and landing instead upon the warriors and horses delivering it, causing them a ghastly and painful death. Men could be seen crawling and running away from the inferno, yet carrying with them the flames upon their bodies.

Meanwhile, Leron dispatched small bands to circle the township and send flaming arrows into Dartell.

All now was in uproar as battle raged.

Within the encampment below Garr's mountain, most of the retained and restricted councillors still slept, oblivious to the nightmare unfolding in their names.

Garr sat with the arms of Idor wrapped around her before a small fire flickering merrily. Garr was cold and tired beyond her comprehension.

A messenger arrived from Leron and stood before Garr with a courteous small bow. She broke the seal and read with dismay the news of the broken plan. For a moment, she sat staring into the dancing flames.

"Idor, we must go to stand by Leron. All is not well. Clark and others can join us there later, when the main force is assembled. We must inform everybody of the situation, but let's leave Knap in his slumber. The children have Sala and Volka with them—they are safe.

"Leron already has good council by his side in Yegor, Nic and Brian, but this is my responsibility. I must stand beside them all."

"Garr, Idor will organise. You here by fire. This will change, listen to Idor."

He removed the wrap from around his shoulders and added it to the one already around Garr. She nodded thankfully, acknowledging his love and caring.

"Idor, please instruct that any of the main force already assembled should be ready to move within the hour." Idor smiled and nodded.

At that moment, a sleepy Luana waddled into the area loaded with endless wraps dragging on the ground and pulled around her. She walked sleepily into Garr's embrace and quickly closed her eyes.

"Hello, my little flower, what's the problem? Where is Aunt Sal and Volka, sweetheart?" There was no answer. Garr picked her from the ground and sat her upon her lap, rocking and cuddling her affectionately while gently kissing her forehead.

"Sorry, Garr," Volka said as he came in, bending to kiss them both. "We turned our heads for but a second. How are things progressing at Dartell?"

"It's not good, Volka, but it will change. Regardless of our precautions, somebody was able to warn them. A message must have been sent to Dartell from here, somehow. Idor and I must join Leron. We can't sit here while he takes all the risks and responsibility. We'll be leaving within the hour."

"Garr, I must come with you, that is true correct, ya."

"No, Volka, please stay and protect these young people. Who else is there that we can really trust? Please stay with them and keep them safe and warm for me."

"Garr, you listen. I a warrior, no a mother. It is hard for me." He paused. "But for you and Idor and all our children, I will be a woman, and I tell Sala be a woman also." He smiled, and, for the first time in a while, Garr also smiled.

Gently, he lifted Luana, who was now a considerable weight and deep in slumber, and walked away with her cradled in his strong arms, humming a soft tune as he went.

As dawn shone its light once again on the landscape, Leron sat upon his horse alongside his generals and watched as large twists and bellows of dark smoke rose from within Dartell. The Western Gate now roared with great flames twelve metres towards the heavens.

The elite warriors inside, now reduced to but fifteen, continued to fight bravely, while archers positioned around the township continued to send their arrows of flame within.

Leron stood ready to charge at the Western Gate but waited, each moment seeming endless. He wanted Garr to arrive with whatever numbers of the main force she brought to back up his own force of around four hundred men. He knew she would support him, if possible.

Within the walls, the tide of opinion had turned against the council supporters, and citizens battled against citizens and fires alike. In the council building, discussion and argument raged whilst a few men of action made difficult choices. Dartell had the manpower to defend itself, but only if it was sufficiently organised and that organisation had to come together immediately. There was not a moment to lose.

They had correctly seen the situation develop. They knew that, at some point, they would face an onslaught on the Western Gate and their defensive tunnels were unavailable. What could they do about it?

Surrendering what they now saw as their sovereignty was unattractive; Jacob, the local council leader, realised that both his own fate and the fate of others hung in the balance. Whatever action they decided upon would have great consequences, and he was amongst the few who sat quietly to consider their defensive and attacking options.

They decided to subdue the Garrtellian force through deceit. First, the council announced that they would offer to surrender to the Garrtellian army and council. Their intent was to hide the re-gathering of all their guardian warriors to the Western Gate area, including some who would stand without the walls, as a protective force, while their comrade purported to negotiate terms of surrender. The guardians within and without would be ready to fire upon their enemy, as soon as the signal was given.

The Western Gate was gone and smouldering debris hung from great hinges.

The supposed peace negotiators rode from Dartell under a banner of peace. As they did so, a substantial force, numbering some seven hundred men, filed out behind them from where the gate once stood and fanned out to either side.

The Dartellians rode with the banner of truce until they were four hundred metres from the city walls and waited to be met.

Leron was unconvinced, yet Nic and Brian felt the chance should be taken to hear what they presumed to be an offer of surrender.

Garr, Idor, and others had arrived, and eight hundred to a thousand men followed with the greatest of haste.

The leaders of Gartellia stood together exchanging ideas and thoughts.

It would be difficult for Leron to use the horse warriors in a wide sweeping charge, as the ground where the guardians stood, affront the walls, was levelled rubble and scrub. It had earlier been the intent to charge the now open gate along the flat, wide, and level track that led up to it.

Idor suggested to the group that their available men should be sent wide of the situation to either side of the gate to face the guardians. There they could spread themselves deeply across a wide breadth, allowing them to fire into the mass of Dartellian guardians with ease.

Leron was unsure for a moment.

"It's a good suggestion, Idor, but let us not move with haste. These Dartellians have made me angry. They have taken their own position against us, Idor. Time and again they have ignored the dictates from the main council, never once spending time to explain or consult. Over the last three or four years, we have compromised and compromised. We must bring them to order if Garrtellia is to have any future.

"They have proved themselves dishonourable by not adhering to one of the negotiated solutions created over that time. Right now, while we consider honour and compromise yet again, they are organising their defences and attack. Our forces within, who they knew to be Garrtellians, are dead. This is all-out war, my friends. We must complete our mission."

Garr spoke up to calm the discussion.

"Leron, I hear your words and I sympathise with your anger. Now let us agree our plan. We do not want to regret what we do. Spilt blood is never forgotten—warriors have families and children."

Garr then, like the others, stood still considering her thoughts, fears, and indecision. They were awaiting ultimate wisdom and guidance from above, but there was none.

An awesome and horrid thought brought clarity to Garr's mind.

"They have brought a small party of leaders to the fore to negotiate, with guardians, roughly twenty I believe. That could be their mistake. We will ride out to meet them with a party twice that size but with no banner of peace, yet we should display peace in every other form.

As we stop before them, we will immediately raise arms and surround them, while sending two banners of peace to the guardians at the wall. At the same time, we will send our warriors to either side of the gate, as Idor has suggested. As many horse warriors as possible should be held back, ready to charge through the gates if battle should start. If there is any resistance, then their lives must be taken, not ours, and may our gods be with us all. Do we agree?"

214

"Garr, Leron, should you not wait a little longer," Idor suggested. "Allow further warriors arrive? Send food and water to the party and say Garr to come very soon. Look with big glasses, if they unrest or begin move, we go meet them."

All slowly began to nod in regrettable agreement—Leron, Nic, Brian, and Garr. Idor placed his hand out into the small circle, and they all followed until the five hands were together in unity. The plan was agreed.

Meat, fruit, and wine were sent forward with tables, seating and shade, and the message delivered.

One plan set firmly against the other.

The warriors were instructed.

Below the rise in the land, warriors moved into positions, ready to move forward at the call. Two observers lay upon hillocks with binoculars, watching the Dartellian party. They appeared to feast, full of their own confidence and importance, possibly relying on their past victories against Garr and Garrtellia and her endeavours to maintain peace throughout the land.

Some spoke of the battles of the past in which they had been as one for Garrtellia against the Kahn and many others.

An hour passed. Unrest began to grow among the leaders of Dartell.

The guardians outside the walls stood in direct sunlight, with no shade afforded them, forcing them to use their shields for protection or to sit on the ground.

Garr, with Idor and Brian, prepared to go forward. Fifteen warriors dressed as councillors fell in around them, flanked on either side by another thirty warriors. To the far extremes, other warriors were poised to ride on further towards the guardians with the banners of peace.

The main body held high the banner of Garrtellia.

They rode out to meet their enemy like ancient gods from on high, with the sun shining brightly between them, creating bright hallows of light.

Back below Garr's mountain, Sala paced back and forth with young Nikolas in her arms. A large group of children, including Luana, young Idor, Holly, and Sonny, sat in turn tossing stones to catch on the backs of their small hands. Sarina and Knap sat with them along with a number of warrior womenfolk.

Volka was not in attendance; he had succumbed to the ancient call of a warrior and had ridden to be next to his brother.

Apart from the children, there were few words spoken. Nobody knew what was happening. They just had to wait.

Occasionally a group of hill folk or nomads would pass through the campsite, clad in their warrior regalia, some on horse and others on foot.

Some had no battle dress in particular and were clothed in their everyday attire, holding but their hunting bows and spears.

Far afield, womenfolk, with or without little ones and old folk, paced floors or sat and stared into the great unknown while the few children played games of tag or camps, and babies clung to their mothers' breasts.

The feeling of fear and anticipation hung heavily in the air.

All were aware that, come tomorrow, they could be lonely and, in any case, the world they had come to know and accept could be changed, perhaps forever.

Some spoke openly of the doubts they felt about the union of Gartellia. It was a difficult balance, of security and community, against the world the older ones had known of tough independence.

In reality, not many would return to those days, but at this moment it felt like an option.

As Garr's party neared the Dartellian leaders, they began to rise from their seated positions. Julius, their leader, walked forward with hands held out in greeting.

"Garr, it is always with respect that I and my comrades stand before you. Today it is with a heavy—wait … what is this treachery!"

At the moment of his first words, Garr's warriors encircled the Dartellian peace party. With bows drawn against them, the guardians reluctantly dropped their weapons and their resistance, while the banners of peace went forward towards the guardians gathered at the township walls where they did not anticipate and were not aware of the Garrtellian plan.

Leron's two large groups of warriors had positioned themselves to the north and south. The formation was intended to confuse; giving the impression that the Garrtellian force had greater numbers than it did.

Julius continued to shout in rage. He turned towards Dartell and pushed his way through his comrades. When he reached the encircling warriors, he halted for a moment, then he proceeded to break through them and walked beyond, still shouting, towards his guardians.

"Are you cowards? Will you not defend your township and your families? We outnumber them. Fight and save your souls. Fight for Dartell."

While eyes were diverted, there was an eruption from within the encircled councillors. Guardians grabbed at their weapons and, in response, arrows flew at them from all sides.

As horses backed away, the flight of arrows continued. At such close range they penetrated deep and through bodies. Men staggered, looking like pin cushions, but still some attempted to attack the mounted archers.

Garr's horse nervously stepped backwards, lifting its front hooves from the ground. An arrow had entered at her side, below the ribs, where the leather plates were laced together. Garr grabbed instinctively at her side in excruciating pain, her fingers spread out on either side of the deadly arrow deep within her flesh. Her head dropped for a second and then regained its upright position, but her eyes told the story.

The arrow from one of her own warriors exited at her lower back. A single tear of awareness ran down her cheek.

Idor saw the pain but not the arrow. He was on foot and moved quickly towards her with his hands reaching forward to take her to himself. As he reached up to take her from her horse, a staggering guardian slashed at him with his sword, cutting him at the neck and opening a great gash. Idor felt his strong right arm go limp, he tried to turn but nothing would happen. He waited for eternity or for the following strike of death.

As Garr looked down upon her Idor, more tears fell; she slowly dismounted and went to cradle him within her arms. As he gasped and turned his back into her embrace, he saw his brother Volka withdrawing his own sword from well within the guardian, and they both smiled a smile of love as Idor's eyes closed.

On the plain before the township of Dartell, archers let fly against archers. The guardians were fine archers, as were the warriors, but the odds had turned against them due to the formation of their opponents and their discomfort with the need to improvise.

As the warrior arrows thudded home within the massed guardians, they fell in droves. From within the walls of Dartell, further guardians tried to aid their comrades, but now they too had to deal with battle on two fronts because arrows now flew towards those upon the wall defences from within Dartell, as the remaining elite Garrtellian warriors within the city now truly showed their worth.

The sight of man or woman falling dead or wounded was abhorrent to all, but there was no time for fancy thoughts, morals or principles in the middle of battle.

Then the thunder of hooves commenced, as a hundred mounted warriors charged down towards the open Western Gate of Dartell.

The sun was now low in the western sky, throwing the horse warrior's shadows into gigantic shapes. Stone, grit, and dust flew side-wards from the thud of heavy hooves, creating billowing clouds of orange dust.

Behind them, two hundred warriors ran through those orange clouds towards the gates. As they reached it, they turned left and right, hacking and slashing with sword and axe. Limbs dropped to the already blood stained ground and bodies were split like dry timber from top to bottom.

The warrior groups of archers at either side of the gate now laid down their bows, withdrew their swords, and ran towards the gate, joining the slaughter of the now disorganised guardians.

Sala and Sarina stopped their activity and looked at one another with a knowing stare. Their inner senses somehow made them aware that blood was flowing. They embraced for a moment. One of them was shaking violently.

Knap looked over at the two women and shared their intuition and pain.

With some aid, he stood and hobbled to them, wrapping his arms around them.

"My dearest daughter and beloved friend, you should not be afraid. Our loved ones are strong and, above all, they are right. The spirits will be with them whatever happens, and I feel positive and hopeful that they will return to us.

"Pay attention to your children and show them no fear or doubt."

He squeezed them the best he could, then kissed them both tenderly, and returned to sit close to the fire and await the news which would not be good, even if attached to victory.

He wouldn't sleep until the outcome was known.

The horse warriors thundered through the tracks within Dartell. Guardians and simple folk alike scurried into doorways or leapt through windows to avoid the slaughter by sword or hoof.

From afar, Leron watched his victory grow. Yet, it was with sorrow in his heart that he watched both the growing number of slaughtered lying upon the ground in front of the walls and the smoke of many fires within Dartell.

The horsemen reached the central square, where they found crude flags and banners of white being waved desperately at them on all sides. Realising that they had now reached those citizens resisting the council's move against Garrtellia, Nic and Brian dismounted and spoke to the people. At this point within the township there were no guardians remaining as all were either dead or at the Western Gate attempting to hold off Garr's warriors and protect what was now left of their sovereignty.

The horse warriors gathered at that place and, for a moment, were treated like saviours of the world. But there was no time to wallow in appreciation; the task needed completion.

"The battle is nigh over, save your buildings and your township, we will return to assist you. Are there others that stand against us or are all at the Western Gate?"

"They are all at the Western Gate or running via the Great Gate to the north. All behind us are for Garr and Garrtellia."

"We say again—save your buildings and your homes. Is the library safe?"

"The library is sound as are most of the main buildings. The children and the old have been moved to buildings in the eastern section of town. They are in safety and comfort even though filled with fear."

Brian and Nic divided their warriors into two. One party turned to the north, the other south. As the horse warriors swept to encircle the western quarter, guardians, now seeing the futility of the battle, were laying down their arms in surrender. By the time the western quarter of the township was subdued, with the gaping entrance once again in view, they could see that battle was all but finished.

The cost had been a heavy one to both sides. Dartell would take many months or even years to rebuild.

It was with great sadness that Teo and Vora rode alongside of Big Brian viewing the devastation that was now Dartell. As they rode through the gap where once stood the greatest gates in the land, they looked in silence at the many bodies that covered the rough ground. Around where the great gates once stood, bodies torn and broken were piled high to either side, the blood of one running over his brother below. Lives had been wasted because of the unwillingness of but a few to forego ego and vanity.

Such is the cost and ways of war and foolishness.

Their sadness would be compounded when learning of the wounded Idor and Garr.

The Old Guard & The New Land

It took a few years for the wounds created with Dartell to heal sufficiently to say that all was well in the land.

Of course, for those loyal to Garrtellia there was no problem, and the younger people, in general, were keen to move forward. That is the way of the world.

It was in those rebel families and the older members of the township that dangerous resentments still lurked.

The battle for Dartell had destroyed families. Those affected were only left with their memories and stories of injustice to focus their lives upon.

Nevertheless, in the land as a whole, harmony improved, and, to aid it, new laws and systems were slowly generated to bond together the land of Garrtellia.

There was universal acceptance of the official coinage as the main means of payment. A tax was applied to all which, though almost impossible to impose and collect, was the beginning of undertaking tasks for the common good.

A new and tighter system was established for the election of council leaders.

A new system of justice, with a uniform approaches to judgement and punishment, was put in place.

One of the most important developments was education. Townships, larger villages and nomadic tribes were actively encouraged to initiate schooling for anybody able to attend and to gather any and all books into one place for the benefit of all at the places of learning. The main council redistributed the gathered tax to assist, encourage, and enforce the fulfilment of their plans.

However, none of these actions were started or maintained easily. The resistance was immense.

Nomadic peoples and the hill folk found the changes most difficult to accept. The new social developments seriously restricted them and impacted on their traditional lives. Since their lifestyles required independent thinking, the new laws seemed irrelevant most of the time; they were simply an unnecessary imposition.

Change would take them a good deal longer to get used to than others who willingly and regularly interacted with others. For this majority, it was an exciting time full of new concepts and opportunities.

It certainly didn't replicate yesterday's amazing world way back before the big disaster, but they were moving dramatically, for the first time in many generations, towards a culture in which all could live with a relative lack of fear.

Garrtellia was becoming a land where the intellectual and the physical attributes of all could be respected, allowing people to prosper and develop.

Knap lay on his bed looking very small and grey, he was bent to one side in half slumber, breathing heavily. His wispy white hair straggled in all directions. Beside him sat Sala, fearful of the outcome of this long period of illness.

She hungered for another year or two of his warmth, his loving smile, and his touch.

How could this fragile bundle be the same man of strong back and arm that had cradled her and her brothers once upon a time? The man who had always loved, cherished, and protected her and her family—a man of great fame, whose reputation would probably sustain her own family for generations to come.

How did all that happen so quickly? Where had all that precious time gone?

While Knap slept, Sala rose from the bed, needing to stretch and move her limbs. She walked through her childhood home, passing a hundred memories at every turn, gently touching the door to the place where she and her brothers had spent so much of their childhood.

Before she went through the front door, she turned and looked back, slowly taking in every detail as if she would never see it in this way again. Her father's existence bonded all those memories together, giving value and sense to all the thoughts she treasured and the very way she had tried to live her own life.

In the winters of her childhood, there were small oil lamps at every corner and a fire glowing. Then it was a place of warmth and comfort. She remembered how she and her brothers would sit in wonderment while their father told them stories of magical adventures; she smiled to herself, turned, then stepped out into the sunlight.

Her sister in law, Jenna, pushed her chair back under the rickety table, then, ducking under the low branches of the apple tree, walked towards Sala.

"Is he okay, Sal?"

"He's sleeping heavily. I just needed to move around. Are you okay?"

"I'm feeling tired like you, that's all. The others should be here soon. Do you think Garr will be able to come?"

"It would take heaven and hell to stop her, Jenna. You watch, she'll be here alright, with all the children in tow and an army supporting her. She would cross an ocean to comfort my father. Ever since they met, she's been his surrogate daughter. They love and respect one another, it's very simple."

"Has that ever bothered you?"

"Strangely, no. She was always fun and interesting to have around. "When I was younger, she seemed so large, such an adventurer—a warrior woman. I idolised her. She was everything I ever wanted to be. Now, so many years later, I still idolise her and love her.

"Now Volka, that's different. I think I love him. I certainly think he's wonderful, and he is the father of all my children, I think."

"Are you sure about that?"

They both smiled a knowing smile. Jenna winked at Sala and went in to sit next to Knap.

Sala walked over to the old apple tree and patted the trunk, addressing her arboreal companion.

"Well, old friend, we've seen some fun together, have we not?"

The apple tree never answered with words. But she felt it was also sad and steadfastly keeping its own counsel.

She sat and once again looked back at the large domed hillock that formed her old home. It was but a humped meadow of grasses and wild flowers, with the occasional flap extending lower down that protruded to form a window. Two metal tubes stood out above the top of the mound through the grasses, one with white whispery smoke floating away from it. The entrance had a large flat grassy roof with stout trunks supporting it. It was large enough for the whole family to sit under these days. A lot of meals had been enjoyed and time spent around the old table where she now sat.

The home had been formed over years of work from a natural hillock. This originally had allowed Knap to dig out the bottom half of the house. Knap had visited the site for a month now and then until it reached completion or was complete enough to install his growing family—a family that was an unexpected rarity in those days.

In her childhood there had been no fences around the place, as it wasn't advisable to advertise your presence, just some odd trees and bushes to disguise its existence. Nowadays, there were paddocks for pigs and goats, areas allocated for vegetables and many more fruit trees—all a little neglected now.

To the far right was a tree house perched within the boughs of a large cherry tree. Unsurprisingly, it was where the grandchildren congregated whenever they were around.

All that was missing from the scene was her mother, Mara. And it seemed that her father would soon be leaving her also.

She felt lonely already and hungered to be in the embrace of somebody she loved. With her head upright, being brave and strong, tears rolled thickly down her face.

Contradicting her emotion, the mottled sunlight that penetrated through the apple boughs bathed her face in warmth, and her eyes edged themselves closed.

She wanted to escape from the memories and the pain of that moment.

The cart that Idor had given them both was never a comfortable choice, but it was a convenient one.

Keppa, now a loyal old friend, was still always ready and willing to pull the little cart anywhere that pleased his mistresses.

He spent most of his time in a meadow close to home where he could plod and munch to his heart's content. A companion for the very old Monster, he would sometimes play a game from yesteryear or just watch the clouds go by, which was a lot more appropriate these days.

Just occasionally, they might be joined by an old and tatty looking cat; Garr's large white tom, who would hobble and scramble down the rock track from the cave to see what was going on. Once he had located Keppa and Monster, he would, as always, impose his presence by sitting upon Monster throughout his cloud watching or standing inconveniently under Keppa, using him as a shield from sun or rain. As Keppa would move, so would Wiz—a truly strange and funny sight to behold. Garr, Sal, and Idor knew that all these creatures had somehow outlived their expectation of years, but they seemed to still be hanging onto life somehow.

Garr regarded herself blessed by all those around her. Her life's journey had changed from horror and disaster to amazing happenings, unbelievable love and friendship, and adulation. She never planned on or wanted the reverence of others, yet now in the position she found herself, she understood its value. Her life had certainly never been boring or average.

A messenger had arrived requesting that Volka, Idor, and Garr attend at Knap's bedside and advising them that his general state appeared low. They understood and Idor had immediately arranged a small party to attend to the preparation for their journey. The warrior women had organised the children, both Sala's and Garr's.

Garr had also sent messages to Nic, Sarina, Clark, and Yegor, all of whom had grown very close to Knap over the years.

It was a quiet party that left to travel to Knap's bedside, all anticipating the worst of outcomes.

The journey would be at least five hours of sad thoughts and great memories, filled with overwhelming emotion and respect. All were aware that they must find the strength to celebrate his life.

"Mother," Luana asked, "are you and Father properly healed now from your wounds? I mean, you won't get ill again like Knap, will you?"

"No, sweetheart, we are well now, strong and healthy. Just you feel your father's muscles—hard as rocks and as big as mountains. You have no need to worry about us leaving you.

"Now listen to me, you too, Idor—stop talking and please listen to me. When we all see Knap, remember that he is feeling very poorly and he might be leaving us all shortly. So if there's anything you would like to say to him, this may be your last chance. Do you all understand?"

"Of course we do, Aunt Garr," replied young Idor. "He will be going to join the unseen warriors. We've already talked about it together, and we all love him, so we have decided we will tell him so. We think it's important to tell people such things."

"This is good! Knap is indeed a great warrior and worthy of your affection," said Idor. "Now enough sadness. You want feel me muscles, ya."

Luana and young Idor laughed while their brothers and sisters huddled around them and held on tight as yet another mighty bump shook the small cart, nearly throwing young Rosy off and over the tail board.

Idor bent forward and grabbed her, then whispered privately in Garr's ear.

"You travel forward with Yegor, Garr. Time maybe no much. Ya, good idea."

Garr called over to Yegor, then climbed upon the rear of his horse, holding on hard as Yegor dug in his heels and drew away from the party, with two warriors following at a short distance.

Garr found the galloping harsh upon her body, but she endured the discomfort and said nothing. She still looked a fine athletic women, her mousy long blond hair as full as it was in her youth, but her body told her a different story.

The old arrow wound taken at Dartell had healed after a time, but when she put her body under stress, the wound could still open once again; there appeared no real solution. The troublesome wound was one thing, but the fact the arrow had hit her spine was the real problem. Without warning and for no apparent reason, she could awaken and not be able to move. It scared her, yet she never seemed to speak of it. After two or three days the pain and paralysis would fade away, and she'd be able to undertake just about anything she wished once again.

The threat of full paralysis lurked within her thoughts every day. It was her biggest dread; the only thing that had ever really scared her.

Just the thought of not being able to hunt or walk through her favourite woods down to the river and watch the trout leap for a fly or two was awful. Would she one day be unable to chase or cuddle Luana, Rosy, and Louis or the others she loved so much? And being left unable to care for her largest baby of all, Garrtellia, also worried her. It still needed her constant love and attention.

She kept her discomfort hidden from all but those closest to her. And thanks to the good fortune of her looks, others had never become aware of her problems. She was called upon and expected to be superhuman, but neither she nor her loved ones had any illusions.

Idor had also not fared so well in this respect. The wound that he had taken at Dartell had left an ugly scare. He was no longer able to stand with his head held high. The tissue had healed but had pulled together the muscle around his right shoulder, leaving his head to fall a little to one side. For a long time his right arm was also useless. It had taken him a year and a half of daily exercise to rebuild some strength and dexterity.

An hour later, in severe discomfort and with sweat dripping from her brow, Garr slid from the rear of Yegor's horse. She held tight to the leatherwork and regained her breath for a moment.

"Yegor, will you walk with me please? I'm not yet steady on my legs, I'm sorry."

"Never say sorry to me, Garr. Tu never problem, it me pleasure, me honour. Is much pain you?"

"I'll be okay. In a while the pain will be gone."

Yegor dismounted with a leap and, subtly taking Garr around the waist, escorted her to where Sala sat at the table with her eyes closed in half sleep. Yegor placed a hand upon Sala's shoulder and gently roused her. She awoke fully with a start, then, realising who was before her, relaxed with a thankful and happy smile. The emotional strain showed clearly on her bronzed face, and both Garr and Yegor were surprised how poorly she looked.

"Sal, how is Knap? And what of you? You look so tired."

"I'm fine, I'll survive. Dad's not good. He mostly sleeps—he's truly tired and has lost enormous amounts of weight. Jenna is sitting with him."

"Should I go straight in to see him?"

"No, I need the both of you two first. I know that's selfish."

She stood and wrapped her hungry arms around them, holding them tight and close. When she was done, she stood back, a tear appearing in her eye.

"The children, are they ok?"

"Of course, they'll all be here in a while. Don't you worry about them. If possible, take me to see your father. We've been so very concerned about all of you."

Standing alongside Knap, Garr looked upon him remembering.

She thought of how he enjoyed just being alive and the pleasure he found in all things around him; the delight he found in thought, his sons, daughter and grandchildren, and each flower, bee, and bird. Garr could not remember a time when she had seen Knap unhappy. Even throughout the great floods and frozen winters of the past or when the land they lived upon burned each and every day until they thought all would die, he had found a smile and a positive word.

She continued to stare down, not really able to take her eyes from him in case the pain she now felt erupted or he magically disappeared.

Her emotions broke through and, without realising it, she spoke aloud.

"I love you so much, it hurts me so to look upon you in this discomfort. I wish I could take your pain, Knap, I truly do."

Yegor stepped close behind Garr and placed a light hand upon her shoulder. Sala sat down alongside Jenna. All were silent.

Garr shook herself back in control and continued to remember. She thought of the journey to Dartell: the encounter with Yegor and Yazzy, meeting Deck, Clark and Gable, the leopard by the stream.

There were so many wonderful things that she should and would remember.

Her mind went back further to the many hunting trips they had both taken in the days when Knap's legs would carry him at speed and his bow would send forth arrows straight and true. She remembered how their long evening conversations had assisted

Garr in developing her thinking and self-esteem; she was so very, very grateful for this man.

With difficulty, she turned from these pleasant memories in her mind, knowing that her emotions must be set free. She walked from the bedchamber into the outer room, and instantly the tears rolled freely while she sobbed for the pain of her friend.

Both Sala and Yegor followed her automatically to the doorway in concern; she raised her hand to stop them.

"I'm okay, really, let me be, please."

She remained there in the dullness, working hard to deal with her feelings and memories and then, as if from nowhere:

"Garrtellia has so very much to thank this wonderful man for. He is my hero." Then, again, she fell silent.

Soon, Idor arrived with the children. He set his warriors around the outskirts of the smallholding to avoid insensitive interruption and to protect the members within from any harm.

With all his family and friends gathered around his bedside, Knap amazingly raised himself, calling upon his failing body strength. He smiled and spoke to them the best his voice would allow.

"Help me outside. This is all too dull and miserable in here. I think we all need to see the sky, the hills, and trees; I want to feel the sun and the breeze upon my face." He paused, raising his hand a little and shaking his finger. "I always meant to change this dull old house. Still, I guess it's a little late for that right now! All of you listen to me, maybe one more time. I want to see my grandchildren, I want to see them laugh and play. I want to see my beloved family and friends happy and strong before I leave. There's no need for sorrow, for I have been privileged to have known great love, friendship, and adventure. How many do we know that have been so lucky to have a family like this? I have no regrets. Life has been so kind to me."

At that, he touched the hands of those close to him.

"Now let the children play, and find us a musician who can play a merry tune, and then, very soon, I shall want to be with my Mara again. Will you let me sit under my old apple tree? I guess we're about the same age, that tree and I. Then you can pass me a beer and let only tears of laughter be seen, none of sorrow."

They did his bidding.

Through the tight circle gathered around him, Luana and young Idor wriggled their way to his side. Luana took his hand, and Idor wrapped his around them both. Knap smiled fondly at them.

"We've had some fun between us. Just you two remember that and to be fair and true in your lives. Do you both hear me?"

Luana spoke up. "Knap, we don't want you to leave us. We love you so much. What will we do without you by our side?" She started to cry and young Idor placed his arm tighter around her shoulder.

Knap struggled to wrap both arms around the two of them.

"We'll always be together in one another's hearts, always. Now don't you cry, little ones. If I do leave, remember, I'll be watching you always. You dry those tears. Go play and be happy and proud that we are and were the greatest of friends."

He managed to kiss them both.

"Can you find that little smile for me, Luana?"

She did find a smile, accompanied by a great sniff, and young Idor, still with his arm around her, led her back through the crowd.

In the background, somewhere, other children were laughing, so Knap closed his eyes to enjoy the sounds of that laughter and the birdsong. Slowly he allowed his peaceful spirit to float gently beyond the wispy clouds and the deep blue sky, to somewhere far above, where we are all destined.

Many commented that they had never seen such a bright funeral pyre and never known one to burn for so long.

Sala and her brothers had insisted that all gathered should stay and celebrate his life.

They drank, ate, and danced while laughing and crying.

For three days, while the fire still burned, they partied the best they could. Knap's memory and name would be passed forward by history, and the folks of Garrtellia would tell their children endless tales of the great wizard Knap for all time to come.

The First Rays of Sun

At forty-three, Garr was putting on more weight than she wanted, but, all things considered, it wasn't so tragic. The majority of folks never even reached that age, let alone display her youthful looks and movement.

The loss of friends and creatures around her weighed heavy on her mind and soul.

Due to the assistance afforded her by the women folk of Idor's tribe, she still managed to maintain a reasonable lifestyle; a little hunting with Idor or the children, numerous trips around Garrtellia, and many council meetings were still managed with little difficulty.

The delegation of responsibilities over the years had been a great success. The intention was purely to lessen pressure upon herself and her family, which it had done, but the effect was also to heighten her status to a regal one. She wasn't happy with that, but there was no escape. The people of Garrtellia needed somebody to look up to, and circumstances had chosen her. Garr's strength of commitment, her honour and principle, all added perfectly to their vision, and if ever somebody naturally looked regal, it was Garr. Luckily, she possessed humility beneath her confidence, and she never hesitated to listen to other points of view and never shied away from making a difficult decision when called upon. She was blessed with the common touch, which was also a regal gift, and, whether or not she was aware of it, those around her felt it and were willing to live within its comforting shadow.

Luana was now the image of her mother, but a little taller and with the charm and dignity of her father. Wherever she wandered, admiring eyes fell upon her. They were obviously eyes of desire also, but she was untouchable and unapproachable to most. Being the heir and the princess was a difficult duty.

She had flirted with the odd warrior at the Big Gathering and fiestas around the land, but for Luana there would only ever be young Idor and her father.

Young Idor was her knight, her warrior, friend, and lover.

They belonged to each other and always had, from the very beginning of their lives.

Young Idor had at last grown way beyond Luana in height, and the timing was perfect for she now needed his chest to nestle against and his strong young arms to embrace her. He was now also taller and bigger than his father in his youth, and was looked upon by all as both the prince of the realm and a young man with humility and honour.

He looked very much like Sala, with a great bush of black hair, a strong, straight nose, long fingers, and straight limbs. When they stood together, Sala and young Idor looked like twins, which pleased Sala immensely.

"He's a lucky young fellow," Volka would comment, "the looks of his mother and the heart and brain of his father. Well, I think I'm his father."

"One never really knows about these things, Volka," Sala would tease him back, "so many years ago, so many men, so many."

Both Luana and Idor had learnt well, with the endless guidance and devotion of Yegor and Knap, before he had left them. They were knowledgeable young people, as well as skilled in warrior ways. They had all grown up with horse travel available to them and thought nothing of using their bows from a saddle or bareback, but if required their strong young legs would take them flying across the grasslands with hardly the need to draw breath, mile upon mile.

Now they had begun to occasionally sit at the main council, representing Garr or Idor when not available. Their personal counsel was seriously listened to and their words were considered with due and genuine respect.

Garr and Sala rode unattended towards Prallian.

It was a rare situation and they both felt fully aware of the oddity. They felt naughty, as if somebody would be chasing them to threaten them with some awful punishment. They both felt extremely free, as if they were a part of nature itself.

It was so different from the feelings generated by the yoke placed upon their shoulders.

On their arrival, there would be council business to be discussed with Nic, Brian and Clark, documents for Garr to place her seal upon, and final decisions to be declared.

The matters of Gartellia must be the priority and be maintained. It affected so much and so many.

Thereafter, they intended to have some social and private time.

The anticipation and excitement that Garr was feeling was immense. Although she had not said that to Sala, she guessed she was feeling the same.

Their relationship had never waned through all the difficult years of battle and problems, or when time had been at a premium. Children, which she had never expected to produce, were demanding, and their menfolk had on occasions confused the feelings they felt. But, somehow they had held on to each other, their friendship, and their relationship. Neither understood the how and why, and, thankfully, it didn't matter to anybody. Love and comfort were taken wherever and whenever they were found.

Some things had not changed.

It would have been quite normal for Idor or Volka to take other womenfolk into their family but neither of them had done so. Possibly there was simply never the time or the desire.

How strange are the ways of the world?

The middle of the day had been reached. It was bright, yet fresh, and the track had taken them into the dark shadow of the hills above them; a chill was creeping into their bones. They chose to trot towards the sunny side of the narrow valley. There they dismounted, then walked up the grassy slope until they reached the lower rocks and could sit upon a large flat boulder facing the warmth of the sun.

Sitting for a moment or two, they drenched themselves in the warmth and rarity of their freedom—just themselves, no children, and no Garrtellia. It was so very peaceful and oh so very rare.

Lying back and spreading their arms above their heads, they watched a lonely white cloud drift through deep blue, slowly breaking into smaller wispy patterns and shapes, then disappearing from their view over the sun covered mountains.

It was pure ecstasy and escapism—the first time in many a year they had felt so blessed. They watched an eagle float gently by and for the hundredth time, marvelled at its effortless flight.

Garr dragged herself free of the decorated clothing, removed her boots, and lay back into that ecstasy.

The two horses stood under an adjacent Mediterranean pine, munching contentedly on meagre pickings. Garr wished

Monster were laying alongside them, yet thankful for the young mastiff, Kia, that these days fulfilled Monster's old duty of guarding his mistress. Monster was probably deep in sleep back at the cave.

Then breaking the moment with a sudden twist and turn, Sala dived and attacked Garr.

The sudden and unexpected change of pace scared Garr.

Not thinking of Garr's old injury, Sala thrust her fingers deep under her arm pits and tickled her ruthlessly. It was Garr's weak point, and she liked to give rather than receive, especially since the nightmare at Dartell.

They rolled in laughter mixed with pleading and then crashed off the edge of the flat rocky ledge and onto the downward grassy slope.

"Stop that, Sal! You know I hate that, please, please. Okay, I give in, I surrender."

"No chance, oh great leader—you need to be punished because you're wicked."

"I'll get you back. You know I will. Oh no, STOP it please, please, please."

They tumbled down the slope, while the mastiff ignored them, looking away with disgust at their childish fun. Some four metres down the slope, Sala suddenly remembered about the old wound. Feeling a little guilty now, she relented and sat upright as if nothing had occurred.

"That was good fun, I enjoyed that. I'd like to get you again later. It's not often one has the opportunity in life to tickle a queen's fancy. But I'm seriously sorry, Garr, I completely forgot about the old wound."

Now they both sat upright on the grass, both exhausted from the game and taking deep breaths.

Garr pushed at Sala, knocking her sideways.

"I'll get you back, I promise, but it was good fun, Sal. When was the last time we had a laugh like that? I never know when that wound will cause me a problem, so don't worry, no harm done."

She stood and moved back to her clothing and sat once again upon the flat rock. Both women still had firm bodies and hid both the years and motherhood well. Garr was the taller by quite a gap, and still the more athletic, despite being the elder of the two by far.

The remainder of the journey contained other expressions of their newfound freedom. They chased and they raced, with their black and blond hair flowing behind them, as both dug their heels in deep, as hooves pounded the soft ground of the valley bottom.

"Garr, I still feel a little guilty about this day," said Sala.

"We'll be working, why should you?"

"No, I don't mean what we are doing. I mean the tickling and racing. You really should not do that kind of thing these days. Obviously, it was fun, but it could have easily turned out badly."

"Sala, there's no chance of me living life in a chair or a bed. Really, I'm okay. Please don't worry about such things. Suddenly, the pain will start again. There's nothing we can do about it."

They trotted into Prallian with heads held high and displaying a little of the dignity that some expected of them. But here in Prallian, most were close and knew them both as simply Garr and Sal, as Nic's sister and friend. None could imagine that in the hands of these two women was the power and future of the land.

The old cobbled streets and stonework of Prallian caused their entrance to echo their arrival. The sight of Nic and Sarina's great oak door was a welcome one. Sala leapt from her mount and pushed it open. Kia wandered in feeling it was but home from home and planted himself duly exhausted in front of the empty fireplace, pleased he was at the journey's end.

Sala returned to Garr, seeing now that she was in some discomfort and assisted her to dismount. It was a painful process and when both her feet were on firm ground, she sighed heavily and limped in through the open door, placing herself immediately into a comfortable chair.

By the time Sala had rustled up a drink and food, Garr was sound asleep, not looking at all regal, with mouth open, arms and legs in all directions.

Sala watered and attended to the horses and provided for Kia likewise, then sat patiently upon the arm of the chair next to Garr, one arm placed gently around her shoulders.

She then also drifted into a worried and guilty sleep. She knew in her heart that the two of them had overdone the fun throughout the day. Nevertheless, the exhaustion of their journey, with the sun and frolicking, had taken the energy from her.

Nic, Sarina, and the boys entered through the still open doorway, with Nic expecting the normal affectionate greeting from his sister. Instead, they were greeted by sleeping bodies, heavy breathing, and Kia's snores.

They unloaded their produce and tiptoed around their sleeping guests, preparing a meal. It had been a hard and long day in the fields, and they had only returned home when the light had faded and made work impossible.

Despite their own weariness, they erected a table outside, within the square, around which all would be able to eat and enjoy the coolness of the evening.

It was the custom in Prallian. Mostly tables were left erected and the whole village would sit and share this time together, either in family groups or in little gatherings, some moving from one table to another. But on this occasion, it was going to be a sleepy affair due to the exhausted guests.

Sala awoke first and then gently awoke Kia and Garr. They sleepily embraced and greeted one another, with Kia nestling his great head into them both.

Garr, catching sight of her brother for the first time since arriving, called out to him.

"Sorry, brother, I guess your old sister has overdone it somewhat, but we had some fun on the way here. I think I won everything."

"Oh no, you didn't," Sala insisted. "I thought I did."

"Aah! Don't be silly, Sala. Monster and Kia could whip you in most competitions standing backwards, but I still love you, even if you do tell lies."

"Creep."

"Stop bickering you two. Go have a wash and join us in the square. It's a beautiful cool evening, and you'll feel better in the fresh air."

Nic watched his sister limp to the washing stand and realised that she was not quite the athlete she used to be. He stared at her for a moment, noticing the lightening of her hair, and realised again that her beautiful blond hair was beginning to turn whitish, possibly ash-blond. The curve of her shoulders made her look a little shorter, and, possibly for the first time in his life, he saw his sister as a mother, as the leader of the land he lived and fought for, and as the one that held life and death within her power for all within Garrtellia.

How strange he hadn't seen her like this before; how incredibly strange.

"Nic, come on, please help some. Even your sons are doing something for a change. Get Sala and Garr out here. They'll feel a little brighter in this cool air."

Ban joined in the chatter.

"Mother, I heard that. It's not true, both Jac and I sweat blood and tears every day so you can live a life like a princess. Ever since Aunt Garr's been viewed as royalty, you've this extra little air about you—"

Before he could finish his words, a splendid shot with the jug of water drenched him.

"You see what we poor children have to endure every day, Aunt Garr."

"Yes, darling, I guess your mother is really wicked."

Garr, with some difficulty, ducked behind the chair, ready to receive the second giant splosh she knew she deserved.

"Love you, Aunt Garr, glad you're here to protect us."

When the jesting had died down and all were within the square, a happiness floated over those gathered. Garr and Sala were normally obliged to exchange words and greetings with everyone in the square before being able to join their family and eat. It was a task they were used to and it was expected of them. On this occasion, Garr decided to address them all from the centre of the small square.

"Friends of Prallian, will you forgive this humble servant for not speaking to all our friends this evening. It's been a long day and both Sala and I are weary from our journey and desperately in need of food. We will be staying with you for some days, so we're sure of lots of conversation and hopefully some decent gossip, which we most definitely are looking forward to. Please forgive these bad manners."

As Garr sat down at Nic and Sarina's table, there was clapping from the people of Prallian. Garr rested her head upon her hand, looking down at the wooden table under her elbows.

"I don't require all that—it's so embarrassing. I guess I should be used to it, but I'm not. Isn't it strange? I appreciate that they are clapping their leader, and yet they all know me as a friend, surely. It just makes it seem wrong, somehow. I will never understand how our minds work."

Sala attempted to assure her friend. "My dearest, Garr, of course you understand. A few are the hunters and the others are the hunted, or is it the haunted. In-between are the ones you have to be aware of, those that flip and flop and swoop around. Then some take the short view and can only consider this moment and this day, while others take the long view, the bigger picture. You only think you don't understand here and now because, for you, all that simply comes naturally, instinctively."

"Sala Billings, you have your father's head that's for sure."

"I haven't heard my other name for a thousand years. Now, that felt strange. What's your second name?"

"I really have no idea. I don't think I've ever heard it or thought about it before. Now that is even stranger, don't you think? Nic. Do you know or can you remember if we have a family name?"

"No idea, but I guess it should be Tellia. Nic Tellia and you can be Garr Tellia. Does that help?"

"No, but it sounds good. Garr Tellia. I like that. Sala Billings meet Garr Tellia."

"Pleased to make your acquaintance, Garr Tellia, friend and lover for a thousand years, and, oh, great leader."

They laughed heartily and indulged in more food and alcohol. The gathering slowly picked up a relaxed, happy and merry mood.

Nic interrupted their chatter.

"Come on sister, let's dance. Prallian needs a little fun and you and Sala are the excuse. Jacob, some music please."

He took his sister's slightly reluctant hand and led her towards the centre of the square, where a few groups stood talking. Understanding their intention to dance, the groups drifted towards the sides of the square. They began to move to the rhythm of the music as the tempo slowly increased, Garr moving cautiously even though the alcohol had now dulled the discomfort she was feeling a little earlier.

Folks around the square, started clapping and hooting. Nic was already moving in rhythmic turns and hops.

A few other couples took their lead, and, with the upbeat rhythm still growing, a crazy dance began. Feet pounded upon the old flagstone floor, as possibly many had done hundreds of years before them. Nic was now jumping and twirling around Garr; she hadn't danced since the battle with Dartell and wasn't yet completely committed to the idea. She knew she would be risking far too much for the third time that day.

More couples piled into the centre of the square, leaving the food until later. A few children, keen for a change of activity, jigged around the edges of the tables, with one daring the other to run across the centre through the dancing adults.

Garr was nearly there, and, with the alcohol flowing deeper into her body, she wanted to enter Nic's rhythm and placed a hand upon his waist, pulling him closer, connecting with him, his spirit. They slowly started to spin in unison, the dizziness of the pace taking them into the growing volume of music. Others still seated drummed upon the tables to the beat, throwing in occasional hoops and shouts. Older ones nodded with approval and patted out the tune upon their knees.

It seemed that everybody had needed this release of energy. Nobody wanted to stop, except to swig back another jug of vino, beer, or cider before returning to the dance.

The musicians and the dancers fed on each other's enthusiasm, with the pace seeming to increase even more. Garr was passed to Brian, and soon everybody was changing partners. Then Garr found herself spinning and whooping with Sala before her. Slowly, the exhausted musicians wound down the pace and let the music slowly fade into the noise of jolly and happy people.

All were now energised and hungry for more; the buzz of loud chatter floated around the little square, mixed with the clung and chink of jugs, plates, and tankards. Garr found Nic back at their table and wrapped her arms around him in love and gratitude.

"Oh, brother, that was good fun. That dancing took me back to our youth when there was that long, long summer of nothing but alcohol, then festival after festival. Do you remember?"

"I certainly do. We have some good memories tucked away from our past. That summer never ended really."

For a second they both flashed those thoughts through their minds.

In reality, their good thoughts were often clouded over suddenly by bad memories, and both had trained themselves to cut away from bad energy. They reappeared from their thoughts and returned to the square with the chatter around them and smiled gently and knowingly at one another, then turned to engage others in chit-chat.

Garr wandered over to speak with Clark on the far side of the square. His wife had passed away some time back and it had aged him terribly. Now he sat, once again looking happy with his world, with a bonnie granddaughter bouncing upon his knee and another tugging at his sleeve.

Garr placed caring kisses upon each cheek.

"You okay, Clark? You look rather busy this evening."

"Aunt Garr, Aunt Garr, grandpapa won't dance with us. He says he's tired."

"Well, shame be upon him, girls, but your Aunt Garr will. So, come on, let's have a party. See you later, Clark."

"Garr, you're seriously too crazy for a woman of your age. I have seen you hiding your pain. Now, please slow down. I'm worried about you."

By the time the next dance had finished, Garr was seen amongst a group of four children, all doing the new and sensational Uggy Googy dance, which involved complicated hops and skips and the essential holding out of the ears and blowing of loud raspberry noises as they all jumped around the dance area. It was serious and tiring stuff.

Back at Nic and Sarina's doorway, Kia sat head on paws, watching his mistress with his usual red-eyed look of disgust he managed to generate on such occasions. Beside him, Monster's old friend Regge lay contentedly snoring.

The night flowed on; children slowly disappeared to sleep wonderful dreams, and some of the older villagers followed, no doubt wishing they could recapture those youthful dreams.

There was many a skipping, swirling dance in the square before Garr reached over and whispered to Sala, "I think I'm ready for bed, Sal. Suddenly I'm feeling really tired or am I drunk? No, it's tiredness, Sala. Are you staying up for a while or are you wilting?"

"I'm wilting. I'll follow in a couple of moments after I've finished chatting with Sar and Maggie."

Garr wandered off to say her good nights to everybody; it was another hour before she was able at last to lay her weary head upon a clean and fresh pillow. It smelt of lavender, and the fragrant smell mixed gently with weariness and total bliss.

She lay for some time thinking of her and Sala's children, of Idor. She thought of Knap. Her eyes and her mind grew suddenly heavy and a little swirly, and she gave way willingly to sweet thoughts and to the end of an exhausting, yet wonderful day. As she sunk down into slumber, she could visualise across her valley to those white-cap mountains she loved so dearly.

The following morning, all in Prallian awoke later than intended.

It was a satisfied awakening.

Sala stretched long in bed, the light forcing its way through the wooden shutters.

Garr still lay in half sleep, with dreams mixing confusingly with wakening thoughts.

"I need water, my mouth feels like a bullock's."

"You don't look too good either, sweetheart."

"Cow."

Sala leapt from the bed and, grabbing a wrap, wandered from the room, only to return a moment later with a large tankard of reviving water.

"Thanks, Sal. Sister, my damn back doesn't feel too good this morning."

She tried to raise her body, but it did not want to oblige.

"Oh no, this is going to bugger up all our plans, Sala." She cursed profusely.

It took two days of lying fairly still, enduring pain and aching, before the paralysis eased. But she didn't waste the time. She spoke in detail to Clark about his intention to stand down from the main council. So many members of the main council were considerably older than Garr, and many were experiencing the effects of age. The majority were now long established friends, but their slow and steady withdrawal from their public duties presented Garr and the younger members with the reality of a changing world. It was a world of new ideas and sometimes extreme points of view.

Jac had always taken a keen interest in the affairs of Garrtellia, and both Garr and Clark agreed that he should be recommended to stand in his place. Although it was well within her power to install a main council member, it was nowadays politically correct to go with a council vote accompanied by a consenting vote from Garr herself.

Meanwhile, a messenger arrived from Garr's mountain.

The seal was broken upon Garr's lap amongst odd paper and scrolls, orange peel, and plates, while she still lay upon the bed, propped up by four large pillows.

The contents from the letter the scribe wrote for Idor were not pleasing.

"My Dearest Garr, I send you my deepest love and very sadly, some bad news. We have received reports from Daniel that Bayon has been attacked from the south. Previously, a small number of scouting and raiding parties had been experienced, but the word from other sources is that a considerable force is being gathered, presumably with the intention of a serious full-scale attack against Bayon.

I have already instructed, in your name, the assembly of an immediate support force, which will be ready to leave in possibly two days. I have also dispatched riders and pigeons to any and all towns and villages in the region known to have a reliable and sizeable force and instructed them to move to the aid of Bayon with immediate effect.

Garr, there is something else I must tell you. Monster appears very unwell. He is hardly moving and just lays curled upon your sleeping platform. I fear he may be ready to join others we have loved. I dare not move him. Is there anything you wish that I do?

Always with Love, Idor.

Upon a second sheet, Idor had written:

Garr, I have just received your message stating the need for you to extend your stay due to your back.

Under these circumstances, please keep me well informed of all your intentions and any needs you may have, darling, and please take good care of yourself.

As I know you're in good hands, I shall try not to worry, although I shall be with you in spirit every single moment.

The children are happy and well, but we all miss you and hope to see you and Sala soon.

I will take care of matters here and keep you informed of everything. Monster is still holding his own, but more and more I believe he is leaving us. Shall I have him brought to you?

As always and forever.

That evening a substitute council meeting was held around Garr. Opinions and thoughts were exchanged. Under the circumstances, a little alcohol was taken and a kind of jollity entered the frame. Idor had the matter fully under control, and, in many ways, he was second to none in such matters, hence the relaxed atmosphere.

Suddenly, a growling voice was heard echoing through the house, shaking all to alertness.

Brian and Nic moved swiftly to face the threat.

But laughter was then heard from them, along with jovial talk and the sounds of greetings.

Teo, Vora, and Garta stood at the bedroom doorway.

Arms raised, Teo moved towards Garr, patting Sarina affectionately upon the hip as he squeezed through the crowded room.

"Oh great Garr, what you do in bed, this is no possible. Very good see you. It very, very good see you not with problem, yu. I send for medicine warrior straight now. Garta, ride my brother and fetch Morro. Our great leader needs his wisdom and care."

As Garta left, Teo placed his great mass upon the bed causing further disarray amongst the growing clutter that had built up there. He placed his heavy arms around Garr, who humbly endured his well-intended greeting of affection and the odious smell that rose from his every movement.

"Now, Garr, tell of you problem."

"Teo, it is as always wonderful to see you and Vora. This may indeed be good timing. Is the tribe close at hand?"

"Ya, half day walk. Medicine warrior be here tomorrow, you see. No problem tomorrow. Teo's true word, Garr."

"No, Teo, that isn't the problem I speak of. Garrtellia is being attacked to the far west in Bayon. Could you possibly help us with your warriors? Time is always of the greatest importance with such unpleasant issues."

"Ya, this is no problem, Garr. You are the sister of Nic and the leader of our Garrtellia. We always ready help Garr and Garrtellia."

"How many horse warriors could you spare, Teo?"

Teo looked at Vora, and the two of them spoke for a moment in a language that none in the room could follow.

Sarina reappeared, passing tankards amongst the group and placing a large plate of meats, cheese, and bread upon the ever growing pile which once looked like a bed but now resembled a rubbish heap.

"Garr, think two hundred horse warriors, maybe two hundred fifty could ride tonight if you says. That good, ya?"

"That would be wonderful, Teo. Please, let it be done. I thank you so much. We must send a messenger to Idor immediately. Brian, would you ride with Teo? We should have at least fifty from this area. That would add up to about six or seven hundred who would be at the scene by tomorrow with the main force a day or so after that."

The bulk of the party moved outside, leaving Garr where she was. She had by good fortune created a good result, yet she felt frustrated. She was beginning to feel she needed to see Idor, her cave, the children, and especially Monster, who now occupied her thoughts as much as the affairs of state. She simply needed to be able to move.

"I should have gone also, Garr," Nic said to his sister. "I shouldn't let Brian go alone."

"No, Nic, I need you here for Sarina, Sala, and me. Ban is going, and Brian has Anton with him. They'll be fine. None of us can fight every battle and you shouldn't feel you need to either. Don't you think we've given enough to this land?"

"Yes we have, Garr—you especially. But it's been our choice and we do have privileges for our troubles."

"You're right, I'm sorry. I'm speaking selfishly. Forgive me? I am so very worried about Monster. If he was to leave us now without me being by his side, it would break my heart. I dare not think about it for it would bring tears to my eyes."

In the square, Teo, Vora, Brian, Ban, and Anton, Brian's eldest son, mounted and rode out into the still night to meet the others before heading west to pick up the tribe warriors. It was a night of stars, pleasantly cool, and not even the slightest breeze. They didn't look like men going towards battle as they spoke quietly to one another. Hopefully battle and bloodletting could be avoided.

The morning came. Sala was lying with arms and legs wrapped around an already awake Garr, whose head was buzzing in all directions.

"Sala, are you awake? Sala, I feel okay this morning. I can move everything. Come on, Sal, wakey, wakey. Did you hear me? I feel okay today. Thank the heavens a hundred times over."

Garr cautiously slid her legs towards the floor, doubting her own feelings. Everything seemed sound—no pain and no stiffness. She sat on the side of the bed and turned a little in all directions to double-check once more. There was nothing, not even a twinge, absolutely nothing; it was a wonderful, wonderful feeling.

She thought how strange and annoying it was that this happened to her body.

"You stupid, stupid body," she said to herself repeatedly.

The clutter from the bed was now spread around the room. She tiptoed through it and found Sarina sitting with Nic at the large old table, talking quietly. They turned to look towards Garr.

"Ah, sorry you two, forgot about the wrap."

"Don't worry, Garr, sit and have a drink. It's really good seeing you up and around again. Nic was just saying that it hasn't quite turned out to be the rest that you and Sala planned, has it?"

"You're very right there, Sarina, but that's life in Garrtellia. I am so sorry about using your home like this, Sarina. You've been wonderful as always."

"Hey, you don't say that, we are all family here."

With a grunt and a groan, Sala stumbled from the bed and stood at the doorway.

"Garr! Go and put a wrap on, you're such a hopeless woman at times. This isn't your cave, you know."

"Okay, okay, sorry to offend you."

She stood and, almost in defiance, stretched tall. Her body had those scars and a little extra covering these days, but she looked magnificent. Her hair still hung down her back, maybe a little lighter than it used to be, but still thick and youthful. She was tanned all over and, these days, even the scars and scuffs around her calves, hands, and forearms had healed over. There was no sign of wasting or sagging. Only her feet showed the passing of time due to years of running over tough terrain and boots that let in water. But, internally, it felt different and her back reminded her daily of the passing of time.

Sala couldn't resist her, here amongst family, in this air of rare freedom.

She walked over to where she stood at the table and gathered her in her arms once again.

"I love you, Garr Tellia. Now go and put a wrap on before you frighten the children, the old folks, and the dogs."

Nic and Sarina's laughter at the two of them echoed around the room. Then Sarina turned to cut sausage and threw it in a pan for breakfast.

"Jac should be down shortly. He's very pleased at being selected for the main council, Garr, thank you."

"No need to thank me, Sar. He's earned it, plain, true, and simple. More to the point, he'll be very good at it, Sarina. I'm sure of that. He is naturally wise and cautious. They're both wonderful boys, but you would know that I guess."

The journey to Bayon was to take the warriors a full day, even at the extreme pace they employed. The optimism of the earlier night's talk had shaded their judgement but nevertheless, good time was made. By the time they were picking up local warriors, far to the west of the land, it was once again dark. Here, in this part of the land, you could occasionally smell the salt of the sea in your nostrils, depending on the prevailing wind, and feel a freshness upon the wind which the warriors of Prallian never normally experienced. This night, if you listened carefully, you might even hear the sea, as the waves dragged over a million tons of shingle, the sound of each receding wave was caught by the wind and carried to their ears.

Alternatively, the warriors may not have heard anything at all. They made camp upon the edge of a pine forest, sleeping soundly in their exhaustion, with the prospects of yet another battle ahead.

Such thoughts threatened and haunted their dreams. Their lives, their blood and bodies, and their futures were all at risk once more.

The gift of life was indeed precious. No matter how difficult it appeared at times, it was undeniably a miracle.

In spite of their weariness, most woke with first light. They were greeted by the sight of womenfolk from the local area bearing loaves, sausage, and all variety of fruit and nuts.

These warriors, both men and women, were indeed coming to be their saviours, and, although not known to the locals, were being duly treated and honoured as such.

This side of battle was no hardship.

Back at Garr's mountain, the work of organising a small army had been completed. The men, the transport, arrows, and all other supplies were all ready. It was a task that Idor, Volka, and Yegor were used to. Preparing to leave, they thought again of their womenfolk, who they were missing badly.

Idor had been sleeping in Garr's cave; it gave him comfort to be there with the children rather than far below in his own encampment. Luana was now a woman in her own right and a council member with a voice that was listened to as she gave sound counsel. She was generally clear-headed, if occasionally a little impulsive, but there was always young Idor by her side to smooth and calm that side of her nature. Their relationship was so similar to that of her mother's with Idor. The other children, as usual, were schooled, herded, and fed by Idor's tribe's women and old folk; it was a tried and tested system and it worked well for all.

A messenger arrived advising Idor of Garr and Sala's intention to return to the mountain and making him aware of the small army that Teo and Brian had led to the west. They had arrived outside of Bayon, where they would await further instructions while reconnoitring the area.

Idor was much heartened by both items of news as they were read out to him.

Back in Prallian, despite the growing crisis, Maggie was leading Garr, Sala and Sarina on horseback down a winding, rocky track riddled with great roots like dark serpents from the deep. The track travelled parallel to a small murky stream and gradually took them deeper into the mixed woodland.

In places it was an ominous and threatening woodland, with ugly creepers hanging from many of the trees, a heavy dark canopy with little light breaking through, and a dank smell lurking everywhere. The heavy silence was loud enough to place all on alert.

The waters within the stream seemed thick, like dark treacle, appearing to slither slowly over rocks and under thick waterside plants, which hung over like evil hands, ready to grasp and devour.

Within this place were famed wild boars with heads over half a metre in length and tusks that could rip the innards from a horse or a woman. These were creatures that understood their weight and power and had no fear of warriors, carnivorous cats, bears, or packs of wild dogs. This wood was their world, yet the human was possibly their greatest threat.

Sarina now led the four hunters cautiously, ducking under occasional low branches and passed gnarled and twisted old trees that could have been there for centuries by the size of their girth. These trees were the guardians of this evil feeling place.

Occasionally, something black or dark would scurry amongst the undergrowth, quickly vanishing from their peripheral vision. It was unsettling, causing nerves to flutter and doubts to rise.

Slowly they moved forward, waiting for more open woodland to come into view and looking carefully to left and right for threats and hog trails. None of this party were novices at boar hunting, but the tales of disaster in this place were known within the community and generated great caution. That caution transferred to the horses, whose nervousness also took some controlling.

It was with some relief that the woodland eventually began to thin a little and sunlight rained down once again upon them through the higher and more open canopy.

Here, great beech trees began to dominate, and, although this was not the best hiding terrain, it was the main feeding areas at this time of the year when large families of hogs would forage and doze in the sunbeams.

The four gathered closer for a moment and drank from flasks, discussing their plans with an air of nervousness; the wild wood had affected all their nerves.

They were always aware of the other risks that lurked within such a terrain, such as packs of wild dogs, a bear, or one of the large cats. However rare, they existed and all knew tales of misadventure and terrible disaster.

Splitting into two parties, they followed a figure of eight pattern, crossing at the centre point every so often. They looked and listened at each and every crack of a twig or rustle of a leaf. Alertness was everything when hunting these wild boars.

An inner silence settled within them.

Then suddenly, with no warning, it was there—that moment they had been fearing, yet waiting and looking for.

A great scurrying to the left of Maggie and Sala sent leaves and other woodland debris into a cloud of confusion and movement amid grunts and squeals.

Great shapes moved through the woodland dust and beams of light. Maggie's horse bucked in fear, while Sala turned her mount to join her, blowing her horn to alert the companions to join her at haste.

The whole family of boars ran at speed past the rear of Maggie, and she flew up and back from her mount, crashing to the ground with a resounding thump. She regained her poise quickly, ready for whatever came at her. But she was lucky, these boars simply wanted pastures anew and the sweet still of their homeland.

Sala reached her in good time, taking hold of the loose reins and calming her unnerved mount.

"Come on, Maggie. Stop sitting around, sister. Let's get to it."

"Cheers, Sala."

She remounted with one leap, and the chase was on.

Heads down, they charged, swerving and ducking between and under tree after tree, leaving great clouds of leaves and dust behind them.

They chased on through a thickening woodland once more, the two pairs coming together, all with an eye to the quarry. Garr was riding low upon her mount, bow loaded and ready in one hand, while the other held tight the reins. Both heels kicked and knees held firm. The chase was fast and furious.

The excitement pumped rapidly through their veins whilst sweat pumped from their bodies.

Then, before they could react, the chase took on a new form. The massive male boar came straight for them, while his family took cover; he alone would face the tormenters, the pursuers, the destroyers of his peace.

Like an oxen with short legs, he ran amongst them, tossing and swinging his great head whenever near a horse. Sala went down, crashing her shoulder into a trunk and bouncing several times before she could regain her feet. The hog was at her, head down with intent to do her retaliatory harm. Maggie crossed between them, grabbing at Sala's desperate arms; half on and half off, she clung on as best she could, the tusks just missing her dangling legs.

Now Garr crossed the chase to divert the beast's attention, and the creature instantly followed her lead. She turned for a second swing around a large trunk and let fly an arrow that sunk home into the boar's hind quarter.

Not for a second did the beast's pace slow nor did he make an utterance.

Garr turned her mount sharply once again, mast and leaf litter showering the area and filling the air with so much debris that, for a second, the beast was lost amongst it.

Sarina entered the onslaught, and, from where she stood high in her stirrups, she let fly three arrows rapidly into the flying debris. Nobody knew if they had found their target as the ground settled back onto the forest floor.

There was a nervous moment of fear and excitement as they awaited the expected charge, all breathing heavily, eyes flickering from left to right.

Horses jigged in nervousness and riders continued to breathe heavily.

Yet there was nothing to see.

It was almost worse than the terrifying charge they had expected.

"Are you all okay?" someone asked and they all called out in response.

"He must have gone north or gone to ground somewhere—every other direction was covered. Come on, let's finish this, girls, a great lunch awaits us."

Sala remounted her horse, a little winded but still game. She trotted after the others thankful for the short rest. They spread out, knowing their quarry was here somewhere.

Tracking was a waste of time in such woodland and circumstance.

He was out there for sure, whether running hard or laying low to nurse his wounds, and readying himself to charge and rid himself of his aggravating foe. Maybe he was watching them. No doubt he'd done it before and expected to do it once again. For sure, he wouldn't stay down for long; they all knew that. Two of them were already badly bruised and one bloodied, at least. And their quarry carried at least one arrow. The battle was about equal so far.

They travelled on cautiously and nervously.

The tension gathered, sweat dripped from nervous brows, horses jigged and twitched in parallel.

Suddenly a whispering voice broke the concentration.

"That's him ahead, I think. There he is, Garr. He's in front of you, Garr, right in bloody front of you, woman, behind the bushes."

Garr slowed her horse further, which then immediately turned sideways, nearly running into Maggie's. Garr circled her mount quickly. Maggie kicked and rode on past the bushes, hiding the beast, and looked back.

He stood there panting, still as still, and then, in an instant burst of energy, he was off towards Garr. Sala let fly two arrows rapidly, one appearing to find the target just before he swept the rear of Garr's horse. She flew through the air, her horse tumbling hard, rolling and complaining. Maggie and Sala stood their positions, letting fly arrow after arrow, but the debris and confusion of horse, rider, and hog made accuracy impossible and dangerous.

The creature stood breathing heavily once more. Confused and now in obvious discomfort, he took to running once again; anywhere now away from the torment.

In his confusion, he scrambled over Garr's horse, causing it to leap up once again and cry in pain. Then his stout heart resurged, and he turned unexpectedly upon his pursuers once more, running amongst them with his great head swinging those awesome tusks to left and right. In one moment three of them lost their mounts. They climbed trees, swung from branches or froze to the ground hoping the gods were with them. The moment passed and the quarry trotted gaily away into the forest, appearing well satisfied, head held high. In truth, battle was taking its toll and pride faded as the beast stopped at the calling of pain throughout his body. It breathed harder now and then his foe were once again behind him.

Relentlessly they pursued the giant, now able to take better aim.

The giant beast tumbled, front legs giving in to the pain and exhaustion. Then he struggled again to stand. He ran yet again, a zig-zaggy run with no direction, crashing into trees and shrubbery; his life was now draining away, his running nearly done.

He lay with four arrows deep in his body, breathing heavily, unable to repeat the enormous effort needed to challenge his four large adversaries, unable to resist or challenge destiny any further.

In the past, he had probably seen off other hunting parties, large cats, and packs of wild dogs, but never again would that happen.

A thought ran quickly through Garr's mind: 'What did this great creature think in his final moments? Was it of family or of sunbeams, butterflies and bird song?

'Would he be full of sorrow or pride in saving his family? Would he have anger and hatred towards his foes, or did he understand fate?'

He took a last difficult breath, not quite filling his lungs with fresh air, the air of his homeland, and then closed his weary bloodshot eyes. Slowly his heart relaxed, then slowed, then stopped, and his soul floated into the blue far above and his body took on another purpose.

The battle was over. The journey to death had taken time, and yet actual death was quick and peaceful.

By the time the carcass had been butchered, three hours had passed them by.

The meat was thinly salted and stuffed into eight large leather pouches, which would hang as panniers upon each of the mounts; dripping a trail of blood from forest to Prallian.

The site of the butchery was left for those of the forest to clear.

The great majestic head, which still deserved respect, was tied between the two panniers upon Sala's mount and now rocked from side to side with the movement of the horse—a head without a body, staring straight into the evening light.

As Sala led the small party of hunters from the forest, the boar's fixed stare seemed to be upon each one of the trailing three. His tongue hung sadly to one side, and yet upon his face there was a cynical smile as he wobbled along ahead of his foe.

'I hope his family isn't watching this,' Garr thought to herself. 'How would they deal with such a vision? I'm not so sure

I like it, either. I've seen too much blood. Was it all really just? This creature received, no, deserved our respect; and maybe he deserved his life in these woods, carefree.'

For a few moments, her thoughts flew through the blood and battles of her past. She remembered her early years, when she and Nic were very different people. Yes, those were tougher times, and a lot more conflict and aggression existed between all peoples. But, as she reflected, guilt entered her mind.

She and Nic were then deadly and arrogant young warriors, giving not an inch in conflict, justly or not. Possibly their childhood experiences had generated that aggression or maybe it was youthful bravado or innocence and ignorance. But, looking back, she felt that it could not be excused, and she hated and regretted that period in her life. So much death and so much blood had been spilt. Their reactions had been instant and instinctive, without consideration, and never with regret. Maybe it was the factor that had allowed them to survive, but did that make it acceptable as well as understandable?

It was by meeting Knap that had made her the person she now was.

At least her youthful experiences had given her the wisdom in later life to balance situations more carefully and wisely.

She knew that her public support now did not justify all those actions of her past.

Nothing really was sure or true; possibly having the courage to make decisions, knowing that all those doubts existed, was the key to leadership. But now, she wasn't sure about that either. Life had only taught her that she knew little to nothing with certainty and that decision-making was always a risk.

Her thoughts changed directions as Luana entered her mental wonderings. She loved all the children dearly, but to herself she could not deny that Luana she loved the most. Maybe it was because she was her first, maybe because she saw herself in Luana—a youthful creature, full of positive thinking, with no doubts to contend with and total belief in all her thinking and actions.

Then she thought of Luana running through the grass, her long blond hair flowing behind, her long legs stretching further with each stride. She moved with grace and ease, always with young Idor next to her. She was indeed so very beautiful. A tear of happiness formed in each eye.

She shook her head clear and again found herself staring at that great boar's head, still wobbling from side to side with that spooky look upon its face.

"Are you back with us now, Garr?"

"Sorry, I was miles away in another land. Luana brought me home."

"What are you talking about, mad woman?"

"Oh, just things. Nothing really, yet everything."

In Prallian, they dismounted. Everyone was drained and exhausted.

Garr knew that she would remember this hunt above all others for the freedom and the great companionship and the lack of her personal responsibility. It was so wonderful to find others taking the lead. Possibly, until this day, she had never fully realised the enormous load she had been carrying for so many years. For better or worse, in that tiny moment of reality, she had seen something as she had never seen it before, and it disturbed her. She understood that once knowledge or experience of anything was gained, it could never be dismissed and would forever be part of one's thinking and consideration. This created a feeling of concern within her, but, in spite of it, she knew she should smile and display happiness together with the expected festive air.

A small crowd gathered, wanting to share in the adventure, admire the result of their trip, and harass them for all the details of the hunt.

While others unloaded the bags of meat, a small number of children pointed their tongues at the great head now sitting proudly upon the floor. His staring eyes and great tusks still instilled fear in the little ones. His head rocked slightly, causing squeals and dashes for safety.

Tonight there would be a village feast.

The small group of hunters stood amongst the villagers, telling their stories. Garr, not feeling so well now, leant against the wall, beads of sweat upon her brow.

Sala broke from her conversation to look at Garr.

"You okay? You're not looking so good."

"I feel really awful, Sal. I need to lie down. Walk with me, please."

As they walked slowly to Sarina and Nic's, the colour of her face completely disappeared. Her knees gave way and she crashed to the hard stone floor.

Immediately, she was lifted by the concerned villagers and carried to her bed, obviously in some kind of faint.

That evening, the villagers ate together in the square, but the joy of the hunt, for the hunters, was dulled by the wounds and exertion of battle and, particularly, by the fact that Garr still lay motionless upon her bed. A heavy sweat covered her as she slept uneasily.

The following day, her health had not changed.

A messenger was sent to Idor with the worrying news, and her physician was sent for.

When, after three days, she awoke still covered in moisture, she could hardly move.

Her first words were typical.

"How does it go in Bayon, and where is Idor and the children?"

"It goes well, my princess. Peace has been made, but now to the important things in life. Can you explain how you feel? We are all so very worried about you."

"The children—where are the children?"

"They here, you see them later. They are well but have much worry for you Garr."

Sala, taking Garr's hand, spoke up.

"Garr, you must try and explain how you feel. Eldred is trying to work out your symptoms. He wants so much to be able to help you get better. Is it your back that is causing you this problem and pain?"

As she started to speak, her eyes closed once more and Sarina applied a cold swab to her forehead.

Between them, they had cared for her both night and day.

The children had visited her many times, but, as yet, had not been able to talk with their mother as they took turns holding her hand or touching her arm. Luana had kissed her mother gently upon the forehead, whispering words of love and encouragement and hoping she might hear them.

Eldred, the medicine man, was perplexed by the symptoms.

He had laid healing herbs beneath her and dribbled potions gently through her sleeping lips. There seemed to be no progress. He had called upon Morro, the medicine man from Teo's tribe.

They consulted together. Both were recognized as amongst the greatest of medicine men throughout the land but, as yet, they had not healed their illustrious patient.

Idor was now openly worried and inwardly in despair. Standing nearly to his old height, he raised his voice. This was a rarity that drew attention, instant respect, and a little fear from those around him.

"We built you people a land, defend you from foe fed you when you be hungry. We do our work. It not the work we would have chosen. Right here and now, do it, before I see to it that you can't. Earn you keep or deal for my actions. Do you understand? Do you hear me?"

He paused for a moment of reflection, somewhat surprised by his own outburst, and then decided to continue.

"Ou've grown fat and lazy on people's trust; *do – not – generate – my - wrath.*"

His pain and rage were deep causing him to stutter a little when he spoke.

His head ached and throbbed from the anger and frustration. At his temples and neck, his veins stood proud, and his cheeks flushed red.

All about him froze at the outburst.

Only Luana moved; she went to her father, feeling his fear and his love, and taking his hand like only a daughter could, they walked slowly from the room.

Outside, in a shaded corner away from the eyes of others in the square, Luana said nothing; it wasn't required. She simply wrapped herself around her father, both to share and take away some of his pain.

As she indeed absorbed some of that pain, it turned to soft and salty tears that trickled down her cheeks and onto her father's shirt.

The other children had heard their father's outburst and instinctively followed their sister, slowly gathering in embrace as the family shared a moment of deep communion.

After maintaining the family embrace for some time, the mood changed. Now recharged a little, Idor stood tall once again.

He kissed his children's foreheads with great tenderness and gratitude.

Until that moment, not a word had been spoken.

"Come my children, your mother is made of tough stuff. With our caring, she will recover good, I sure of this. Now have been weak, we must be strong like giants, that how the people must see, always strong. Your mother want this."

They returned once again to Garr's side, together and strengthened.

It was on the eighth day that Idor decided that Garr should be moved back to her home. Many resisted and disagreed with his decision, but Idor was not in the mood for dissent.

The arrangements were made, and those close to her elected to travel with the party, not wishing to have Garr too far from their caring and love.

Lying upon new bedding at her cave, Garr appeared to sleep well. After her first night, she half roused at first light to familiar smells and feelings that stirred contentment within her.

Her arm drifted over the edge of the bedding and instinctively felt for Monster. This dog of antiquity nestled to her touch, then shakily stood and pushed his nose gently against his mistress, showing affection whilst sniffing at her state of health. He understood that all was not well and was inseparable from her, as indeed was Kia, who had now learnt the ways of Monster and somehow understood that he was a prince in waiting that must keep his position.

For the first time in over a week, Garr stretched a little and opened her eyes. The corners of her eyes were dry and crusty from sleep and illness.

Two warrior women rose to aid her in standing and carrying out the functions of life. They wiped her face gently and plumped the pillows, before letting her gently down once again.

Sala and Luana had slept adjacent, and now awoke to the pleasure of a soft smile.

Their hearts leapt as if spring had suddenly broken through, and, at that moment, within the cave, the early light appeared golden.

"Good morning, Garr, you look wonderful this morning"

"Mother, you really do look so good today. How do you feel?"

"I feel good, if a little slow and wobbly. How is the world? Where are the others, Luana? And your father?"

Luana looked towards the womenfolk.

"Be here soon princess, very soon," came the answer. "You no worry, everything look good at last for our Garr, very soon Idor be here."

"Thank you, Gena, you are so wonderful. What would we ever do without you and Mari and all the others?"

Luana leapt towards her mother and embraced her. Then, as she passed Gena, she embraced her also. She quickly moved to the entrance to view the day for a second, her naked body silhouetted against the early morning light. Jigging up and down on her toes to fight the early morning chill, she then dashed for the lower areas of the cave.

On her return, she passed Sala, now in a similar state. She went to embrace her but timing would not allow Sala to stop.

"One moment please Luana, one moment."

When Sala had returned to the main area, looking somewhat relieved and moving more casually, Luana was already seated again upon the bedding next to her mother. Sala moved to join them but Gena's old and wrinkled hand shook in their direction.

"Clothes, oo two, clothes now. Tu no children, tu respecta your father here one moment. Go go, now, shoo, shoo."

"Yes, Gena, alright, Gena. Keep your hair on, Gena."

Like two naughty young girls, Sala and Luana did as they were bid.

When Gena's heckles were up, queens and princesses were of no consequence to her, the only words she would heed would be Idor's, her rightful leader. A tribal and nomadic upbringing had set her ways, although her affection for them was edging upon devotion.

Idor, Volka, and Yegor stood together at the cave entrance, and, after seeing Garr looking so well, broke into happy smiles.

Garr's thick hair spread over the orange colour of the pillows and tumbled down over the bedding, with one of her hands still upon Monster's head and the other upon the blue hue of the bedding cover.

Sala and Luana, now dressed, stood still in their little girl guise at the far end of the sleeping area.

Gena and Mari overlooked the scene while preparing food and drink for Garr and the others now present.

Idor felt vindicated by the result of his insistence that Garr be moved to her mountain. He organised comfortable seating at the entrance for Garr, for he knew well this was her favourite place. It wasn't the warmest of weathers, but sitting here, whether she was awake or drifting to and from sleep, would make her as happy as she could be, and there was nothing more important to him than her happiness.

He was right. With her eyes upon her valley, she relaxed and felt as content as she could under the strange circumstances of her temperature rising and falling erratically and her limbs being unable to support her.

Eldred and Morro, the two great medicine men of the land, had worked endlessly to resolve the condition that Garr was in and continued to treat her in the very best way they knew. They had recovered from the onslaught of Idor's frustration and continued labouring endlessly in their care and attention. Neither of them were young and the effect of their tireless work could be seen upon their faces.

They had sent messengers across the land to fetch healers of differing types—faith healers and magical healers. All were sworn to the secrecy of Garr's illness, but none could resolve the situation satisfactorily.

In private, they spoke to Idor.

"My dearest, Idor, we fear that we are dealing with the wear and tear of time. Over the years, our Garr has endured many injuries and an endless flow of pressure and stress. With love and care, she should recover her full health, but we must but be patient."

"Is there nothing else we can do for her?"

"Just love and care, Idor, just love and care. We wish we had greater magic. We have raised our hands to the heavens hoping for a miracle and for inspiration."

Over the following days, Garr drifted in and out of sleep, her temperature rising and falling. Some days she found that she could stand, and, with care from those around her, she almost enjoyed a little social life.

In those more lucid times, she would sit with a clutch of children around her, telling them stories of the great warriors she had known, the battles and endeavours to create the land of Garrtellia, and the great mixture of peoples and tribes that had been brought together.

With the influence of Knap still upon her, she had gathered a large collection of ancient books now, and these had become her treasures.

Between her stories of Garrtellia, she would pause—normally with the phase, "did you know that once upon a time"—and then take her audience, which often included adults, on a journey of ancient history, geography, or science. For the children alone she saved *Wind in the Willows, Treasure Island, White Fang,* and *Huckleberry Finn.*

She was somehow growing into a situation which she both liked and hated.

There were bad times. She would feel low and depressed; normally these periods were followed by fever and delirium. She would rant and cuss, normally talking of her youth, wild days full of violence and youthful violation.

In these periods, Nic would want to be with her, holding her hand and mopping her brow with cool water from the stream infused with herbs. His head hung downwards, his face damp with the sorrow of bad memories and yet rejoicing in their togetherness after all this time.

He loved her deeply and was forever grateful for the gift of his salvation from purgatory, and her wisdom in setting him free into manhood.

All but the closest had now let their dreams for her full recovery fade away.

That was not what they said, but the sorrow upon their faces and their body language told the truth. The drooping shoulders and the heaviness of their brows spoke volumes. They expected and feared the day when somebody would rush to them in tears with the announcement of sad news.

The others dreamed of revisiting old haunts once again, when they would be trapping or hunting together.

They must not and would not let all their dreams desert them.

Within their minds, they walked along the river's edge with the summer sun shining upon the gently rippling waters whilst pulling at grass seed heads and listening to bird calls.

They pointed out the great dragonflies and kingfishers, and, together with Garr, they felt the excitement as the trout leapt high into the air, before twisting and tumbling back into the fresh water with a great flick and splash.

But more than this, they dreamt of sitting close together and just feeling the warmth and presence of Garr's body, with no speech required. They simply wished her able to smile, laugh, and cry with them once more.

Garr now journeyed into her worst nightmare.

She was rarely able to stand now; her body simply too weak, and, even with all the care around her, she felt so very, very lonely.

Her only joy was her escape into stories, both magical and from the past, and let her failing body once again enjoy all those pleasures of life.

"And as the queen passed her crown forward to her eldest daughter and kissed her tenderly, she said to her, 'You will be the finest of queens, my little one. You have earned the love of the people. Love them back with honesty as you have loved your father, and be always true to yourself.' Princess Sirreena held tightly the magic broach, and, without realising, rubbed it. Within moments, she noticed, standing by the entrance, a tall figure. It was Prince Marco. She ran to his arms and he readily embraced her."

"And so children, that is nearly the end of another story. I'm so sorry, but I must sleep a little now. My eyes need rest, and they will not stay open a second longer. But we will see what happens in the story tomorrow."

As Garr's eyes closed, the children began to leave, each kissing her as they left, all chattering away to Idor, Luana, and Sala; now Garr could sleep.

"When this story ends, will you tell another? Please, Garr?"

"Oh yes, Mummy, please say you will. Please, please."

"Of course, my treasures. Tomorrow and the day after there will be many stories."

She looked out across the valley to those far away mountains, and so many memories flooded into her thoughts.

Monster stood up slowly on those shaky legs and stretched a little.

His silvery grey fur caught the failing sunlight.

He looked at his mistress through those great red eyes and nestled his head in close, sniffing and then licking her ear softly.

As Garr slid into a deep sleep, Monster dragged himself upon the bedding. It was no longer an easy task for him. Lying close to his mistress, he too closed his weary eyes and willingly joined his oldest of friends on their final adventure together.

After a long day of work and worry, Idor sat alone in his tent amongst his tribe.

A lone warrior was making his way slowly down the rocky track from the cave to deliver the saddest of news, his face damp with sorrow.

Before the messenger entered the settlement, Idor could feel an emotional tension rising within himself. He knew in his heart that Garr had left him, and he wasn't by her side. He knew also at that moment that he wouldn't be able to bear the loss. Even their beloved children were not compensation enough.

Across the encampment, a stillness grew as others listened to their hearts.

A telepathic emotion spread like an invisible cloud.

Luana had been walking with young Idor when, for no apparent reason, they stopped simultaneously and looked straight at one another. An overpowering weight filled their hearts, and they also knew that Garr had left them.

There was no doubt.

They moved close and clung to each other, without saying a word, and cried quietly in one another's arms, right there amongst the tall grass, as a gentle breeze conveyed the sad news to them.

At that moment, Sala's heart fluttered and a few beats seemed to be missing—taken by another.

She placed her hand to her struggling heart, gulped, and took a long deep breath, before staring blankly into the evening sunlight and staying stock still. Then she buried her face within her two shaking hands while her mind took flight to another world of loneliness, foreboding, and despair.

As Idor walked his solitary walk towards the track he'd trodden so often, his people turned towards him in heartbroken respect, standing silently, hands clasped, or dropping to one knee. Some already shed tears, others placed their hands over their hearts, as was their custom.

Alone he trod the longest walk of his life, within a lonely cloud, with no earth beneath his feet or sky above him—singular, detached, encased in sorrow he would never be able to shed.

From differing corners of the camp, the close and loved ones also walked alone and in silence, all moving simultaneously towards the small track leading them towards Garr's still and silent body.

The solemn procession moved up through the boulders, all twisting and turning as the path demanded, each one with their heart invisibly connected to that beautiful women lying still and peaceful, her hair still flowing wide and wild.

Before her lay the valley, mountains, and Garrtellia.

Beside her, Monster nestled peacefully.

Around her, on this solid earth, existed the results of her effort, caring, and love over her forty-three years of wondrous living.

Now her spirit flew freely.

Never to desert her beloved people, it would flow amongst them for centuries to come. It slowly and simply blended and danced delicately with the final rays of the sun.

Epilogue

As Idor reached the top of the track, he looked over towards the entrance of Garr's cave, where he saw his princess lying still and at peace, covered in golden sunlight. He couldn't move any further.

Luana and Sala joined him. Their hands met naturally and it was good to feel one another's warmth.

Sala, like Idor, was frozen by the moment; she just looked on in sorrow, unable to believe Garr's passing.

Gena and Mari stood shakily to one side, with bowed heads, slowly shuffling backwards into the darkness and shadow of the cave, their task complete.

Luana was the first to move forward. Everything within her told her to go to her mother; she couldn't resist the internal call.

Her body was shaking, and her cheeks and chest were damp with fallen tears. She crouched beside her mother, then slowly bent forward and tenderly kissed her forehead, whispering words of love into her ear.

As she did this, a strange rush of great energy seemed to enter her being, engulfing her and filling her almost beyond capacity. She was suddenly scared of being overloaded with such power, and yet it was strong and good, like nothing she had ever experienced before. She stared at her mother as the force held her still, and then, suddenly, it was finished and gone. She was at peace, total peace, feeling as though a new being was within her. The spirit of Garr would live on.

It was her experience alone, and she would not be able to share it with anybody on this day. She also knew that now she was not only the daughter of Garr, but that she had also been chosen to receive her great spirit.

For Luana, this was a unique gift beyond comparison, and she was deeply humbled by the magnitude of the honour.

Luana, with a shaking hand and voice, ordered that Garr be moved back within the cave, and then, slowly, the others who still appeared paralyzed upon the spot where they stood, were able to move within. Each displayed their grief and love gathered around Garr's bedding platform.

Kia looked on with a mystified air, whilst Monster slowly dragged himself with great difficulty upon the bedding, laying next to his mistress, his great nose snuggled in close to Garr's body, where he relaxed into a deep sleep from which he would not awaken. It was as things should be. A love and devotion firmly attached to the very end.

Idor was still within a daze and would be for the rest of his lonely time upon this earth. Even the children, whilst dealing with their own pain, could not console him. While Luana spent so much of the following days weeping privately, all the rest of her time was devoted to her father. Young Idor gave constant support to all. There was only pain, confusion, and broken hearts.

Yegor and Volka organised from dawn until dusk.

To the west of the valley upon a gently rounded hilltop grew the largest pyre ever seen. It looked like a new settlement, a fortress, and a crown. Around the outer circle of angled timbers was draped red fabric. At the centre, a great pyramid rose to over six metres.

The valley floor filled with tents and makeshift camps for as far as the eye could see.

By the third day, all were gathered.

From all points of the land, people had travelled. Dignitaries came in sombre draped robes, displaying their ribbons of authority upon their arms, while simple folk arrived in the only clothing they possessed.

The mountain was solid with people looking towards the crowning pyre, and then the time arrived for the final salute.

Idor struggled to rise to address the great crowd and say some words to her people.

Young Idor placed a gentle hand upon his.

"Let me, Uncle."

Idor stared up towards this handsome young man—tall, straight and strong. He took his hand and nodded his approval.

With a hand resting upon Idor's shoulder and the other squeezing the hand of Luana, he took a deep breath and raised both arms high above himself, appealing for hush from the multitude.

"With our sorrow and heartbreak, we say a sweet farewell to one who may not be here in body, but within whose spirit we will abide forever."

Messengers, located throughout the masses, carried the words onwards.

"She, our queen, our leader and friend, is with us still and her deeds will be forever told. Tomorrow our land steps forward into the unknown, into shadows and sunlight, and we must now choose the way forward with the help of Garr's spirit.

May Luana, our new and worthy queen, travel and guide us safely forward towards the sunlight, with that spirit of Garr, our mother and hers, and the spirit of our land Garrtellia."

When at last the great pyre was lit late on that third day, a very grey and old Monster still lay by Garr's side. They placed her arm around him for mutual love and company on their last journey.

Throughout the valley, a thousand small flames flickered, as folk stood or knelt in silent respect, with disbelief still in their hearts, facing the great leaping flames as they licked the darkening sky—a flaming crown upon a humble hill. The world of Garrtellia would move onward. As the sun dropped to the horizon on that evening, all knew that with the new morning, there would be a new sun.

When that new sun rose in the eastern sky, it began to blaze from around the sides of the hilltop, mingling with the still blazing pyre, and so heralding the sad passing of a great spirit and yet announcing a new beginning.

The End.

Ideas for Discussion

1. Real survival is harsh. Is human goodness and spirit given generously in these conditions or is it only given in exchange for something needed?
2. When everything precious is taken from an individual, spiritually and materially, are they able to hold on to their values in life?
3. If laws did not exist, how would you maintain or create order?
4. Assuming all humans desire love and affection, is it right to take it from anywhere or anyone that can offer it?
5. Every form of government falls short of perfection: can you think of an overriding statement that should govern all laws and actions?
6. Are all actions taken by Garr selfless?
7. Do you believe that 'good intent' is an adequate justification for action?

Email johnbrooksy@outlook.com

'Yours Reviews and Comments on this story are very much appreciated'.

The Little Green Thingy Thing

Garr loved telling and making up stories for the children that often gathered around her wherever she travelled across Gartellia. This is just one of her bedtime stories.

Now, this is a true and strange story and you should listen carefully in case you ever have this experience yourselves, so if you are all quiet and comfortable, I will begin.

Thingy Things are mystical and magical creatures.

Sometimes you are able to see them and sometimes you are not.

There are some folks that never see them, and, *even worse*, they refuse to believe they even exist.

So, I think I have been very lucky.

I have seen them in many places. In fact, wherever I have travelled throughout Gartellia, I have seen Thingy Things.

You cannot talk about them generally, because some people think you are nuts and crazy.

Some I have seen, have been red Thingy Things and some, brown Thingy-Things.

Some have displayed great floppy, elaborate crests on their heads and spiky tails that were very, very long. Others were smooth all over and looked like worms with legs.

In some places, they are very large and dangerous, and they roar like lions, while generally they are small and friendly and normally will say, "Good Morning" with a little Thingy Thing smile and in their own very special way.

I am not really sure what Thingy Things eat, but I guess some eat apples and some grapes, while others probably enjoy nuts and grasses and yummy sweet things all mixed up together.

I think most Thingy Things grow up very fast, a lot quicker than little boys and girls. And, they don't go to school either because their mums and dads teach them everything they need to know in life. I know this is true as I have never seen any Thingy Things with any books, so I guess it must be correct.

I also think they live in the rocks, just like me. I guess they must make little houses and rooms deep inside the rocks and under the ground.

Once upon a time, I was living on the plains, in the far south of Gartellia, where the weather is sometimes very hot. This is a country where lots of eagles and wild boar live. A place where there are lots of hills and lots of open countryside but not many people. This is called wild country.

In the wild country, there are lots of rocks all over the ground and lots of cactus plants with spikes all over them; if you fall on a cactus, the spikes might stick in your bottom and you would very soon jump up again, probably saying, "Oooh, ooh" and "Ouch".

The people there collect lots of citrus fruit, like oranges and lemons, which look very pretty on the trees with all their dark green leaves as you know.

This particular day, the weather was lovely and warm and the sky, very blue.

Little Mols, Josh, Cam, and I were out walking amongst the hills, picking our way between the rocks and looking at the little birds singing high up in the bamboo plants, which as you know is like very tall grass.

"What is that, Garr?" Mols said in an excited voice and pointing up at the rocks above us.

Cam and Josh did not hear this as they were both busy inspecting the many beautiful little rocks. Some were shiny gold, some silver, and some striped.

I immediately looked in the direction that Mols was pointing, but I saw nothing.

"I cannot see anything, Mols. What did you see?"

"It was a—it was a green thing!"

"Was it a bird, Mols?"

"No, Garr, it was a Thingy Thing, a green Thingy Thing, like a doggy Thingy Thing. Like in the stories you tell us."

"Aaaah! A doggy Thingy Thing; a green doggy Thingy Thing. I have seen a red doggy Thingy Thing before, Mols, but not a green one. Are you sure it was green?"

"Garr, it was very big, but just like an apple, a green apple."

"A green apple! It looked like a green apple, Mols?"

"No, Garr, you're being silly. The same colour as an apple, green, like grass."

"How do you know it was a Thingy Thing, Mol, or was it just a dog you saw?

"Sometimes, Mols, the light makes things look very different, the colours and shapes. I think we will have to keep our eyes open and hope we can see one again. It certainly sounds very different but, I guess it was a dog, and the sunlight made it look green."

"Was not," said Mols.

Josh and Cam came running over to where Molly and I were discussing what she had seen, both carrying loads of wonderful little rocks, which we all had to look at very carefully, turning each stone over many, many, times and reflecting that each was possibly millions and millions of years old.

When we had finished looking at all the little stones, I told the two boys what Mols had seen.

"Wow and double wow! Shall we go and have a look, Garr?" asked both Cam and Josh.

"I think that is a great idea, boys. What do you think Mols?"

"Yes, but you have to carry me, Garr, cause I am only little and the rocks are big and I am a little girl and Cam and Josh are big and you are very big."

"Okay, Miss Mols. First, we will eat our lunch, then climb into the rocks and have a look for Mols green Thingy Thing. But, only if you two boys promise to stay with me and do as you are told because rocks can be dangerous. Is that a deal?"

We all shook hands, and that sealed the agreement. As you know, that is also a secret code for adventurers when climbing rocks and hunting.

Lunch was excellent. All our favourite things were wrapped up in our leather bag.

After we had eaten, Cam picked some fresh oranges off a tree, and we all had one each. Then we all agreed that lunch was yummy, yummy and sat for a while just looking around at the beautiful views around us.

"Come on, Garr, let's go hunting," said Josh.

So, after making sure there was no rubbish left lying on the ground, we started to climb up the side of the hills and between the rocks. It was steep in places, but both the boys were good climbers and made sure that they always had a good grip on something solid. Mols just clung on tightly to my ears and hair while pointing in the direction where she had seen the Thingy Thing, maybe!

Of course, she was the only one that knew what to expect, and I have to admit that even I felt a little nervous as we approached the area where she had seen it, maybe! We moved slowly, not making a sound. I was not expecting to find anything at all as everything was very still and quiet apart from birds chirping happily. Both Cam and Josh were now also very quiet and wanted to stay in line behind Mols and I.

It was all really rather scary!

Suddenly from nowhere we heard a noise. A sort of rumbly-grumbly, low and mumbly noise, a sort of *GooooMoorrrnnnng*. We all stopped where we were and looked around to see from where the noise had come and what the noise was.

The two boys moved in close behind me, both hanging on and making scary noises, "Eeeerrrh."

"What was that, Garr?"

"Sweetheart, I don't know yet, but I hope it's very small."

Nervously I peered behind the adjacent rocks and boulders. Nothing here, nothing there at all. Strange, we all thought! Then suddenly!

G Moorrninna, gmorninngy, moorning.

"There was the sound again! Garr, what - is - that?"

"I'm real scared," said Josh.

Suddenly I remembered that sound; it was clearly the sound of a Thingy Thing trying to communicate with us.

I had heard it before in different places, but never in that area. This was exciting, and it seemed that Mols was correct. She wasn't tricking us after all and that was unusual.

It did not sound too large or too fierce. In fact, it sounded friendly. And, Mol and the two boys appeared to automatically feel the same way about the noise.

G Morningng, g moorning, g m morning

Now the noise was becoming louder, clearer, and more regular.

GooMornin, GoooMornin, Goomorning, Godmorninng

Suddenly, behind a large square boulder just ahead of where we were standing, was the Thingy Thing. A kind of silly smile on its face, green and kind of wobbly like jelly. It had a long neck and a little round body with little arms and large flat feet.

In size, it was similar to a medium-sized dog or sheep but with very long ears that bent over at the ends.

It was indeed the most unusual looking creature the children had ever seen, and, for Mols, Cam and Josh, their very first meeting with a Thingy Thing.

The Thingy Thing now seemed to be relaxed, and confident that we were friendly and suddenly stood up very straight. That made us all jump back a little.

"Good Morning," the Green Thingy Thing said, and then it repeated itself, over and over again.

"Goood Morning, Goood Morning, Goood Morning, Good Morning, Good Morning, Good Morning, Good Morning, Good Morning, Good Morning," he said until we were all laughing out loud, while the Thingy Thing continued to make the *good morning* sound, possibly because it was making us all laugh so much and so loud.

In our food bag, we found just one last apple we hadn't eaten. We had now all sat down comfortably and we passed the apple to the Thingy Thing, who reached out very gently and very carefully, took the apple, and tasted a tiny piece. Then with a kind of silly smile upon its face again and large open eyes, it started to munch away at the apple making a mixture of the strangest noises, whilst pieces of apple flew all over the place.

MmmmGGooGooing, Ummygoo-goo, Ummy Ummygoogoo

After he had eaten the apple and core, his big green tongue licked all around his face and hands, and then, leaning back against a rock, the Thingy Thing gave out a great sigh.

"Gooooooo," followed by a very loud belch, "Burpppp."

Then, once again standing on his very large flat feet, he started to climb further up the hill. Before he disappeared behind some rocks, he turned around to look at us once more. It was a long happy look, then, he sort of smiled, waved his paws and called out, "Good morning, good morning."

"Good morning, Thingy Thing," we all shouted back. "Hope we see you again, take care of yourself and be careful." And, with that it was gone.

"Double wow, incredible," said Cam. "Was that a dream or was that real?"

"Ooh, nope," said Joshua and Mol together. "That was a real Thingy Thing like Garr has told us about in her stories from everywhere."

"Garr, we did not really believe you about the Thingy Things in your stories before, but we will always believe you from now on. Honest and double honest, Garr."

"Is that so, my little ones?"

As we all walked back home over the hills, I suddenly remembered about the *Gotuss* I had seen high in the mountains and thought that I could share that story with Mols, Josh and Cam someday. And maybe, then, Pip, Bay and Joe could join us and of course any of the other children who enjoy adventures, that would be real excellent fun.

Indeed, who knows what's hiding around the next boulder.

Sleep tight and kisses, little ones.

Homework

1. Can you draw a picture of a Green Thingy Thing amongst the rocks?
2. Can you draw a picture of a magical creature that nobody has ever seen before?
3. Was the story set on the plains or in the mountains?
4. Who was the youngest person in the story?
5. What other colours had Garr seen on Thingy Things?
6. Can you remember, what was eaten for lunch by the four adventurers?

Review Requested:

Follow the Story of Garrtellia

This story is the first part of a trilogy. If you would like to follow the journey, please look out for the release of the 2nd book; 'The Second Dawning' and the final book; 'Innocent Reflections'.

If you loved this book, would you please
provide a review at Amazon.com?

Lightning Source UK Ltd.
Milton Keynes UK
UKHW021956190219
337571UK00011B/1906/P